### DON PENDLETON's
# MACK BOLAN.
# BLOOD FEUD

## A GOLD EAGLE BOOK FROM
# W⬤RLDWIDE.

TORONTO • NEW YORK • LONDON
AMSTERDAM • PARIS • SYDNEY • HAMBURG
STOCKHOLM • ATHENS • TOKYO • MILAN
MADRID • WARSAW • BUDAPEST • AUCKLAND

First edition August 1998

ISBN 0-373-61461-6

Special thanks and acknowledgment to
David Robbins for his contribution to this work.

BLOOD FEUD

...I therefore believe it is my duty to my country to love it, to support its Constitution, to obey its laws, to respect its flag, and to defend it against all enemies.
—William Tyler Page
*The American Creed*

The Mob is a cancer eating away at the fabric of society. Unless someone is willing to stand up to the wolves of the world, no one is safe.
—Mack Bolan

To the men and women of the FBI.
God keep.

# *PROLOGUE*

### *Naples, Italy*

A bloodbath could begin in the most unlikely of ways.

Vito Scarlotti had been coming to the Lucia restaurant for more years than he cared to think about. The pasta was outstanding, the wine excellent. Best of all, from his reserved table on the terrace he could look out over the deep blue waters of the Bay of Naples and gaze on majestic Mount Vesuvius, its summit crowned by clouds.

The waiter came promptly with the menu. Soon the owner himself bustled to the table to extend his greetings.

Scarlotti was accustomed to being treated as royalty, and in a perverse sense, he qualified. It was safe to say that he ranked as the single most influential person in all of Naples, although none of the people thronging the busy streets below were aware of the fact.

On this golden afternoon Scarlotti ordered linguine and his favorite wine. He faced his two top lieutenants and was about to inquire about a shipment of opium due in from Istanbul when a tall figure abruptly filled the shadowed doorway connecting the terrace to the main dining area. Automatically the man on Scarlotti's right snaked a hand under his jacket.

"Behave yourself, Marchio," the old man scolded, resting a hand on his childhood friend's arm. "Are your eyes so bad that you no longer can recognize my own flesh and blood?"

Marchio drew his hand out, but he didn't relax. In certain circles he was one of the most feared men in all of Italy. "The Butcher," some called him, a nickname earned decades earlier when a brash government prosecutor had tried to put Vito Scarlotti behind bars. The man had been strangled to death with his own intestines. His wife and two sons had also been slain, their bodies slit from navel to neck, their eyes gouged out, their tongues removed.

Scarlotti rose, extending his right hand. "What a pleasant surprise, my son! Where have you been keeping yourself these past few weeks?"

Antonio Scarlotti glided like a great, dark panther to the table and clasped his father in greeting. He was inches taller than Vito, who stood well over six feet. His shoulders were twice as broad. Every movement hinted at latent power. Every motion was precise and fluid. "My apologies," he said as he pulled a chair over next to his father's. "I have been busy."

"Too busy to pay your respects to your own parents? Your mother is very upset. She thinks that you have forgotten all about us. You must stop by and see her soon.''

''I am going to the villa after I leave here,'' Antonio promised.

Vito smiled and patted his son's wrist. ''You will make her old heart glad.'' He studied the handsome features of his pride and joy, features so like his when he had been in his twenties. The same hardness was there, the same fire in the eyes and the same iron cast to the jaw and mouth. At one glance anyone could tell that his son wasn't a man to be trifled with, and that swelled Vito with pride.

''I need to talk to you about America,'' Antonio said.

The special moment was ruined. Vito frowned and straightened. ''Again? How many times must we go through this? How many times must I say the same thing? My answer has always been no. It will always be no.''

Antonio folded his arms and regarded his father intently. ''This is the very last time. I swear.'' He paused and seemed to be struggling for the right words. ''I would not try your patience, Father. But you know how much this means to me.''

Vito made a sharp gesture of annoyance. ''Why that should be, I will never know. The blood feud took place long before you were born. Let sleeping dogs lie, my son.''

''Are we supposed to live with the stain forever? Do we spend our lives deceiving ourselves, acting as if nothing ever happened?" Antonio sighed. "What of our honor?"

It was Marchio who responded. Snorting, he declared, "You are a fine one to talk of honor, cub! You, who betrayed your own best friend just so you could bed his woman."

Antonio swiveled toward the enforcer, his face a marble mask. "You never did show me proper respect. Not once over all these years."

Marchio matched Antonio's flinty gaze. "Respect is like trust, cub. It must be earned. You have done nothing to earn mine." He leaned forward, his right hand close to the flap of his jacket. "All you have ever done is cause your father grief. If you had been just another tough off the streets, we would never have tolerated your behavior. I'd have disposed of you long ago."

"You would have tried," Antonio said.

"Enough!" Vito snapped. "I will not sit here and listen to my son and my best friend bicker over a matter that has already been settled."

A strained silence descended, broken when Antonio draped a hand on his father's shoulder. "Forgive me. I must make one last appeal."

Vito shook his head.

"We can do it, Father," Antonio persisted. "Give me a year or so to organize everything, and two years from now the Camorra will have reclaimed what is rightfully ours. Think of it! All that power! All that wealth!"

"Think of the cost, my son. Think of the blood

that will be shed. Think of the lives that will be lost. And for what? To fight a war neither side can ever win.''

''But that's just my point,'' Antonio explained eagerly. ''We *can* win, Father. The element of surprise is on our side.''

Again Marchio interrupted. ''Surprise alone cannot win battles.''

Antonio scowled. ''Coupled with the will to win, it can. And never forget that they have grown soft over there. All that luxury has made them weak. We will be like wolves in a sheep pen.''

All eyes swung to Vito. He stalled by taking a sip of wine. In his heart of hearts he wished that he could do as his son wanted. It had always been difficult for him to refuse Antonio anything. He knew that some—Marchio included—believed that he had spoiled the boy. And perhaps they had a point. Antonio had grown into a willful firebrand who insisted on always having his own way.

''Interesting that you should mention wolves, my son,'' Vito began. ''Haven't you ever noticed that a wolf's proper place is in the wilderness, far back in the mountains where it can prey on deer and rabbits? For when a wolf comes down out of the mountains to raid farms for sheep and goats, it is ruthlessly hunted and killed. There is a lesson to be learned in that.'' He looked at Antonio. ''All things must stay in their own element.''

''For animals that is true. But we are men, Father. The only limits on us are those we impose on ourselves." Antonio indicated the sprawling city below. "Look at us, Father. The Camorra took root in Naples, yet now we control half of Italy and much of Europe. We have been spreading across Asia for years. What makes America different?"

"Need you even ask? We tried once, remember? It nearly destroyed us."

"We were fewer in number and far less organized," Antonio countered. "This time we will have the edge. This time we will send them running with their tails between their legs." A sneer curled his thin lips. "Those I let live, that is."

Vito looked at his son again. He looked long and hard and saw something he had never seen before, or that maybe had been there all along but he had been too blind with affection to notice. Inwardly he shivered, as if an ice-cold hand had reached into his chest and seized his heart.

"For the final time, Father," Antonio said, "what is your answer?"

"The same as always," Vito wearily replied.

Antonio regarded his father for several moments, then slowly stood. "So be it. I've tried my best to convince you. From this day on, I will not bother you again."

"Give my regards to your mother."

"I will." Antonio went to leave, but hesitated. In a rare display of emotion, he gave Vito a fleeting hug. "I've tried my utmost to please you over the years. You know that, don't you?"

"Of course," Vito said, surprised.

Nodding, Antonio made for the doorway. He paused halfway there and glanced back. "Oh. Before I forget. I would like a word with Marchio in private. That is, if you don't mind, Father?"

Vito absently gave his assent. Refilling his glass, he glumly sat back to contemplate the view.

Marchio followed the younger Scarlotti into the dining area. As was his habit, he had hooked his right thumb under his belt, within easy reach of his pistol. "What do you want?" he demanded gruffly.

A waitress passed close by. Antonio wagged a finger toward the men's room. He went in first and held the door for the enforcer to go on by.

Turning so that he always faced Antonio, Marchio slid past and backed up to the sinks, allowing ample space between them. "This had better be important. I do not like to leave your father alone, even for a short while."

Antonio released the door and casually shoved his hands into his pockets. "Yes, you've always been devoted to him. I want you to know that I appreciate your loyalty."

"Save your flattery for someone who cares," Marchio said. "If you have something to say, get to the point."

"Be patient, old man," Antonio said. "This will not take long." Striding to a mirror, he swiped at a bang of black hair that perpetually drooped over his right eye. "I have a hypothetical question to ask you."

The enforcer tapped his foot.

"Try not to misconstrue what I am about to say," Antonio said, "but if something was to happen to my father, if he was to die tomorrow of a heart attack, for instance, would you be willing to serve under me as my second-in-command?"

"Your father is in prime health. He will last many years yet."

"No one's fate is etched in stone," Antonio replied dryly. Leaning against the sink, he pursed his lips. "I really want to know. While we have not always seen eye to eye, I have long respected your tactical brilliance. You would be an asset to any organization. So be honest. Would you agree to serve me after my father is gone as faithfully as you have served him?"

"No."

"Care to tell me why?"

Marchio exhaled loudly. "Didn't you hear a word I said out on the terrace? I do not respect you, cub, and I never will. You are only half the man your father is."

"How so?" Antonio inquired, taking a step closer.

"Where your father inspires respect in others, all you inspire is fear. Where your father uses his head to combat his enemies, you rely on brawn and firepower. Where your father has learned to think ahead and keep the common good of the Camorra in mind, you act rashly and think only of yourself."

"Still, his blood courses through my veins. I am

a lot like him in many respects. He has told me so himself.''

"True. You have inherited most of his worst traits and few of those that make him the great man he is. Which is why you will never amount to much. I doubt you will last five years after he is gone." Marchio's expression saddened. "It is unfortunate that he never had other sons. Perhaps one of them would have been fit to follow in his footsteps.''

"There is always my sister," Antonio said sarcastically, while slowly advancing another pace.

"Never underestimate Maria, boy. She is a credit to the Scarlotti family."

"Unlike me," Antonio said, grinning to show that he didn't harbor ill feelings over the older man's comments. "Well, you have certainly been frank. Since you will not join me, we have nothing left to discuss." With that, he raised his right arm toward the door. "Feel free to go."

"With pleasure."

The younger Scarlotti stepped back to permit the enforcer to go past. Just as Marchio did, Antonio offered his hand. "To show there are no hard feelings, eh?" he said.

Reluctantly Marchio shook. He started to draw his hand back when suddenly Antonio's left arm snapped out as rigid as a pole, straight at Marchio's head. There was a muffled sound, and a small hole blossomed in the center of the enforcer's forehead. Out of sheer instinct he grabbed for his pistol, but he was dead on his feet before his fingers touched it.

"What a waste," Antonio murmured, catching hold of the heavier man and dragging him into a stall. He smoothed his clothes, left the rest room and strolled from the building as if he didn't have a care in the world.

Antonio's long black limo waited at the bottom of the steps. Without a word to the two men in the front seat, he slid into the back and nodded curtly.

The driver wheeled around the circular driveway, braking when he came to the street.

"Hold it," Antonio ordered. Flicking a switch at his elbow, he rolled down the window. He had to twist to see the terrace. His father caught sight of him, smiled and waved. Antonio waved back. Then he calmly picked up a black box from the seat beside him, held the detonator out so Vito would realize what it was and just as calmly pressed the red button on top.

The explosion was spectacular. The restaurant erupted skyward in perfect mimicry of the famous eruption of Mount Vesuvius. Screams rent the air, but they were few and far between. Most of the patrons died immediately, torn to bits by the incredible violence of the blast.

As the debris began to rain to the ground, Antonio Scarlotti tossed the detonator on the floor and commanded the driver to depart.

And so it began.

# CHAPTER ONE

*One year later*

Luther Rossi killed people for a living. He had a rap sheet as long as both arms, yet he always managed to avoid doing serious time thanks to high-priced Mob lawyers. The Feds had been after him for years, but he had eluded them time and again. Once he had fought his way out of a federal cordon, gunning down three agents in the process.

Mack Bolan, aka the Executioner, was about to save the taxpayers a fortune in legal fees and prison costs. Cloaked in a combat blacksuit crammed with the deadly tools of his trade, he padded toward high brick walls that surrounded a remote estate in upstate New York. His rugged face was smeared with combat cosmetics to reduce the sheen of his skin. Strapped to his right hip was a .44 Magnum Desert Eagle. Under his left arm rode a Beretta 93-R. An M-16 completed his primary arsenal.

According to reliable intel gleaned by Hal Brognola, Director of the Justice Department's Sensitive Operations Group, Luther Rossi had been living at that estate for the past month or so. At least, Bolan *hoped* the intel was reliable. There had been no time to send in an advance team to confirm the tip.

As soon as Brognola had been handed the report, he'd contacted the soldier. "He's yours if you want him, Striker," the big Fed had offered. "Rossi has vowed never to be taken alive, and I don't want to lose any more good men putting his vow to the test."

Bolan had readily agreed to go in. As far as he was concerned, anyone linked to the Mafia was fair game for his own personal brand of justice. Payback, some would call it. Revenge, others might say. Both would be wrong.

Years earlier, Bolan's family had been destroyed by the Mob, and yes, he had waged a one-man campaign against the Mafia for more years than he cared to count. But vengeance had long since stopped being even a tiny part of his motive.

Mack Bolan was waging war.

He would give his life, if need be, in defense of his country, just as he had been so willing to do in Vietnam and elsewhere.

The sad truth was that not all of America's enemies were to be found on foreign soil. Tearing away at the very fabric of American society were parasites every bit as destructive as the most powerful intercontinental missiles. Drug addiction, illegal gambling, graft and extortion, as well as organized criminal rackets of every conceivable stripe, were doing more to bring America to ruin than all the Communists in the world had ever accomplished.

In the vanguard of the spreading evil was a malignant entity ripping at the heart of all that Americans held dear. Until the Mafia was eliminated, American streets would never be safe to walk at night, her parks would be breeding grounds for packs of savage gangs, her once superb schools would be recruiting stations for future drug dealers and hit men. Corrupt politicians would flourish.

The Mafia had to be stopped, and Bolan would do his part. It was that simple.

A cool breeze wafted from the northwest as the Executioner jogged to a high cluster of weeds and crouched to take his bearings. He was approaching the estate from the west. No guards were visible, and the grounds were dark, but that didn't mean a thing.

Near the southwest corner grew a solitary maple. One of its stout lower limbs, Bolan noticed, hung no more than ten feet above the brick wall.

Staying low, the soldier catfooted to the tree. He squatted at its base to listen, but all he heard was the hoot of an owl off in the woods and a distant train whistle. Rossi had picked a prime spot to lay low. The nearest neighbors were more than a mile away, the closest town almost ten miles distant.

Slinging the M-16 over his left shoulder, Bolan shimmied up the trunk. Once on the lowest branch, he found it was a simple matter to work around to the limb that jutted over the wall. Hunkering, he scanned the grounds.

Over four acres were enclosed, the main house covering at least one of them. A wide garage and two outbuildings flanked it to the south. Hedges and shrubs crisscrossed the spacious lawn, and sixty feet from the corner stood a gazebo covered with ivy.

Not a soul was visible. No movement was evident. Bolan, adept as he was at spotting concealed sentries, failed to pinpoint a single member of the opposition. Which bothered him. It was unlikely that Rossi stayed at the estate alone. There should be guards—dogs, perhaps, and electronic surveillance.

The minutes dragged by, but Bolan refused to commit himself. Only a fool rushed blindly into enemy-held territory. He commenced a visual sweep of every square foot of the perimeter and was shortly rewarded with the barely discernible silhouette of a camera mounted on a pivot on the rear wall of the main house. Angled toward the middle of the rear lawn, it wasn't swiveling back and forth as it should be.

Bolan wondered if maybe he was too late. Given Rossi's uncanny knack for staying one jump ahead of the law, Bolan's target might have flown the coop. He studied the windows, seeking proof that someone was home.

The house reared three stories high. Almost all the windows on the lower floor were lit up, as were half of those on the second. Only one on the third floor glowed a pale white. As he looked on, a shadow flitted across the pane.

Bolan wasn't able to tell much. It had been a man, strangely stooped over, and it appeared that the person carried a gun, either a large pistol or a small submachine gun. So there were gunners inside. He inched farther out on the limb to clear the edge of the wall, then looked down.

A body dressed in dark clothing lay sprawled on its back in the grass, arms outflung, the head bent at an unnatural angle. The open jacket revealed a pistol in a speed rig under the right arm. Lying next to the dead man's shoulder was a radio.

The Executioner was more mystified than ever. It didn't take a genius to figure out that the corpse had been a guard, and that someone had disposed of him with extreme prejudice, apparently by snapping his neck with a sharp, skilled twist. The obvious conclusion was that another party had penetrated the estate shortly before Bolan got there. He remembered the image at the upper window. Had it been the killer?

Holding the M-16 in his left hand, Bolan dropped and landed lightly beside the corpse. A quick check confirmed the body was still warm.

Rising, Bolan sprinted to a hedge. As soundless as a ghost, he slipped along it until the surveillance camera was in clear view. It still hadn't moved, and an electronic eye above the lens, an infrared sensor that locked on to targets, was as dead as the gunner by the wall.

Evidently the security system had been deactivated.

Bolan was about to go on when out of the corner of an eye he glimpsed movement to his left. He whirled just as a lanky shape loomed up out of the night and lunged at him, a stiletto glittering dully in the starlight. The soldier pivoted. Razor-sharp steel hissed past his cheek. Before the man could swing again, the Executioner aimed a buttstroke at the gunner's temple. He only clipped his attacker, so he was taken aback when the man folded as if stricken by the plague and didn't so much as twitch after hitting the ground.

Suspicious of a trick, Bolan prodded the curled form with the muzzle of the M-16. He surveyed his immediate vicinity to ensure no other nasty surprises awaited him, then sank onto a knee. The stiletto had fallen from the guard's fingers. Bolan was careful to flick it aside before he clamped a hand on the man's throat and rolled him over.

The soldier's steely blue eyes narrowed. A bloodstain marred the man's shirt from belt to collar. As near as he could tell in the dark, the guard had been shot four or five times, no doubt by the same party responsible for the death of the gunner over by the west wall.

The man had to have revived, Bolan mused, and, with the last of his strength, attacked the first person he saw.

Whoever had penetrated the estate was a fellow professional. Both triggermen had been taken out swiftly and efficiently, the security system rendered useless without setting off any alarms.

A shadow flitting across a lower window reminded Bolan that his mysterious counterpart was still on the premises. He jogged to the hedge, verified the clear space beyond was safe to cross, then raced to a row of low shrubs. No shots rang out.

The rear door hung open a crack. In front of it lay another body, a mafioso crumpled in a miserable busted heap.

Bolan girded himself to sprint to the doorway. As he began his move, something thudded into the soil inches below where his chest had just been. Instantly he threw himself to the right. A burst of bullets missed his head, but not by much. He landed on his side and immediately snaked to the south, using the shrubbery for cover.

The Executioner was too combat savvy to return fire. He had to locate a target, for one thing. Also there might be more than one pro involved, and the blast of his autorifle would alert the rest.

At the end of the row Bolan halted. Drawing the Beretta, he took a sound suppressor from one of his pockets and threaded it onto the pistol. Now he could deal with the shooter on even terms.

Loosening the sling to the M-16, Bolan slung it across his chest. Then, holding the 93-R in a two-handed grip, he sprinted toward a flower bed choked with roses. Just as he flattened, the bushes rustled as if being shaken by an invisible hand. Several tattered leaves fluttered on the breeze.

Bolan suspected that the shooter was near the garage or one of the other outbuildings. His best bet was to circle around and come at them from the east, but that would take time and he wanted to get into the house quickly.

Resorting to one of the oldest tricks in the book, the soldier roamed a hand over the rose bed until he found a stone big enough to suit him. He gauged the distance to an oak tree located near one of the sheds, then hurled the stone in a looping arc. It skimmed through the foliage and clattered from branch to branch on its way to the bottom.

At the first sound, a shadow detached itself from a rear corner of the garage. A silenced pistol coughed twice.

Bolan's reflexes were the equal of his unknown adversary's. He chugged off a pair of shots and was rewarded by seeing the shadow stagger backward, then fold in on itself and pitch forward. He broke for the corner in a zigzag pattern, the Beretta at full extension, his trigger finger cocked. But another shot proved unnecessary.

A stocky man dressed all in black lay facedown on the asphalt. The slug had cored his left eye and burst out the rear of his cranium, spattering brains and gore on the garage. Bolan hastily pried off the ski mask the gunner wore, revealing a shock of jet black hair and features that branded the hit man as hailing from a Mediterranean country. Italy, if Bolan was any judge.

From inside the house came a tremendous crash.

Bolan spun in time to witness several vague forms spirit across a second-floor window. A scream knifed the night. He thought that he heard the telltale muted sputter of a sound-suppressed SMG.

Suddenly the window exploded. Through it plummeted a man who screamed as he dropped. He smashed onto a small white picket fence, splintering it. Stunned and battered but still alive, he managed to gain his hands and knees. He glanced up at the window.

Bolan did the same. A pair of black-clad men holding silenced Uzis was framed by the jamb. One of the SMGs spit a hailstorm of lead.

The man on the ground jerked and thrashed as his body was turned into a sieve. The only sound he uttered was a grunt when the firing ceased and he melted lifeless to the soil.

Bolan brought the Beretta into target acquisition. But then the two men were gone, slipping back inside without a word or a whisper of noise. He scanned the other windows on that side, coiled and sprinted flat-out for the back door. Once safely there, he put his ear to the crack in the hope of hearing what was going on within. The house was as quiet as a tomb.

He was at a loss to explain the firefight. His best guess was that he had stumbled into the middle of a battle between two Mafia factions. Yet to his knowledge there was no Mob war in progress. The Families had been at peace for some time.

What then? Bolan asked himself as he quietly

pushed the door wide enough to enter. He did so bent low, his back to the wall. A broad kitchen led to a narrow hall. A coffeepot bubbled on the stove, and three plates heaped with partially eaten food sat on a table, proof that Rossi's men had been taken completely by surprise.

Bolan stealthily advanced to the hall. It was brightly lit at his end but not at the other. The overheads farther down had been shot out. If someone was lurking in one of the rooms there, the soldier would be fair game.

Hiking the Beretta, Bolan did the only thing he could—he shot out the lights at his end. The tinkle of shattering glass wasn't as loud as he worried it might be, but still loud enough to alert anyone on the ground floor. The moment the hall plunged into darkness, he was in motion, racing to the nearest doorway and ducking into a room that smelled of cigarette smoke. It was unoccupied.

Upstairs there was a distinct thud.

Bolan moved on, searching for a flight of stairs. The next room was a study or den. A closed door opened into a utility closet. Past it was a lavishly furnished living room, and lying in a neat row on the plush carpet were three dead gunners, all slain execution style by a single shot to the back of the head. Bolan guessed that they had been the three eating in the kitchen. Caught off guard, they had been forced at gunpoint to march down the hall to their doom.

A mahogany rail let Bolan know there was a

stairway on his right. He paused on the bottom step, hearing muffled voices followed by what sounded like a slap. He climbed slowly, two at a stride, always gazing up. The stairwell curved to the right, ending at a landing where another dead mafioso bore mute testimony to the thorough job the hit team had done.

Bolan hugged the wall, his tread as light as a feather. The first room he came to was the one with the shattered window. Another man was sprawled over a sofa, his throat slit from ear to ear.

The soldier went on. The remaining rooms were empty. A second stairwell rose to the third floor. As he stepped onto it, somewhere above a man cursed in Italian. Another slap hinted that someone was being questioned by the hit team. A series of thuds tended to confirm it.

When his head was as high as the landing, Bolan peeked over the top. An empty hall stretched before him, bathed by light spilling from a room. Shadows moved across the lit patch. He crept higher, the Beretta fixed on the doorway, every nerve keyed to a raw edge.

"You know the routine, Rossi. Make it easy on yourself. Tell us where we can find Leo Tinelli."

Bolan stopped. Tinelli was the Mafia bigwig Luther Rossi worked for, one of the most powerful bosses in New York City. So Bolan's hunch about a Mafia war might be right, after all.

"Go to hell, bastard! I will never talk!"

That had to be Rossi, Bolan speculated, sounding as if he had a blackjack jammed down his throat.

"Bound by the code, eh?" the first speaker said sarcastically. "The Mafia has always set itself up as so special, so superior. Bah!" A slap resounded. "You are spineless pigs, every one of you!"

Someone said something quickly in Italian that Bolan didn't catch. "He has a point, Rossi. We do not have all night. You will tell us what we need to know or suffer the consequences of your stupidity. What will it be?"

No answer was forthcoming. Bolan heard a peculiar metallic clack that ended as unexpectedly as it began.

"Last chance, Rossi."

"I'd rather die."

"Suit yourself."

Bolan inched closer as Rossi cried out. A couple of steps more and the tableau was revealed.

Luther Rossi had been tied to a chair. Clad in pajamas, naked from the waist up, he was staring, aghast, at his chest. Bent over him was a tall man in a ski mask, the blade of a butterfly knife gleaming in his right hand. As nonchalantly as if he were peeling an apple or orange, the man had sliced the knife into Rossi's right shoulder.

"Damn you!" Rossi clenched his teeth and tried to wrench the chair backward, but he was tied too tightly.

Bolan felt no sympathy for the Mafia triggerman. Rossi was to blame for dozens of deaths, many involving innocents who had unwittingly witnessed

Mob activity and were silenced to prevent them from testifying.

Since the door was only partway open, Bolan couldn't determine exactly how many masked gunmen he was up against. The two by the chair were in plain sight, but his intuition warned him there were more. Seconds later a third appeared and whispered to the man wielding the butterfly knife, who absently nodded. The third hardman then walked toward the hall.

Bolan rapidly backpedaled. He reached the landing and ducked around the corner into a shadowed recess. The man in the mask went by briskly, skipping down the steps without looking back. As soon as he was out of sight, Bolan returned to the room. The odds were now more in his favor. Neither member of the hit team was facing the doorway.

Rossi cried out. A strip of his skin hung limply on his chest, and blood trickled down his stomach. He gasped when his tormentor inserted the tip of the butterfly knife to peel off more. "All right! All right! I'll talk!"

The man with the knife straightened. "So soon? I'm disappointed in you, Rossi. We've all heard what a tough man you are."

"Just don't stick me again!" Rossi pleaded. "I'll do anything you want!"

"Tell us where to find your boss."

"I will," Rossi said, "but first you have to untie me so I can—"

Rossi never finished his statement. The tall man savagely slashed him across the belly, elevated his knife arm and thrust the blade into Rossi's thigh. The Mafia soldier yelped.

"What are you doing? I told you that I'd talk."

The tall man made a clucking sound. "You're playing games with us, Luther. Either that, or you're too stupid to realize that you are in no position to make demands of us. You will do as we say or you will suffer as few ever have. Guaranteed."

"Okay! Okay!" Rossi gulped in air. "Don Tinelli is at his place on Long Island." He gave an address.

Without warning, the tall man speared the butterfly knife into his captive's other thigh. Rossi tossed his head from side and side and bounced up and down, frantic, in utter agony. He screamed when the blade was torn out.

"Why did you do that? I gave you the information you wanted!"

"Like hell," the tall man responded, unruffled. Bending, he tapped the bloody tip of the blade against Rossi's chin. "We happen to know that Tinelli has not been at the house on Long Island for over a month." He traced the outline of Rossi's jaw with the knife. "We're not the simpletons you take us for, mister. Everything has been planned down to the second. By the time we're done, there won't be enough Mob members left to make a soccer team."

"You're crazy!" Rossi declared. "No one can take on the Mafia and live to brag about it! Whoever you are, you'll be wiped out before you know what hits you!"

Bolan knew that he should make his move, but he waited, wanting to learn more, to find out who the men in the ski masks were, to discover who they worked for.

"We have a saying in the Old Country, Luther," the tall man said. "Maybe you have heard of it— 'he who sleeps with dogs gets up with fleas.' It will make a fitting epitaph on your tombstone, don't you think? On yours, and on the grave of all the Mafia vermin we exterminate."

He jabbed lightly, nicking Rossi's neck and drawing blood. "One last time. Where is your boss staying right this minute?"

Rossi looked his tormentor squarely in the eyes. "Kiss my ass."

"How unfortunate."

Bolan saw the knife flash. In the blink of an eye Rossi's jugular was severed. He edged forward, intending to try to take one of the masked assassins alive if at all possible.

In disgust the tall man kicked the chair over. "See how easy he was, Navali? Just as Tony said they would be, eh?"

The Executioner tensed to spring. He was so intent on the men in front of him that he almost missed the creak of a floorboard to his rear. A glance explained the cause.

The other masked hit man had returned and was bringing an Uzi into target acquisition.

# CHAPTER TWO

*Washington, D.C.*

There were days when Hal Brognola fervently wished he had stayed in bed.

He was at his office in the Justice Department building in Washington, D.C., working late on the bane of all federal employees, paperwork, when someone rapped on his door. "It's open," Brognola called without looking up.

In came a subordinate, Agent Clint Jeffers, a twelve-year veteran of Justice who worked in the communications center. He held two messages. "Sorry to bother you, sir."

"I trust it's important?" Brognola said. Setting down his pen, he stretched to relieve a kink in his neck. Secretly he was grateful for the interruption. He needed a break after four straight hours of desk work.

"I really can't say how important it is," Jeffers responded. "A better word might be 'interesting.'"

Brognola had been acquainted with the agent long enough to know that the comm specialist wasn't the kind of man to get concerned over trifles. "What do you have?"

Jeffers extended one of the sheets. "This came in about forty-five minutes ago from the FBI field office in Las Vegas."

It was a routine message pertaining to an ongoing organized-crime investigation. A Mafia *caporegime,* or lieutenant, by the name of Decio had been under surveillance in connection with a kickback scheme involving construction of two federal buildings in Nevada. Decio had paid a visit to a local brothel, and after he had been inside for an overly long time, an agent had gone in to check, thinking Decio had given them the slip. Instead, the agent found Decio dead, slain execution style, as had the unfortunate woman he had been with at the time.

Brognola lowered the message. In and of itself, the report was hardly earthshaking. Mobsters were rubbed out on a regular basis. "Is there something more?"

"Just this."

The second report was from Miami, marked Urgent. Twenty minutes earlier Mafia Don Giadone had been about to board his private jet for a flight to Cuba when the aircraft had been blown apart. Giadone, his wife and two children, four triggermen, plus the pilot and two other crew members had all been killed in the explosion. Seven bystanders had been injured severely enough to merit being rushed to area hospitals.

The big Fed placed the second report on his desk beside the first. "Strange," he mused aloud.

"That's what I thought," Jeffers said. "I hope you don't mind that I brought them to your attention right away rather than send them up through normal channels." He coughed as if somewhat embarrassed. "I know you have a long-standing interest in Mafia activities."

"That I do," Brognola replied, but in reality the Mob was just another festering cesspool of crime as far as he was concerned, no different or worse than the Triads, the Colombian cartels, the Yakuza, the Jamaican posses or any other established criminal organization. His undue interest in the Mafia stemmed from his close friendship with Mack Bolan. Often his access to information enabled him to pass on timely tips.

"Do you want to hold on to them, sir?" Jeffers asked.

"Might as well," the big Fed stated, adding, "I appreciate the favor, Clint. Thanks."

"Any time."

Left alone, Brognola reread the messages. It couldn't be a coincidence that two top mobsters had been put out of commission in so short a span of time. If he didn't know any better, he'd swear a war had broken out. But there had been no indication of unrest in Mafia ranks for quite some time.

Was there a common link between Decio and Giadone? Brognola couldn't see how. They belonged to different Families. The businesses they ran were completely unrelated. He scribbled a note to remind himself to have the files on both men pulled first thing in the morning, then went back to work on the mountain of forms he had to sign or initial.

Ten minutes later another knock relieved the monotony. At Brognola's bidding the door was flung wide, and in rushed Jeffers. Without saying a word, he slapped a sheet of paper on the big Fed's desk.

"We just received this, sir. I have to get back."

Just like that, the agent was gone. Brognola picked up the report. It seemed that a meeting of mafioso heads in New York City had been disrupted within the past hour by an explosion that destroyed the hotel in which the council had taken place. In addition to the four prominent mobsters and a dozen bodyguards, twenty-seven innocents had been pulled from the rubble. More were missing.

"What the hell is going on?" Brognola questioned aloud. It was as if someone had declared open season on the Mafia and was systemically eliminating its top men all over the country. But that notion was preposterous. Who in his right mind would dare to take on the Mafia? No one had that much muscle.

Brognola set the new report beside the others. Then a disturbing thought struck him. That very afternoon Mack Bolan had left for upstate New York to deal with a top Mafia killer.

Brognola shook his head. The odds were against

it. Luther Rossi wasn't high enough up in the Mob to deserve a special hit by whoever was to blame for the other deaths.

Or was he?

"Striker," Hal said pensively, "I pray to God that you're all right."

*New York*

MACK BOLAN DIVED to the floor of the third-story hallway in Luther Rossi's rented house as a man in black opened up with a mini-Uzi on full-auto. Boasting a cyclic-fire rate that matched a full-size SMG, the Uzi stitched the door frame and would have shredded Bolan had he been a shade slower.

The Executioner fired from a prone position, the Beretta bucking twice, each impact jolting the hit man. He went for the head rather than the chest on the off chance the assassins wore body armor under their blacksuits.

As the gunner's knees gave way, Bolan threw himself against the opposite wall. Not a moment too soon. A pair of SMGs opened up inside the room. Slugs chewed the door to pieces in a matter of seconds and did the same to the floor near it. Through a jagged hole in the bottom panel, Bolan spotted one of the men in black. His forefinger stroked the trigger twice more.

The next moment the room was plunged into darkness; the leader had shot out the lights. Glass shattered when a window was broken, shards tinkling faintly as they fell to the earth below. Then silence reigned.

Bolan wasn't about to rush in. The leader wanted him to think that he had gone out the window, but they were on the top floor. To jump would be suicide. The Executioner could afford to wait the man out as long as no reinforcements arrived.

The soldier was cautiously rising when shoes drummed on the steps, stopping well shy of the landing. Now Bolan had two approaches to cover at the same time. If the leader and the gunners in the stairwell were in radio contact, they might mount a concerted rush to catch him by surprise in a cross fire.

But Bolan had a few surprises of his own in store for them. He swiftly holstered the 93-R, unslung the M-16 and flicked the selector lever to semi. Unfastening a side pocket on his blacksuit, he extracted a small, roughly oval grenade. It was a Mk1 illuminating hand grenade, usually employed to light up portions of a battlefield at night.

From another pocket he retrieved another grenade, but this one was different. It was cylindrical and had four holes in the top. The AN-M8 HC smoke hand grenade contained nineteen ounces of HC filler that produced dense white smoke.

Bolan crawled along the baseboard until he was close to the doorway. Yanking the pin on the AN-M8, he rolled it into the room. The igniting fuse had a two-second delay. There was a pop and a hiss, and a swirling white cloud billowed from the floor, filling the room in moments.

Certain that the leader couldn't see him, Bolan hurried past the doorway, keeping an eye on it in case the leader rushed out.

Eight feet from the landing, the soldier halted again. Somewhere below, voices whispered. Bolan plucked the pin on the Mk1. It had a seven-second delay, long enough for an enemy to pick it up and hurl it back if it wasn't thrown just right. He mentally counted to four, then hurled the bomb over the edge.

Bolan heard it thunk twice as it bounced from step to step. One of the hit men voiced a sharp cry, and feet thudded on the stairs. The Executioner buried his face in the crook of his right arm and closed his eyes. Even so, when the Mk1 went off, it was as if a sun had gone nova. The light was so bright, it lit up his eyelids.

Someone screeched in mortal anguish.

The Mk1 emitted 55,000 candlepower for about twenty-five seconds. In a confined space, such as a stairwell, it was enough to temporarily blind anyone caught with his eyes open.

Bolan ticked off a twenty-count in his head. Then he darted forward, tucking the M-16 to his shoulder. The light was fading but still able to illuminate a lone hit man ten feet down. The man staggered as if drunk. His eyes were wide open but unfocused, tears streaming from their corners.

The assassin stumbled against the wall, rotated and nearly tripped over a higher step.

The soldier could hear the footfalls of retreating gunners as they hurried down the stairs.

He still wanted to take one alive and started toward the man he had blinded, who abruptly froze as if somehow sensing his presence. Bolan did likewise, all too aware that his back was to the hall—to the doorway—and that at any moment the leader would come hurtling out of the room to escape the choking smoke. He had to take down the blinded hit man quickly.

Suddenly his quarry lifted a mini-Uzi and swung it from side to side. "Who's there?" he asked in Italian. "Talosi, is that you?"

The Executioner heard a shuffling sound from the direction of the room, and the skin between his shoulder blades prickled as if jabbed by hundreds of tiny needles.

The gunner had also heard the noise. "Talosi?" he repeated. Then, out of the blue, he unleashed a short burst, raking the steps from right to left.

The only thing that saved Bolan was being several steps higher than those the hit man blasted. He stood stock-still, waiting for the man to lower the Uzi. Instead, he hiked it higher as if to unleash another burst.

Bolan ripped off a 3-round burst that echoed like thunder off the stair walls. The rounds drilled the gunner's chest, catapulting him down the steps.

The Executioner whirled. The leader hadn't yet

appeared, but he would soon. Roiling smoke filled the room from bottom to top. No one could stay in there for very long.

But to Bolan's surprise, he heard no coughing, no wheezing. Either Talosi, if that was in fact the man's name, could hold his breath for an incredibly long interval, or something was wrong. The soldier moved toward the doorway, hugging the right-hand wall.

Outside, a man barked commands, the voice sounding like that of the tall leader.

Bolan realized that he had made a critical mistake. Talosi *had* gone out the window. The soldier descended the stairs three at a time, vaulting over the disjointed body of the gunner. At the bottom he angled across the living room to a door that flanked the driveway. Someone had done him the favor of leaving it wide open.

Shoulder to the jamb, Bolan peered out. Dangling six feet from his face was a black nylon cord, knots spaced a foot apart along its entire length.

There was no sign of the tall leader or any other hit men. Bolan bent and shot from the doorway, the M-16 wedged against his side, ready for anything. He came to a lilac bush and ducked behind it. The hit team was either lying low or effecting its escape.

Bolan sprinted to the corner of the house. To the north the night wind carried a scraping sound, much like metal rubbing against stone. Or against brick.

The soldier sprinted to the northwest corner. A figure in black was going over the top of the wall.

No others were evident, so Bolan gave chase, threading through the hedges and shrubs to a point directly below where the assassin had disappeared. He looked up, and his face brushed another nylon cord, nearly invisible in the gloom.

Slinging the M-16, Bolan scaled the wall. He paused at the top to scour the woods beyond. The hit team was gone, but one of them made the mistake of stepping on a dry twig.

They were heading due north, toward a secondary road four miles off.

Bolan heaved onto the wall, took but a split second to make sure no obstacles were below and dropped to the ground. The moment he alighted, he headed out in pursuit of the hitters.

The woods were mostly pine and oak, thick with brush and dotted with boulders. Bolan made a beeline, leaping logs and dodging low branches that clawed at his face and eyes. He traveled hundreds of yards and still didn't spot the men in black.

Suddenly the undergrowth ended at the verge of a lush meadow. Almost across the meadow were three dark figures, jogging at a steady pace. Bolan brought up his rifle, but they vanished before he could acquire a target.

The warrior forged on, running flat out. The next tract of forest was more open, with fewer boulders and thickets. He glimpsed the trio far ahead. As yet, they had no idea he was after them, and he exploited that for all it was worth. Legs flying, arms pumping, he gained on them bit by bit.

They had to have traveled more than a mile from the estate when Bolan came within two hundred feet of the unsuspecting trio. He slowed, pacing them, catching his breath. There was plenty of time now to confront them. All he needed was the right spot.

Then, inexplicably, the hit team halted.

Bolan flattened and fixed a bead on an ebony silhouette. They had huddled, and one of them—Talosi, Bolan guessed—was gesturing back toward the estate. The soldier wondered if they suspected he was on their trail, or whether they were waiting for another hit man to catch up. He glanced over a shoulder, just as the Rossi estate went up.

The explosion was spectacular. Spumes of flames, sparks and fiery debris gushed high into the crisp air. Despite the distance, the countryside was lit by an artificial twilight.

Now Bolan knew why the assassins hadn't bothered to drag off their dead. There wouldn't be enough left for the authorities to identify. He looked toward the trio and saw the tall man stiffen.

The dim glow was to blame. Thanks to the false twilight, Bolan was faintly visible. He flipped to the right as the three men loosed a volley, then he returned fire, triggering short bursts as they streaked into the trees. One of the men in black tottered but didn't go down.

Pushing up, Bolan pursued them, zigzagging from tree to tree. Ahead a sound suppressor belched lead, and rounds peppered the soil inches behind the soldier.

Dropping behind a log, Bolan fired a burst into a thicket, but no one retaliated. He stayed there for all of ten seconds, until convinced by the crackle of brush that the hit team had moved on. Launching himself over the log, he sought to overtake them before they reached the road.

For a while the only sounds were those of Bolan's heavy breathing and the rhythmic slapping of his soles on the ground. He estimated another mile went by, yet he never once spotted the hit team.

A knoll rose up before him. The soldier bore to the right to go around rather than risk outlining himself against the stars by going straight up and over. The turn saved his life. On the crest, a suppressed Uzi cut loose. A burst of 9 mm lead tore into the turf, spitting up chunks of earth and grass.

Bolan had to fire on the fly, from the hip. For most, it was next to impossible to score while speeding over rough terrain, but to him it was second nature. He had been in so many running firefights that he reacted without thinking, his instincts serving him in better stead than if he took precious seconds to ponder what to do.

A bulky mass at the top had to be the shooter. It didn't resemble a boulder or a log and it certainly wasn't a bush. He cored it, or came close enough that the hit man flipped back out of sight.

Bolan never slowed. He raced around the knoll and spotted a figure lurching down the slope. The assassin spun, the Uzi rising. The M-16 crackled first, and the man crashed to the ground facedown, sliding a half-dozen feet before his descent was arrested by a small tree.

The soldier hurried forward bending low to see the holes lacing the gunner's chest. There was also a wound on the left leg, just above the ankle. Bolan figured that it was the assassin he had winged a while ago. The man had realized he couldn't get away and had stayed behind to slow their pursuer.

Only two to go.

The Executioner pressed ahead, always on the lookout. For over two miles they had sustained a breakneck pace and were bound to be tiring. Even he, as superbly conditioned as he kept himself, was beginning to feel the effects of the prolonged exertion.

A plane buzzed overhead, slightly to the northwest, its lights flashing in a standard pattern.

The soldier paid it scant attention until it veered to the east and the throaty growl of the engine slowed to a purr. His suspicions mounted when the craft banked low over the woods about a mile and a half ahead.

Bolan reached into the wellspring of stamina that had yet to let him down and poured on the speed. The plane flew at a leisurely rate to the east, tilted in a wide loop and came in again, lower than the first time. He wasn't surprised when it abruptly dipped below the trees and disappeared. He knew why.

The aircraft had landed on the road.

He had to hand it to whoever had planned the raid on Luther Rossi. The mastermind had foreseen every contingency. If not for Bolan's unexpected presence, the hit team would have wiped out the mobsters and gotten clean away with no one being the wiser. Bolan's showing up when he did had been a sheer fluke.

But that was always the way in combat. No matter how carefully a man plotted, no matter how experienced he might be, there was no predicting the whims of fickle chance. If crystal balls were as reliable as crackpots claimed, the military brass of every country on the globe would have resorted to them ages ago.

At last a pair of ghostly specters materialized. Bolan estimated they had a three-hundred-yard lead. He tried to increase his speed, but he was at his limit. His lungs ached, protesting the strain. His temples pounded to the beat of his pulse.

Someone shouted, and the men managed to increase their speed a fraction.

For tense minutes the chase continued, Bolan gaining yard by yard. Blinking lights appeared in the near distance. It was the plane, parked on the rarely used road. The sight apparently inspired the hit men to greater effort. Bolan wasn't able to narrow the gap any more.

Suddenly the aircraft's engine revved, as if the pilot was preparing to make a quick getaway. Bolan was sure that Talosi had radioed ahead. His prospects of stopping them were growing slimmer by the moment.

The two men in black shot from the underbrush. They were on their last legs, so winded that they staggered the final twenty feet to the plane. A man in a suit held the cabin door open for them. Talosi and his companion piled in, sprawling onto the floor.

Bolan was almost there. He brought up the M-16, but had to seek cover when the suit produced an autopistol and fired eight shots in swift succession in his direction. The cabin door slammed shut. The engine increased to a whine, and the plane hurtled down the road.

In a last-ditch effort, Bolan broke into the open, slanting to intercept the craft, but he was too late. The pilot knew his stuff. Nose tilting almost straight up, the aircraft flashed into the sky and fled to the northwest. In moments it was out of range.

The Executioner came to a reluctant stop and stood with his hands on his hips, inhaling deeply. His comment summed up his feelings perfectly.

"Damn!"

# CHAPTER THREE

*Atlantic City, New Jersey*

Once a quaint seaside resort famous for the length of its boardwalk and the purity of its beaches, Atlantic City was now a bustling tourist trap notorious for its casinos and crowds.

Antonio Scarlotti stood on the balcony of his room in the Grand Hotel and gazed out over the sparkling panorama of the thriving city. America! he thought to himself. He had been in the country only a short while, and already he was passionately fond of it.

America possessed a raw vitality that Scarlotti found fascinating. He could feel it in the frenetic energy of city street life after the sun went down. He loved to take strolls through the seamier districts, to mingle with ravishing hookers and young toughs, to let the always present threat of violence wash over him like a welcome cold shower.

It was an added bonus, this feeling. Scarlotti had come to America to carve out an empire. He had never anticipated finding the wild, reckless atmosphere so much to his liking.

In the Old Country, everything was so different. The way of life was as sedate as that in a monastery. People were never in a rush. They went about their daily tasks with a plodding thoroughness that Scarlotti had always despised. Even his peers calmly took whatever life had to offer in stride, as the Americans might say.

Maybe tradition had something to do with it, he reflected. For thousands of years, the good citizens of Europe in general and Italy in particular had been doing things just as their fathers had done them, and their fathers had done them just as their fathers before, and so on and so on all the way back to the dawn of recorded history.

America was unique. She was a relatively young country. Traditions were cast aside as if they were chains. Each new generation wanted to live life its own way. As a result there was a sense of newness about everything. Newness, and a vitality that Scarlotti found mesmerizing.

A car horn punctuated the drone of traffic, bringing Scarlotti's musings to an end. He strode into his room, where nine members of the Camorra waited expectantly.

"Talosi is not here yet?" Antonio asked, annoyed.

Guilo Falcone, a young lieutenant whose appetite for viciousness matched Scarlotti's own, answered.

"He should be here soon, boss. The plane went to pick the boys and him up on schedule."

Scarlotti grunted and stepped to the bar. The Grand Hotel prided itself on providing every luxury that money could buy, and its staff was almost successful. A sauna, a swimming pool, a weight room and a dance floor were just a few of the extras. There was even a restaurant, open twenty-four hours of the day.

Pouring a whiskey, Scarlotti faced his soldiers. "As you all know," he intoned gravely, "it has begun. Even as I speak, our soldiers are spreading out across America to strike their assigned targets." He glanced at a trusted lieutenant named Giovanni. "What is the status?"

The beefy Neapolitan consulted a notepad. "Don Giadone has been taken care of. Our boys in Vegas report that they have disposed of three top men in the Saladina organization. On the West Coast the top Mafia kingpin just lost his lawyers and two capos."

"And that is just the beginning," Scarlotti assured his underlings. "Before this week is out, the Mafia will be leaderless, in disarray. By the end of the month we will be in complete control." He pounded the bar, declaring, "The shame of our ancestors will have been erased!"

No one so much as whispered. They hung on his every word, as always, each and every one handpicked, each and every one as loyal as a devoted Doberman and just as fierce. Scarlotti had surrounded himself with men just like himself, men whose violent natures couldn't be held in check by the flimsy restraints of law and morality.

"Our next big strike will be right here, in Atlantic City. It will let the world know that the Camorra is a force to be reckoned with. It will send a signal to the Mafia Dons that their days are numbered, and it will demonstrate to the American authorities that they had better leave us alone, or else."

One of the younger lieutenants, a sallow scarecrow considered a wizard with a switchblade, remarked, "I just hope we have enough soldiers to get the job done right, boss. There are supposed to be over two thousand Mafia members in the United States."

"And we've only snuck in one hundred and eleven of your brothers over the past year?" Scarlotti said. "Is that what worries you?"

The scarecrow nodded.

Scarlotti was too shrewd to laugh, although the idea that the Camorra couldn't handle ten times its number elicited his abiding scorn. "Perhaps some of you feel the same way," he said. "If so, you are forgetting two things. First it is not necessary to chop a viper into tiny bits in order to kill it. All you need do is chop off the head, and the rest of the snake is useless."

He let his words of wisdom sink in while he indulged in more whiskey. "The second thing to remember is that in any fight, brains are more important than brawn. So what if we are outnumbered? If we outthink them, we win. It is as simple as that."

"I'm not worried, boss!" Falcone boasted. "You've never let us down yet, and I know you never will."

Coming from anyone else, Scarlotti would have dismissed the flattery as so much manure. But Falcone had never been one to lick boots, not even his. "Another point to keep in mind is that the Mafia has grown too confident over the years. They strut about in public like peacocks, not caring who knows if they are connected. Some even act as if they are movie stars, bedding starlets and holding press conferences and the like."

Many in the room snickered or otherwise showed their contempt.

"They have made our task easy for us," Scarlotti went on. "For the most part it has been child's play to find out where they live, where they work, where they go to eat every day. They are creatures of habit, and now that we know what those habits are, we can slay them at our convenience."

The mood among the lieutenants was upbeat. Scarlotti could see it in their hawkish features, see it in the hungry gleam in their eyes. They were like a pack of ravenous wolves eager to be at their prey. *His* wolves. A sensation of pure power washed over him, tingling his spine.

At that juncture the telephone rang. Giovanni answered, covered the receiver and looked up. "What time do you want it set for, boss?"

Scarlotti consulted his watch. "It's past midnight now. We know that Castellano likes to personally oversee the counting of receipts at two." He calculated and said, "Tell them to set it for 3:00 a.m. exactly. Got that? Exactly."

Carrying his glass back onto the balcony, Scarlotti stared at the garishly lit casino to the north. It was open day and night, and word had it that every room was filled thanks to a convention of dentists. So even at three in the morning, the toll would be staggering. He smirked, pleased with himself. Everything was going according to plan.

Scarlotti gulped the last of his drink, savoring the burning warmth that spread down his throat to his stomach. It felt good to be alive. But then, killing others always had filled him with invigorating zest. Much as great painters were inspired by majestic scenery, and great poets by sublime thoughts, so did snuffing out lives thrill him as nothing else could.

By that time tomorrow, he would be in ecstasy.

JOSEPH CASTELLANO took his private elevator from the penthouse of the Blackjack Casino to the basement. Flanked by four bodyguards, he walked down a narrow hall to a door marked Restricted: Hotel Personnel Only. The security guard on duty snapped to attention and greeted him with proper deference.

"Good evening, sir. Allow me."

While the guard unlocked the door, Castellano flicked a piece of lint from the shoulder of his tailored gabardine jacket. It pleased him to think that his suit cost more than the security guard made in three months. The rings on his fingers cost more than the worthless little man made in an entire year. Why, one ring alone, a ruby as wide as Castellano's thick thumb, cost more than the President of the United States earned.

"Hurry it up," Castellano grumbled when the guard fumbled with the key ring.

"Sorry, sir."

Castellano sighed. Putting up with simpletons was the price he had to pay for being one of the most powerful men on the Eastern Seaboard. He wasn't about to use his own soldiers for petty casino duty, so he had hired a local security firm to guard the vault and police the grounds. Of course, he had kept it in the Family, more or less. The security firm was owned by his pathetic excuse for a brother-in-law. Ordinarily he would never have done business with the fool, but it made his sister happy and put food on her table. So the sacrifice was worth it.

At last the ponderous steel door swung inward, and Castellano strolled inside. The staff was busy, as usual, preparing to tally the evening's receipts.

It was no secret that one of Castellano's private pleasures was to watch all that money being sorted, stacked and counted. Some of the staff privately thought that he was simply a greedy old bastard who kept track of every penny he made. Others assumed that he wanted to skim his cut personally.

The truth was much more simple than that. Joseph Castellano *loved* money. He loved the feel of it, the smell of it, the sound of cash being riffled, of coins tinkling. A psychiatrist might say that he was compensating for the pathetic poverty he had suffered in childhood. All that mattered to Castellano was that caressing a pile of crisp greenbacks was the next best thing to fondling a woman.

This night, as always, the Blackjack's manager was on hand to welcome him. Eddy Fazio had been scraping for a living on the mean streets of Teaneck when Castellano took the boy under his wing and steered him up through the ranks. Castellano had even gone so far as to finance the kid's college education, requiring only that Fazio major in business administration. Even back then, Castellano had been thinking ahead.

"Good evening, sir," Fazio said warmly. "I have a fresh pot of coffee waiting, and those jelly doughnuts you like so much."

Castellano smiled and patted the manager's cheek. "I swear. You take better care of me than my wife does."

Fazio had heard the same joke many times, but he dutifully laughed as if his boss were as witty as the comedians who performed seven nights a week in the Blue Room. He led the way to a low platform at the rear of the room. Walled in by bulletproof glass, it was a small room in itself, decorated with the finest furniture money could buy. That included a small refrigerator.

Castellano sank into the cushions on his easy chair and drank in the sight of the mountain of money the staff was about to sort. Everything was just as he liked it. "Bring me some coffee," he commanded.

As Fazio obeyed, Castellano's private phone rang. It was mounted on a stand beside the chair. Very few people knew the number, and those who did were under strict orders never to use it unless it was important. Frowning, Castellano picked it up. "Speak."

"Joe, this is Gaito."

Castellano straightened. Don Bruno Gaito was the premier godfather in all of New York City, a close friend and a secret partner in the casino. Gaito's tone was more eloquent than any words could be.

"What is wrong?" Castellano asked.

"Giadone sleeps with the fishes."

It was a pet Mafia expression, meaning in effect that the person spoken of was dead. Castellano went as rigid as a board. Don Giadone was a close ally of theirs. Many times he had been Castellano's houseguest. "Who did it? The Tatalias?" The Tatalia Family had been at odds with Giadone for some time over who should control Miami's waterfront rackets.

"His wife and children were also killed."

Right away Castellano knew that the hit hadn't been instigated by any Mafia rivals of Giadone's. It was an ironclad part of their code that wives and kids were never, ever touched. During a Mafia war, only the soldiers and the leaders were fair game. No one would ever lay a finger on innocents. "An outside job, then," he declared. "Any ideas who?"

"Not yet. My people are making inquiries," Gaito said.

"Maybe it was the Cubans," Castellano speculated. "Giadone told me that he was having trouble with an upstart in Havana."

"I'll let you know as soon as I hear anything."

The line went dead. Deeply disturbed, Castellano hung up.

"Something wrong, boss?" one of the bodyguards asked.

"Shut up and let me think," Castellano snapped. Sinking back into his chair, he idly watched the tallying, his enthusiasm gone. Losing Giadone was like losing a brother. No, it was worse, because his brother was an idiot and Giadone had been one of his few peers, a made man, someone deserving of the highest respect. There were few of the old school left. Each loss was irreplaceable.

Fazio returned with the coffee, but Castellano waved him off and stood. "I'm going out for some air, Eddy. Have the books brought up to the penthouse after you're done and wait for me there."

Castellano couldn't exactly say why he felt compelled to leave. The tragic news aside, he felt a strange restlessness, an urge to get outdoors for a while. Buttoning his jacket, he departed, his bodyguards glued to him like fleas to an old hound dog.

He used his private exit to the parking garage. One of his soldiers slid in behind the wheel.

"Where to, boss?"

Castellano had no idea. "Just drive around the city awhile. I'll let you know when to stop."

During his youth, back when Atlantic City had been a collection of cottages and frame houses, Castellano had idled away many an hour on the long boardwalk, gorging himself on fudge and cotton candy. And now? He could never get over the change, never quite get used to the small metropolis that had sprung up in the wake of the casinos. He had liked things as they were. Yet he'd had no qualms about turning the town into the equivalent of Las Vegas East. It was just another sacrifice he'd had to make on his way to the top.

Castellano had the driver pull up at an all-night diner he had favored years earlier, back when he was a capo for a New Jersey boss. He treated himself to several cups of delicious black coffee and a chocolate-covered doughnut. For old times' sake, he gave the plump waitress the biggest tip she had ever received in her life. She gushed her gratitude.

It was close to three when Castellano left. The limo cruised slowly toward the casino. He admired the towering structure with its glittering lights and blazing blue neon arch. His baby. His masterpiece.

A block from the Blackjack the driver had to brake for a red light. Castellano rolled down his window and caught a whiff of tangy salt air. He was reaching into his jacket for a cigar when he heard a peculiar rumbling, such as a subway train in the distance might make. Only there was no subway in Atlantic City. Besides, he was aboveground.

Castellano looked up, and gaped. His breath caught in his throat. He wanted to scream, but his vocal cords were paralyzed. All he could do was sit there, helpless, as his world, quite literally, came crashing down before his eyes.

MARTHA GATES WAS GIDDY with glee. Her cheapskate of a husband had finally agreed to take her to one of his conventions. Two days earlier they had arrived in Atlantic City and booked into the Blackjack Casino, along with hundreds of other dentists and their families from around the country.

For two days Martha had played the slots and tried her hand at blackjack and poker. She had caught several shows. She had eaten in the fancy restaurant where a single item on the menu cost as much as a family of four would spend back in her hometown of Suttons Corner, Georgia.

It was a dream come true.

Earlier that evening the Gateses had attended a banquet. She had pestered Bob into dancing until well past midnight. Now they were back in their room, in bed, Bob snoring loud enough to rouse the dead, Martha reading a magazine about how to keep the romance in a marriage. She was so keyed up that she couldn't get to sleep.

Martha glanced at the clock on the nightstand. It was almost three in the morning. She read another paragraph and snickered at the notion of trying to entice her husband by wearing lacy negligees. Knowing Bob, he'd be more apt to laugh at her than get aroused. When it came to making love, the man had all the finesse of a bull and all the sensitivity of a clam.

At that moment the bed gave a little shake, as if someone had bumped against it. Martha looked around, puzzled. From deep within the casino came a faint sound, sort of like the pop of a balloon, only barely audible. It was followed by three or four more bizarre popping noises.

Shrugging, Martha buried her nose in the magazine. Suddenly the whole room seemed to shake. She sat bolt upright, wondering if an earthquake might be the cause. But that was ridiculous, she mused. New Jersey never had earthquakes.

A new sound fell on Martha's ears, a steady rumbling that grew steadily louder, as if she were in the middle of train tracks and a train were coming closer and closer. She started to rise, to go to the window.

With an ear-shattering roar the floor under the bed buckled and split. Martha screamed and clutched at Bob as their bed and all the other furniture plummeted into open space. Her husband pushed up onto his elbow, shaking his head to clear it, too shocked to say anything.

Martha's scream rose to a strident shriek of mortal terror when she saw large chunks of the ceiling falling toward them. It dawned on her that the entire casino had to be collapsing, that it really was an earthquake. Either that or the end of the world.

"Bob!" Martha wailed, flinging her arms around her man. He embraced her. They locked eyes. It was the last sight either of them ever saw.

Countless tons of concrete and steel reduced the couple from Georgia to human pancakes in a fraction of a second. Their flesh was pulped, every bone in their bodies splintered. It happened so quickly that they felt only a twinge of pain, and then nothing.

Had anyone been able to ask them, they would have said that it was small consolation.

*Washington, D.C.*

AT 4:00 A.M. the phone jangled. Hal Brognola struggled up out of deep slumber, striving to jumpstart his brain. His tongue felt as thick as molasses when he said, "Brognola here."

"Good morning, sir. You asked to be notified if any other unusual Mob reports came over the wire?"

In a flash Brognola was fully awake. It was the agent in charge of the night shift at the Justice building. "You have something new?"

"Turn on your television, sir."

"What?" Brognola said, not sure if he had heard correctly.

"CNN, sir."

"Hang on." Brognola set down the receiver and

shuffled to the set in the corner of his bedroom. Yawning, he flicked it on and manually selected the right channel. It took a few moments for what he was seeing to sink in.

A reporter stood in the foreground, microphone in hand. She was disheveled, as if she had been roused from sleep and sped to the scene of the disaster behind her. For it clearly was a disaster. In the background was the rubble of an enormous building, smoke and dust still rising from the ruins. Part of one wall still stood, but little else. Brognola concentrated to catch her comments.

"—as yet have no idea what caused the collapse. A gas leak was initially suspected, but that has now been ruled out. Emergency personnel are searching for survivors, but they are not optimistic."

Brognola didn't see what any of this had to do with the Mob. He began to go to the phone but froze at the next words out of the reporter's mouth.

"Police have refused to confirm a source that links the owner of the Blackjack Casino to organized crime. Nor will they confirm speculation that a bomb was involved, although CNN has learned that the bomb squad has been called in."

The full implication hit Hal Brognola with the force of a baseball bat. The next remark barely registered.

"It will be days, perhaps weeks, before the final death toll is known, but already officials are privately saying that it will be higher than Oklahoma City, possibly the highest in U.S. history. Practically every room was taken. And many gamblers were still at the tables and slots—''

Brognola scooped up the phone. ''I'm back, Davis,'' he said, a lump in his throat. ''I want you to contact all department heads. They are to be at my office in one hour. No exceptions.''

''Yes, sir.'' Davis paused. ''Do you think we have another Mob war on our hands?''

''At this point I don't know what the hell to think,'' Brognola confessed. ''All I do know is that it's bound to get a lot worse before it gets any better.''

''God help us, sir.''

''You can say that again.''

## CHAPTER FOUR

Mack Bolan took one glance at his friend and said, "You look like death warmed over."

"Flatterer," Hal Brognola groused while sinking onto the bench. He rubbed his tired eyes and barely noticed when a pigeon scared by a jogger fluttered past. They were in East Potomac Park, not far from the Jefferson Memorial. "It's been a long day," he said.

Bolan had shifted his gaze to the cherry trees, which were in full bloom. "Have your people come up with anything concrete yet?"

"Tidbits here and there," Brognola said. "It's like trying to put a jigsaw puzzle together when most of the pieces are missing. The only thing we know for certain is that someone has declared open season on the Mafia. Our informants all agree that it's not an internal affair. The top bosses are worried. Apparently a big meet has been called, but we don't have any idea yet where it will be held."

Bolan looked at the big Fed again. Really looked. It occurred to him that he had seldom seen Brognola so haggard, so transparently upset. "Have you learned any more about the casino bombing?"

"Only that Joseph Castellano wasn't in the building when it came crashing to the ground. Word is that he's gone underground and pulled the rug in after him. His people are on a war footing, prepared to go to the mat against anyone and everyone."

"What about the hit man I brought down in New York?"

A glimmer of hope etched Brognola's face. "We're still working on it. He wasn't carrying any identification, not even a phony driver's license. A computer check of his fingerprints failed to turn up any stateside priors, so I've sent them overseas to see whether Scotland Yard, the Sûreté and Interpol have anything." The big Fed's brow puckered. "Our best guess is that he's Italian."

"The Italian Mafia, you think?"

Brognola shook his head. "It wouldn't make sense. The Italian Mafia and the mafiosi in our country have always gotten along well. If this is a power play by an Italian hothead, you'd think someone in the Mafia here would know about it. Yet they are all as stumped as we are."

A high-pitched squeal drew Bolan's attention to several children playing tag. They reminded him of the news coverage he had viewed before Brognola called and requested a meet. The camera had caught a fireman in the act of pulling the body of a little girl from the wreckage. "How high is the body count now?"

Brognola folded his hands and bowed his chin. "The last I heard, it was seventy-three and climbing. Unofficially they believe the final total will be over four hundred. Probably closer to six."

"It gets worse every year, doesn't it?"

Brognola didn't need to ask what his friend meant. "What sort of animal could do this? Even by Mafia standards, it's sickening. All those poor innocents snuffed out, just because someone wanted to waste Castellano. It has to be a bona fide psycho."

"With a well-oiled organization at his beck and call," Bolan added. "He's hitting targets all over the country simultaneously. And judging by what I saw at Rossi's estate, these people know their business. We're not up against amateurs."

"Who, though?" Brognola voiced the question that had been plaguing him for hours. "Who has enough manpower and firepower and a big enough bankroll to butt heads with the Mafia?"

Bolan had no answer to that one.

Running a hand through his hair, Brognola asked, "Do you want in on this one or not?" Long ago they had established that Bolan only handled those jobs he wanted to handle. The soldier was a freelance operative, able to pick and choose as he desired.

An image of the little girl who had been pulled from the rubble popped into Bolan's mind. "Need you ask?" he rejoined. "Whoever is doing this has to be stopped before a lot more bystanders lose their lives.''

''I just wish we had a concrete lead you could work with. I know how much you hate to sit around twiddling your thumbs.''

As if on cue, Brognola's pager chirped. He checked the digital display. ''It's the office. I'll check in and be right back.''

Bolan contented himself with watching the boats on the Potomac River. He hoped that it wouldn't take the Feds long to develop solid leads. The longer it did, the more people would die.

There were times, such as now, when the status quo bothered him even more than it usually did. The senseless loss of those who had never done any wrong was an outrage. Those poor conventioneers at the casino hadn't done anything to deserve their grisly fate, other than being in the wrong place at the wrong time.

Part of the reason Bolan waged his eternal war against those who committed such atrocities was to spare future victims. Unless there was someone willing to stand up for those who could not stand up for themselves, the wolves of the world would go on slaughtering the sheep to their heart's content.

It wasn't fair.

There were some who might claim that Bolan was no better than those he hunted down, that he was as much an ogre as they were for taking human life. But anyone who would make such an accusation had no idea what the world was truly like. They had deluded themselves into thinking that brotherly love was the rule rather than the exception.

There had always been two-legged rabid wolves. Unless human nature changed drastically, there always would be.

It fell to Bolan, and those like him, to keep the man-eaters from devouring the flock.

Hal Brognola appeared, walking briskly, a new spring in his step. A grin spread from ear to ear. His whole demeanor had changed, and he started to talk before he had sat down. "You must be my lucky charm."

"A break?" Bolan said.

"Interpol came through. The deceased is one Paolo Borsellino. Born and raised in Naples. Arrested twice, once for strong-arm stuff, again for robbery. Both charges were thrown out by the same judge."

"Naples?" Bolan repeated. "So there is a Mafia war going on?"

"Not quite. Borsellino was a known member of the Camorra."

Bolan pondered a few moments. The name rang a vague bell, but for the life of him he couldn't recall why. "Why do I have a feeling that I should know who they are?"

"You've never gone up against them before, if that's what you're thinking," Brognola clarified. "Odds are that you heard about them back when you infiltrated the Mafia."

It came back to Bolan then, a jumbled remembrance of a criminal organization a lot like the Mafia but based in Naples, Italy. "They only operate in Europe. Or so I was told."

"Back then they did, but they've branched out in recent years. Since they've never made trouble here before, I only know a little about them."

"I'm all ears," Bolan urged.

The big Fed was being too modest. He knew more than a "little." Half an hour later the Executioner had a much better appreciation of what they were up against. The information was unsettling.

To all intents and purposes, the Camorra was their worst nightmare made real.

*Ocean City, New Jersey*

OCEAN CITY WAS another tourist mecca but without the casinos. It retained a small-town flavor except during the summer months, when hordes of sun worshipers transformed it into a madhouse.

A quarter of a mile south of the town limits, an isolated cottage sat on a barren point of land that jutted into the Atlantic Ocean.

Lying on top of a sand dune sixty yards to the southwest, Mack Bolan studied the darkened structure for sign of life. There was none. No lights were on, no vehicles were parked on the gravel driveway.

Bolan wore a brown sports jacket, a dark shirt and jeans. His blacksuit and most of his lethal gear were in his duffel, which at that moment was in the trunk of the rented car he'd driven from Philadelphia International Airport to Ocean City. The car itself was hidden several hundred feet up the road from the sand dunes.

There had been a break in the case. A minor one, to be sure, but one Brognola felt Bolan should personally investigate.

All day the Feds had been poring over passenger lists, checking passport records and doing everything else in their power to try to find out exactly how many members of the Camorra were in the country and who they were.

The FBI had taken over the investigation of the Blackjack Casino bombing and its agents were sifting through the debris with a fine-tooth comb. Teams of agents had spread out across the city, following up every lead, no matter how insubstantial.

But local police had to take the credit for the tidbit that lured Bolan to Ocean City.

It turned out that just that morning, the Ocean City Police Department had received a complaint from a tourist, a fisherman who had been casting at dawn near the barren point. He had seen three men target shooting with what the fisherman swore were automatic weapons.

The Ocean City dispatcher had quizzed him and learned that the men hadn't endangered the fisherman in any way. The tourist doubted that they knew he was there. When she pointed out that no crime had been committed, that some citizens were licensed to own automatic weapons and could use them on private property with legal impunity and that, in any event, the cottage was outside the jurisdiction of the Ocean City police, the tourist had done what irate tourists always did and called her every name in the book.

When the desk sergeant saw the report, he'd had the presence of mind to contact the FBI. He'd seen the news reports about the bombing. He'd heard the rumors that organized crime was involved. Any link to the target shooters was tenuous, but he felt the Feds should know.

The Bureau had done some digging and discovered the cottage was being rented to three foreign tourists. "Italian fellows," the landlady was quoted as saying. "Quiet bunch. Very well mannered."

So here Bolan was, at ten-fifteen at night, his fingers sunk in fine sand, the ocean lapping at the shore to his right, a stiff wind from the northwest rustling scattered pockets of tall grass. The Beretta was nestled under his left arm, the Desert Eagle in a custom holster on his right hip.

The soldier stared off up the highway. No cars were coming. None had gone by for quite some time. Taking a gamble, he rose and jogged to a sandbank that bordered the cottage to the south. No sounds came from inside.

Drawing the big .44 Magnum pistol, Bolan climbed over the bank and crossed the gravel driveway. The door was locked. So was a window. He went around to a small patio that faced the sea. A sliding door resisted his tug.

On the north side of the cottage was another window. Bolan pulled on the bottom rail without really expecting it to budge. To his surprise it did, and in another moment he had eased a leg over the sill and was crouched in the dark in what had to be the living room.

A sofa lined one wall. Chairs had been pushed back against another, and a table had been shoved into a corner in order to make space in the center of the floor for a huge pile of boxes and crates.

Bolan checked the other rooms. The single bedroom and a cramped kitchen were empty. A large stack of dirty pots and dishes hinted that the so-called tourists very rarely ate out.

Back in the living room, Bolan examined the pile. The first box he inspected contained ammunition. One of the crates had been pried open, the lid left on the floor. Inside were enough Uzis to outfit a regiment. Or a regime.

The tip had paid off. It had been a one-in-a-million shot. Now all Bolan had to do was get back to his vantage point and wait for the Camorrans to return.

But as he rose, the growl of a car's engine heralded the arrival of the renters. He rushed to the window as gravel crunched under heavy tires. Slipping out, he closed the window, hearing brakes squeak on the other side of the cottage. Then voices murmured.

Bending, Bolan sprinted to the northeast corner, intending to dash past the patio to the beach and work his way around to the sand dunes. He assumed the Camorrans would enter though the door fronting the driveway. But he was wrong. Their muted talk grew louder as they grew nearer.

The Camorrans were coming around to the patio.

Bolan squatted, an eye pressed to the corner. Five men appeared, not three. Two of them carried grocery bags, while another had a newspaper. With their dark hair, their similar features and their identical builds, they could have been brothers of the hit man Bolan shot in upstate New York.

The Executioner was as still as a statue as one of them unlocked the sliding door and entered. Two others trailed him in, but the last pair settled into beach chairs on the patio. Bolan couldn't get past them without being seen. His only option was to slink back under the window to the west end of the cottage and from there sneak off into the dunes.

He started to do so when one of the Camorrans spoke.

"It goes well, Carlo, don't you think?"

"Yes," answered the other. "Just as he said it would. I tell you, Lucci, he is the greatest leader we have ever had. He could be a general, this one."

"Did you see how mad he was at Talosi? I thought he would rip him apart with his bare hands!"

"Do you blame Tony? Talosi lost five good men and was almost caught himself." Carlo snorted.

"Then he had the gall to claim that it wasn't a Mafia pig who killed Ligrani and the others, that it was someone who could move like a ghost and see in the dark like a cat."

Lucci joined in the mirth. "If I did not know Talosi better, I would say that he lost his nerve. But he has never let Tony down before."

"That is the only reason Tony spared him this time," Carlo said.

Bolan was no longer in any hurry to leave, not when he might learn valuable intel. The way they talked about the man named Tony indicated that he might be their leader.

The Camorrans were quiet for a while, listening to the hiss of the surf, until Lucci coughed. "I would not want anyone else to hear me say this because word might get back to the boss, but I do not like being here. I miss the Old Country."

"What you miss is that ravishing woman of yours," Carlo joked. "Be patient, my friend. We all have a job to do. Once it is over, I'm sure you will be given permission to go home."

"But what if I'm not? You know yourself that Tony plans to have most of us stay on to take over Mafia operations. By the end of the year he plans to bring in seventy more of us." Lucci shook his head. "It is a mistake to divide us up like he is doing."

Carlo glanced at the patio door. "Be careful no one else hears you talk like that. He doesn't like to have his decisions questioned."

Lucci ignored him. "I don't know about the rest of you, but I never wanted to leave Italy. I was perfectly content there." He gestured inland. "America is so strange, so different. The way of life here is nothing like that we are used to. I miss the quiet pace."

"You miss your wife," Carlo reiterated.

The sliding door opened and another Camorran joined them. "The food will be ready in five minutes," he announced.

"Spaghetti off a grocery shelf!" Lucci complained. "It tastes like paper."

The newcomer patted his belly. "It is filling, at any rate."

He turned to Carlo. "When do we leave for the meeting?"

"Tony wants everyone there by 2:00 a.m."

Apparently Lucci was one of those people who could gripe about everything. "There is something else that bothers me. Why must we skulk around in the dark so much? In the Old Country we could go right out in broad daylight and kill our enemies."

Carlo had no sympathy. "I swear, you become more like my grandmother every day. She would moan and groan if she broke a fingernail."

Bolan intended to eavesdrop longer, but the man who had joined Lucci and Carlo suddenly came toward the corner of the patio where another folding chair had been propped. Ducking back, Bolan sped along the wall, dropping to his hands and knees when he was close to the window. He wanted to avoid a clash if he could. In a few hours, hopefully, they would unwittingly lead him to their boss.

At the very moment that the soldier crawled under the window, it was jerked upward. "—nice to have some fresh air in here. It is too stuffy."

Bolan looked up into the astonished face of the Camorran who had poked his head out. The man grabbed for a pistol in a shoulder holster, his draw fluid lightning. Since Bolan already had the .44 out, he only had to snap the big pistol up and stroke the trigger.

Kicked upward by the impact of the heavy slug, the triggerman smashed into the window, cracking the bottom rail and breaking the pane. His brains and a good portion of his skull splattered the room behind him.

Bolan stood and ran, followed by shouts and bullets. Lead bit into the wall at his shoulder. He reached the far corner and dodged around it.

The Executioner sprinted toward the dunes, the only available cover, but he had to cross the gravel driveway first. The front door was flung open when he was halfway across. Acting on impulse, he dived to the right. An Uzi chattered, and miniature geysers of dirt and flying stones tracked him as he flipped off the edge of the road and up against a dune.

"Over here!" the gunner in the doorway bellowed. "I see him!"

The soldier still entertained the idea of shadowing the Camorrans to where the mastermind directing their operation was holed up. To do so, he had to leave at least one alive. Which made the Camorran with the Uzi expendable.

The Desert Eagle roared, slamming Bolan's target to the gravel. Another shooter promptly appeared in the doorway, while Carlo and Lucci rushed from the patio.

Bolan sprinted around the dune and in among other gullies. His feet sank into the sand so deeply, it slowed him. Gruff yells alerted him that the Camorrans were fanning out as they converged.

Passing a half-dozen mounds, Bolan paused to trade the .44 for the Beretta. From an inner jacket pocket he removed the suppressor. Now he could fight back without giving his position away.

Since the Camorrans had no idea who he was, and probably mistook him for a Mafia soldier, they'd expect him to make for the highway to escape. So Bolan did the opposite. He trotted toward the ocean, never once revealing himself. At the last dune he went to ground.

It was high tide. A strip of beach thirty feet wide stretched as far to the north and south as Bolan could see. He was content to stay where he was until the Camorrans stopped hunting, but soft footfalls provided proof that one of them was too close for comfort and coming closer.

Bolan snaked toward the water, relying on the moonless night to shroud him. His jacket, shirt and pants were caked with wet sand when he stopped a few feet from the incoming waves. Lying parallel to the waterline, he scoured the shore.

Through breaks in the dunes he could see Lucci and one other hardman. A dozen yards apart, they signaled using hand motions. Lucci turned to the south. The second hardman cautiously walked forward. He didn't seem to know that Bolan was there; he was scouring the beach in both directions.

Once the shooter was close enough, Bolan would be plainly visible. Silently he slid backward into the surf. The icy water brought goose bumps to his skin. His clothes were soaked in seconds, clinging to him like a clammy second skin. He kept going until he was submerged up to his chest.

The Camorran had halted halfway to the ocean, and Bolan decided it would be prudent to retreat a little farther. He extended his left hand to brace himself, and winced when it flared with pain.

Floating beside him was a huge jellyfish, the kind that could put a man in the hospital—or kill him.

## CHAPTER FIVE

Commonly known as the Lion's Mane, the bell-shaped jellyfish grew to be two feet high and over eight feet wide. A typical specimen had over 150 tentacles. They ranged from the Arctic to Mexico and were often washed in close to shore, where they stung dozens of people each year. Most of the time contact caused severe burning and painful blisters. But anyone stung more than once or twice could count on suffering extreme cramps. In some cases, it became hard for the victims to breathe, and unless they were put on respirators right away, the outlook was grim.

The Executioner had no desire to wind up in intensive care. Drawing his hand back, he was going to slide away from the creature when he saw the Camorran coming toward him. He couldn't move until the man went away.

Hoping his dark clothing blended into the murky water well enough to camouflage him, Bolan attempted the impossible feat of keeping one eye on the gunner and the other on the jellyfish. The Camorran squatted at the water's edge and dipped a hand in. Cupping it, he wet his neck and chin. He gazed at the stars, then at the horizon.

Amazingly the man didn't spot Bolan, who had dipped his face into the salt water to just below his nostrils. Wave after wave rolled over him, plastering his hair to his head.

Suddenly a spasm of raw agony lanced up Bolan's left arm. For a few moments he had been so intent on the triggerman that he had taken his attention from the jellyfish. It had moved toward him and was brushing his forearm.

Bolan sidled to the right. The gunner had stood and appeared to be making up his mind which way to go. Another searing sensation racked the Executioner's left side.

At long last the gunner hiked northward. Bolan waited until the man was out of earshot, then crabbed toward dry land. The jellyfish, incredibly, dogged him, floating nearer and nearer as if seeking to prevent his escape.

The water fell to six inches in depth, then four, then Bolan was out and on his knees, the surf gurgling at his heels. The jellyfish had stopped and was bobbing in the swell, a pale glob against the background of black sea.

Someone shouted up by the cottage. A gunner in the dunes answered, then Lucci came running along the beach. Bolan had to hug the sand or be discovered. The chronic complainer dashed by without so much as looking his way.

Commotion at the cottage attracted the Executioner's attention. The three surviving Camorrans were loading the stash of ammo and weapons into their vehicle. The man whose name Bolan didn't know stood guard while Carlo and Lucci did the work.

"—will be mad that we defied his orders," Lucci was saying. "He's liable to stomp us to death like he did that informer. Remember?"

"Don't remind me," Carlo said. "Just work."

As soon as the trunk was filled, they piled ordnance into the back seat, leaving enough space for one of them to sit. They had boxes of ammo left over, which they stacked in the middle of the front seat.

"We're all set," Lucci declared.

"Are you growing careless? We must wipe everything off to erase our prints," Carlo said. "Come on."

Bolan hurried to his sedan. He had a spare set of clothes in his duffel. After changing, he transferred the duffel bag to the front floor, locked and loaded the M-16 and placed it on the seat next to him, then climbed onto the roof so he could see above the reeds.

The Camorrans were filing out from the cottage. Carlo slid in behind the wheel. He peeled out of the driveway, and turned north toward Ocean City.

Bolan didn't start his engine until their taillights were the size of fireflies. Gunning it, he slewed up onto the highway and rapidly accelerated. There was no need to bury the gas pedal, though. The

Camorrans were traveling at the speed limit, apparently to avoid attracting the unwanted attention of the local police. He could hang well back and not lose them.

The situation changed once they reached Ocean City. Traffic was heavy through the center of town. Bolan had to close the gap to keep them in sight. Wisely he always permitted one or two cars to come between them. Once he was caught by a light change and had to wait for the green. By then the Camorrans were three blocks ahead. It took considerable skill on his part to catch up without being obvious.

Bolan wasn't surprised when the trio passed on through Ocean City and continued due north. He was surprised, though, when they rode through downtown Atlantic City without stopping. He had taken it for granted that they would meet their boss there. His surprise mounted when the Camorrans turned onto the Atlantic City Expressway, bearing west, toward Philadelphia. In a few miles they took the Garden State Parkway north.

He concluded that their leader was hiding out in a small town along the north coast, just as they had hid in Ocean City. They passed exit after exit. When they went by Toms River, he began to wonder. When Lake Riveria and Parkway Pines fell behind them, he guessed the truth. And when the bright lights of Staten Island dominated the skyline, he knew for sure.

They were heading for New York City.

Bolan had to notify Brognola as soon as possible. Trailing the Camorrans across open country was one thing. Keeping tabs on them in the heart of the crowded megalopolis without being spotted would be a lot simpler if he had a team of federal agents to back him up.

Fortunately the Camorrans stuck to major arteries. After crossing the bridge, they took the Richmond Parkway into Staten Island. They slowed at the Arden Avenue Exit, but it proved a false alarm.

Bolan's chore was compounded by their sedate speed. They never went over the limit and hugged the slow lane as if their lives depended on it.

At the Staten Island Expressway they turned right. Bolan frowned, since it meant they might cross into Brooklyn. Sure enough, they did. The traffic became heavier, forcing Bolan to stay not more than a single car behind them at all times.

Then they got lost.

It became self-evident when Bolan followed them around the same block three times. Afterward they circled in ever widening circles, searching for an address. Twice they pulled to the curb, and Lucci got out to check building numbers. Bolan had to hope that they were so busy trying to find their destination, the driver wasn't paying much attention to the rearview mirror.

This went on for forty-five minutes. Finally the Camorrans got smart and stopped to ask directions. They wound up in South Brooklyn, north of Gowanus Bay, in a seedy waterfront district no sane person would be caught dead in at that time of night. They parked in the lot of a run-down warehouse and hustled inside.

Bolan had hung back when he saw them braking. He killed the engine and coasted to a stop at the curb a block and a half away. They never noticed him. He locked all four doors and glided along the sidewalk until he was abreast of a shabby fence that ringed the warehouse. Light shone from a broken window high on the building.

There were nineteen vehicles in the parking lot. Most were cars, several were vans and there was one pickup.

The soldier was about to slip through the open gate when an orange dot flared near the door through which Carlo and the others had entered. Lookouts had been posted. Bolan casually walked on, acting as if he had no interest in the warehouse whatsoever.

Once past the front, he sought a means of gaining entry. Thirty yards farther on he spied a hole in the bottom of the chain-link fence. Seeming barely big enough for a ten-year-old kid to squeeze through, it had to do.

Scouring the street for pedestrians and confirming there were none, Bolan dropped onto his side, pried at the links to widen them and wriggled his shoulders into the gap. It was a tight squeeze. Jagged links tore at his jacket, and the left sleeve ripped. He had to push hard before he could snake through and rise in black shadows that would hide him.

Moving toward the rear of the warehouse, Bolan discovered another wide lot. This one also contained vehicles, but they were all trucks rented from at least three different rental companies. Some were yellow, others orange and white, others brown. He counted ten of them, four of the trailers over thirty feet long.

What did the Camorra plan to do with so many? Bolan asked himself. What could they possibly have to transport? Weapons and ammunition, maybe?

He went on to the rear. A stone wall flanked the structure. There was a door, but like the one out front it was guarded. A hefty gunner stood with his back against the wall, a weapon slung over a shoulder, humming softly.

Bolan crouched and drew a dagger from an ankle sheath on his right leg. His other hand roved the ground and came up with a suitable piece of loose asphalt. Focusing on a spot well beyond the gunner, he threw the chunk in an arc.

Predictably the man wheeled when the piece hit and started to unsling his weapon.

In a driving rush, Bolan was on him. At the last moment the gunner heard him and tried to turn, but the Executioner rammed a shoulder into his backbone and the man went down as if clubbed. He gouged a knee into the small of the Camorran's back even as he yanked on the gunner's hair with one hand and slit the man's throat.

The lookout thrashed and sputtered, but he couldn't throw Bolan off. In less than thirty seconds it was over, the body twitching in a spreading pool of its own blood.

Bolan helped himself to the man's weapon. It was a *lupara,* a special shotgun favored by the Mafia in Italy. Apparently the Camorrans were fond of them, as well. At close range, if loaded with buckshot, a *lupara* could practically blow a man in two.

The door creaked when Bolan pulled, and he froze. When no challenge issued from within, he opened it wide enough for him to slip into a narrow, murky hall. Muffled voices came from the bowels of the warehouse. A lot of men were talking at once.

Bolan hurried forward. The first door he came to was open. Empty shelves lined the walls of a long room. Lying close to the door was an object about the size of his shoe. He looked closer, his brow furrowing. It was a roller skate, covered with dust and lacking laces.

At the end of the hall another door opened onto a wide hall. The voices were much louder here. He moved warily toward yet another doorway to his right, staying to one side to avoid bright light that spilled through.

Bolan had been wrong about the building being an old warehouse. It had been a skating rink. Floorboards once polished to a fine sheen were now caked with dust and footprints. The outer railing was still in place although cracked in spots. Where once the rink would have been jam-packed with happy skaters of all ages, it was now packed with dozens of black-haired men in dark suits, armed to the teeth.

The soldier drew back. He had hit the jackpot. But there were far too many Camorrans for him to take them on by himself. He needed the Feds more than ever.

Bolan headed for the hall. He took only a single step when the hubbub in the rink abruptly died. A few Camorrans clapped lightly, and then it sounded as all of them had joined in. He had to learn why.

Four newcomers had arrived. Three were typical soldiers. The fourth man, though, was tall and aristocratic, carrying himself as if he were a Roman emperor come to review his legions. Something in his bearing and appearance reminded Bolan of a bird of prey, a great eagle or hawk. Here was a natural born predator. It took no leap of logic to conclude that Bolan was seeing the leader of the Camorra.

Here was a golden opportunity. All the Executioner needed was one clear shot, and he could put a stop to the bloodshed and the slaughter of innocents. He frowned when the tall man bore to the right, to a counter clear across the rink.

Some of the gunners commenced a low chant. "Salute!" they called out, over and over.

A hardman produced a chair, which the leader

used to climb on top of the counter. The instant he lifted both arms, the rink fell silent. He exercised total command, absolute mastery of the small army of killers.

Bolan was impressed. There were Mafia Dons who didn't inspire such complete devotion. The man addressed his followers in Italian.

"My brothers, you will be glad to hear that all goes well!" More applause broke out but was promptly stifled when the man motioned. The soldiers hung on his every gesture, his every word. "Yes, you should be pleased. But do not become overconfident. The hardest part is yet to come. Tonight, we cripple the Mafia's Eastern operations. Then it is on to Chicago."

During the leader's pause, Bolan noticed one of the gunners idly glance toward the doorway. He jerked from sight and waited half a minute before peering out. The gunner had faced the counter again.

"Our losses so far have been low," the tall man with the cruel features was saying. "Five of our brothers were lost on the Rossi hit, and one was lost eliminating Donato and his lieutenants."

Bolan had heard that name before. Rudy Donato was—or had been—the top Philly mafiaso.

"On the West Coast," the leader said, "we have not lost a single soldier. Nine Mafia pigs have gone to sleep with the fishes."

Bolan mentally filed the news to relay to Brognola later. It meant there were more Camorrans in the country than those at the rink. Perhaps a lot more than anyone suspected.

The tall man laughed, particularly sinister mirth devoid of any humor. "Our informants tell us that the Mafia bigwigs still do not know who is toppling them like clay pigeons on a shooting range. They have called for a meeting of all the top men, playing right into our hands."

A stocky man who stood near the counter said loud enough for all to hear, "I still can't believe how easy it has been."

A few of those near him visibly stiffened, as if his statement implied not enough faith in their leader. But the tall man took the remark in stride.

"It is the price they pay for living high-profile lives, Giovanni. It is the price they pay for growing fat and lazy. It is the price they pay for not keeping their mouths shut when they should. It is the price they pay for having people in their organization who will sell them out for money." The tall man's contempt was thick enough to cut with a knife. "Our enemies are like wolves that have been domesticated. They have lost the raw edge all wild wolves have. They have forgotten what it takes to survive. They gorge themselves on food and wine and women, their muscles turning to flab, their minds to mush. They delude themselves into thinking they are as fierce as their forefathers, when in truth they are no more fierce than an overfed poodle."

When the leader stopped, a young tough next to

Giovanni pumped a fist upward and shouted, "Death to the Mafia! Long live the Camorra!"

The cry was taken up by every throat. It became a litany of pride and exultation. The tall man let it go on and on, smiling paternally all the while, smiling even broader when the same tough began bellowing, "To-ny! To-ny! To-ny!," making a gleeful refrain of the name which was mimicked by every Camorran.

Bolan had witnessed enough. He sprinted to the narrow hall. If all went well, Brognola could have agents there within half an hour.

Outside, he took the precaution of dragging the dead lookout over against the wall to delay the finding of the body. He made it to the chain-link fence without incident and squeezed through the hole.

The guard out front had disappeared. Inside, Bolan guessed, attending the meeting. He ran toward his car. As he crossed the intersection, he glanced up the side street and saw a phone booth at the end of the block, bathed in the glare of a streetlight. Just what he needed.

The door rattled noisily. One side of the booth had been kicked in, and shards lay on the floor. Bolan raised the receiver to his ear while rummaging in a pocket for a quarter. He went to insert the coin, then realized there was no dial tone. Jiggling the switch hook did no good, nor did punching several buttons. Something brushed his arm as he moved it, and he looked down to find the cord dangling at his elbow. Vandals had ripped it from its housing.

Slamming down the receiver, Bolan hastened back down the block to his car. He was rounding the corner when the front door to the skating rink opened, disgorging Camorrans in a steady stream. For a few seconds he thought they were coming after him, but they bent their steps to the left, going around the rink to where the rental trucks were parked.

Bolan hiked his collar, shoved his hands into his pockets and crossed the street to get a better view. The triggermen were piling into the backs of the moving vans.

A mailbox stood on the corner. Bolan took a wad of bills out and pretended to be sorting through them. From a distance, it would appear as if he were sorting through mail before depositing it.

As the trucks roared to life, Bolan tugged on the swivel door and feigned sticking letters in. Turning away from the rink, he aimed to cross the street to his car, then tail the Camorrans when they pulled out. Once more, nothing went as he wanted it to.

The first truck barreled out of the gate when Bolan had gone only a dozen steps. It turned to the right. The second truck turned to the left. The third came on straight, passed Bolan and rumbled on to the next junction where it, too, turned. One by one the other trucks departed in different directions.

The chance to snare most of the Camorrans in one fell swoop had been blown. They were fanning out across the city. Given their performance to date, Bolan speculated that hit teams were being dispatched to take down various targets. The moving vans were cover, a sly ruse to get them close to their quarry without being suspected.

Since shadowing all the Camorrans would be impossible, Bolan had to pick one truck and stick with it. Intentionally he didn't look up when another went past. By his reckoning, it was the last. He glimpsed a lone gunman in the cab. The Camorran wore a denim jacket and a baseball cap.

The truck wasn't moving very fast. Gears crunched as the driver shifted. Bolan seized the moment and darted to the rear of the moving van. He leaped onto the bumper step, his left hand snagging a handle on the door. Holding on, he steadied himself, then vaulted higher, his fingers catching the rim of the roof, his right foot seeking and gaining a toehold on the handle. Coiling his shoulders, Bolan pushed upward, flipping onto the roof just as the truck took the next corner much too sharply.

Bolan lost his grip on the roof. Centrifugal force propelled him toward the left side. He was a hair's width from the brink when he managed to stop himself by pressing both palms flat and scraping his shoes on the smooth surface.

The truck straightened, permitting Bolan to scoot to the middle of the roof and crawl forward until he was above the cab. Here he was reasonably safe. He could hang on to the edge without being dislodged every time the vehicle turned, and the driver couldn't spot him in the side mirrors.

Bolan could tell that the man didn't have much experience handling a truck. The gunner worked the gears too hard, grinding them constantly. Thanks to the noise, Bolan was fairly certain that no one inside the van had heard him climb on top.

It was now so late that traffic was sparse. Few pedestrians were out and about. The truck had covered six or seven blocks when Bolan spotted a beat cop up ahead. He slid rearward and flattened until the van had gone by.

The light traffic was one of the reasons Bolan had decided to hitch a ride rather than tail the truck. He couldn't risk being detected. Now all he had to do was take it easy until they got to wherever they were going.

Then the driver took a left, and Bolan spotted a sign that read No Trucks Allowed. The Camorran either couldn't read English or he didn't care. The road dipped. Beyond was a train trestle and an underpass. Another sign had been posted to warn motorists of the dangerously low clearance.

To Bolan's consternation, the driver increased speed. Blissfully unaware of the peril, the man barreled along at fifty miles per hour, the gaping maw of the underpass looming closer and closer.

## CHAPTER SIX

The Executioner galvanized into action the instant that he perceived the danger. Scrambling forward, he dropped lightly onto the cab roof and tucked into a ball. A heartbeat later the truck plunged into the underpass. Hardly a finger's width separated the top of the van from the bottom of the trestle. If Bolan had still been on top, he would have been reduced to so much pulp and broken bones. As it was, his head was mere inches below the steel beams.

The driver had the radio on, blaring rock music, while pounding on the steering wheel in time to the music's beat. He had no idea that he had nearly totaled the vehicle.

In no time they shot out the other side. Bolan immediately clambered back onto the van, holding the *lupara* tight against his leg.

Thankfully the only other tunnel they encountered had ample clearance for big rigs.

The route they took consisted mainly of secondary roads. They passed through Queens to Manhattan, from Manhattan to West New York and from there to North Bergen. Tonnelle Avenue bore them northward to a side road, which the driver followed to the west. Presently they came to remote, swampy country bordering the Hackensack River, where the houses were few and far between.

It was essentially flat country with virtually no traffic. Ironically the driver slowed to a crawl. It soon became clear, however, that he did so for a reason.

The winding country road paralleled a tract of marshland on one side and a low hill on the other. Atop that hill perched a grand residence, a house big enough to qualify as a mansion except that it lacked a portico and pillars. A closed iron gate barred admittance. A security camera installed on the right-hand post ensured that no one could surprise the owner, and a high fence enclosed the grounds.

Bolan's watch told him that it was past three in the morning when the truck cruised by the gate. The driver went another two hundred yards, to where a wide shoulder permitted him to laboriously turn the moving van around. This time he approached the gate at a snail's pace, his window rolled down. Every now and then he stuck his head out to scan the perimeter.

The Executioner knew that someone high up the Mafia chain of command had to live there.

Once more the truck went past the gate. At the next turn the driver applied the brakes and hopped out. He ran to the back door, pumped the metal lever that secured the door and pushed the door, which rattled upward on recessed rollers.

By then Bolan had stalked to the back of the truck. Gunner after gunner spilled from the van until there were eight, plus the driver. They gathered around one of their own. The first words out of the man's mouth revealed who he was. There was no mistaking that voice.

It was Talosi, Bolan's adversary from upstate, the man who had slain Mafia enforcer Luther Rossi.

"You all know what to do," Talosi said gravely. "We have rehearsed this many times."

"Are we sure Tinelli is in there?" a triggerman asked.

Bolan glanced at the house. So this was where Leo Tinelli, Rossi's boss, was staying.

"As sure as we can be about information we've had to pay for," Talosi said. "Tony believes our source is reliable, and that's good enough for me."

"Any idea how many soldiers Tinelli has in there?" another man inquired.

"No more than a dozen." Talosi shrugged. "It wouldn't matter if there was a hundred. Our brothers are counting on us to take him out. Tinelli is one of the most powerful men in the Mafia. His council steers the other Dons."

A shooter hefted an SMG. "Let's do it, then, instead of standing around talking."

In a compact group they sprinted to the fence. One man knelt while the rest stood guard. He shrugged out of a backpack and opened it. Pulling out a rectangular black box, he flipped switches, turned a dial and held the box close to the wire mesh. A sound reminiscent of frying bacon filled the air. "Electrified," he announced. "Give me a minute."

The Camorran knew his stuff. He withdrew from the backpack a long wire with insulated clips at both ends, carefully attached one at a specific point on the fence to his right, then clamped the other end to a junction on his left. The wire served as a bypass, conducting the current around the section of fence the man now attacked with a pair of wire cutters.

Soon enough there was a break ample enough for a gunner to slide through. When they were all on the far side, they spread out and advanced toward the hill.

Bolan dropped from the top of the van. He was past the fence before the gunners were out of sight. He rapidly overtook them, the darkness and the brush combining to hide him.

The Camorrans were moving briskly up the slope when a dog commenced barking. It snarled and growled and generally made enough noise to attract the attention of someone in the house. A light came on, and the hit squad went to ground.

A door opened and a man's voice called out, but the words were indistinct. Suddenly a chain rattled, and a huge German shepherd streaked down the hill. It had to have caught the scent of the Camorrans because it made straight for one of them, a man armed with a Model 12 Beretta submachine gun, a weapon in favor with Italian military forces. The guard dog was almost on him when he opened up. A burst of 9 mm manglers ripped into the animal, and it collapsed in a bloody heap at the gunner's feet.

At a bellow from Talosi, the Camorrans charged up the hill, some firing into windows. Glass crashed and shattered. The mobster who had ordered the dog to attack blasted away with a pistol as he retreated to the front door, but he never made it. A line of bullets walked across his back, punching him to the ground before he reached safety.

Bolan sprinted toward the shooter who had slain the guard dog. The gunner saw him, but had to have thought he was a fellow Camorran. Perhaps the *lupara* fooled him. The Executioner triggered the shotgun at point-blank range, driving the man to the grass, a hole in his chest the size of a melon.

Bolan exchanged the *lupara* for the submachine gun. Frisking the man's pockets turned up four 30-round box-type magazines. The soldier swung the folding stock to full extension, worked the bolt and climbed the hill.

The battle raged close to the house. All the ground floor windows had been shot out, and the door had been riddled and knocked off its bottom hinge. Mafia triggermen returned fire from the second and third floors, many with automatic weapons.

The Camorrans had lost the crucial element of surprise, but they weren't about to quit. Half, under

Talosi, weaved toward the rear of the house while their companions laid down suppressing fire.

One of the gunners had taken cover behind a small ornate wall that enclosed a flower bed. Bolan moved toward him, and suddenly had to seek his own cover as one of the Mafia triggermen sent a swarm of lead in his direction. He hit the ground on his left shoulder and rolled into shrubbery.

The hardman stepped back from the second-floor window, but Bolan could still see him. The man was busy extracting a spent magazine and slapping in a new one. The Executioner resorted to his own SMG. The Model 12 was so compact that all he had to do was keep a firm hold on the forward grip to reduce its muzzle climb, and squeeze the trigger.

Rounds punched through the already cracked and blistered pane, drilling the hardman in the chest and head. He jerked about as if he were a puppet whose strings had just been severed, then he toppled forward, his limp arms flinging outward, his head bursting through what was left of the window. Like a swimmer doing a high dive, he sailed out and down, smashing onto a concrete walk with an audible crunch.

The Executioner returned his attention to the Camorran sheltered by the garden wall just as the man popped up and lobbed a cylindrical object at the house. He promptly buried his face in the dirt and placed both arms over his head.

The *crump* of the grenade was louder than thunder, the rain of debris thicker than hail. Bolan held his breath as acrid tendrils of smoke wound about him. Dust particles choked the air.

Bolan heard yells and men running, then the Camorrans were in the house and the gunfire intensified. Men were cursing and shouting, their cries punctuated by autofire and the booming of pistols. Adding to the din was the crash and smash of furniture caught in the cross fire. Upstairs a woman screamed. Then, above the bedlam a high, thin voice yelled, "Mommy! Mommy!"

A child was in there. Bolan heaved erect and sprinted for the front door. The Executioner didn't give a damn about the Mafia kingpin, but the child was another matter. He had to get the youngster out of there. Knowing the Camorrans, they wouldn't leave anyone alive.

The foyer was a shambles. A dead mobster lay sprawled across an overturned chair. Another partially blocked the hallway. Bullet holes dotted the walls, the floor, even the ceiling.

Bolan hurried on. Slowly but surely the Camorrans were fighting their way deeper into the house. He imagined that Talosi and company were also inside by then. Leo Tinelli and his buttonmen were trapped on the upper floors, hemmed in like rats in a cage.

More bodies littered the floor. Bolan halted at a corner. Past it the conflict raged in full force. Wide marble stairs led to the second floor. The Camorrans were trying to force their way up but had met with the stiffest resistance yet. The mafiosi knew that they had to prevent their gaining the stairs at all costs, or their cause was lost.

Bolan drew back. He was fair game for both sides, and couldn't possibly take them all on at once. His priority had to be the child. Retracing his steps to a junction, he hastened from room to room, seeking another means of reaching the second floor. In a house that size, there had to be another route.

The last room Bolan came to was the kitchen. Giving it a cursory scan, he turned to leave—and noticed a dumbwaiter in the far corner.

It was barely big enough for the soldier to squeeze into. He examined the controls to determine if he could operate it from inside, and could. Stabbing a button marked with an arrow pointing up, he folded his arms around his legs and listened to the faint whine of a motor below and the creak of the cable as the small elevator cranked to life.

Bolan tried not to think of what would happen if the power was to be cut off while he was between floors. He might be trapped there indefinitely, or the place might burn down around him.

There was a more immediate concern, as well. Bolan had to hope that every last mobster was busy resisting the Camorrans; otherwise one of them was bound to notice the dumbwaiter and blast away before it came to a stop. If that happened, Bolan wouldn't stand a prayer.

The elevator slowed, then jolted to a halt. Bolan pushed against a small door. He was in an empty bedroom that faced a closed door across the hall.

On the other side, the war went on. He started to slide out when, upstairs, the same child cried, "Daddy! Come quick! Mommy's hurt bad!"

The Executioner stabbed the control panel again, ducked into the dumbwaiter, and quickly yanked the door shut as it resumed its ascent. The higher it climbed, the slower it went. Concussions buffeted the walls, shaking the conveyance. The cable creaked louder than ever.

Bolan was impatient to reach the third floor. From the sound of things, the hit squad had gained the second floor and continued to batter the mafiosi. It wouldn't be long now. The outcome was inevitable. He could only pray the child was still alive.

VICTOR TINELLI WAS twelve years old and more scared than he had ever been in his entire young life. Tears streaking his cheeks, he crouched over his mother, shielding her with his body, saying, "Mom! Mom! Mom!" over and over.

A spurt of gunfire out in the hallway caused Victor to quake. He didn't know what was happening. He had no idea why bad men were attacking his house, why they were killing everyone, why they had shot his mother.

It compounded the boy's terror, his fear so potent that his gut was balled into a knot, his every breath a frightened gasp.

Minutes ago Victor had been sleeping peacefully in his comfortable bed, dreaming of the bullfrog he had caught down by the marsh. Harsh sounds had awakened him, and he had sat up as his mother darted into his bedroom. It had seemed like part of his dream, at first, a dream gone bad—the fear on her face, her frantic yank on his arm, all seemed unreal.

Victor hadn't understood when she was knocked backward, hadn't made the connection between the holes that had punctured his window and the holes that materialized in her chest. Not until she collapsed and blood oozed from every one of those holes did he realize his mother had been shot, just like people were always being shot on television and in the movies. Only this was real. It was real blood, warm and sticky, that had spattered his face. Real bullets had made a pale waxen figure of his mother. He pulled at her nightgown, pleading with her to get up, but she wouldn't respond. Her eyes were closed, and try as he might, Victor couldn't get her to open them.

The whole room shook to an explosion. An acrid odor made Victor cough. He blinked tears away, nearly jumping out of his skin when a hand fell on his shoulder.

"Son!"

It was Victor's father, but his father as Victor had never seen him. Clad in smudged underwear, a smoking pistol in one hand, crimson dots on his neck, a nasty furrow in his shoulder, his father was a shadow of his usual self. The features that had always regarded Victor with the utmost kindness were now almost as waxen as his mother's.

"Dad!" Victor blurted. "Someone shot Mom! What's going on? Where did you get that gun?"

Victor had never seen his father with a gun before, hardly ever seen his father unclothed. His dad always wore the best of suits, always had a ready smile for Victor at any time of the day or night. In Victor's estimation, his father was the kindest, most perfect father any boy could ever have.

"No time for that now," the elder Tinelli said, pressing a hand to his mother's neck. Sadness such as Victor had never imagined came over him.

"We have to get Mom to a doctor!" Victor exclaimed.

"Where's Butch and Louie? They can do it." Butch Ricco and Louie Pesini were two men who worked for his father. They were always around, always running errands, always willing to drop whatever they were doing and play with Victor if his dad told them to.

"It's too late for—" his father began, and stopped, his frame racked by a shudder.

Out in the hall the shooting and yelling had intensified. Victor saw his father glance at the doorway. Behind him there was a new noise that he couldn't quite identify but he felt should be familiar. It caused his father to turn, to gaze past him and start to bring up the pistol.

"Don't," a deep voice said.

Victor twisted. A stranger stood near the dumbwaiter, a peculiar gun trained on his father. There was something about the stranger, a hardness in his face, that fueled Victor's terror. But then the man looked at him, and in the stranger's eyes there was genuine friendliness, real warmth. It confused Victor all the more.

Leo Tinelli had frozen, hatred contorting his face. "If you think I'll crawl, you're mistaken. Go ahead and get it over with, you bastard!"

The stranger glided toward them. Victor had never seen anyone move like this man. It made him think of the time he had visited the zoo and watched a tiger prowl its cage. There was the same grace, the same hint of awful power. He cowered.

"I'm not with the Camorra," the stranger addressed his father.

Victor heard his father's intake of breath. He had never seen his father look so astonished.

"The Camorra? That explains everything! But if you're not with them, then who the hell are you?"

The stranger didn't answer the question. Instead, he wagged his weapon at Victor. "I'll get your son out while you hold them back."

"Trust my boy to you? Do you think I'm crazy, mister? Give me one good reason why I should."

"If you don't, you know what they'll do to him. You must have heard about Giadone in Miami."

Tinelli looked down at his wife, then at Victor. A host of emotions flitted across his face. Victor had the impression his father was in extreme torment.

"I don't want to leave you," Victor said.

"You heard him," his father told the stranger.

At that moment the wall to their left was perforated by half a dozen bullets that zinged over their heads. In the hall a man screamed. Someone else wailed, "Don Tinelli! Don Tinelli!" It sounded like Butch Ricco.

Victor's father straightened, his lips compressed. A gleam came into his eyes, and he suddenly grabbed Victor and shoved him at the stranger. "Go! Now! Before I change my mind!"

"No!" Victor cried. His father looked at him, a look full of all the love they had ever shared and something else that frightened Victor more than the guns and the uproar and the confusion. He had a strong, terrible certainty that he would never see his father again. "I won't go!"

The older Tinelli lunged, hugging Victor. Victor felt moisture on his cheek, heard his father choke out words.

"Don't argue, son! Just remember this night. And when you're grown, pay the sons of bitches back for what they've done! Make the streets run red with their blood! Never forget your mother and me!"

Then Victor's father was gone, dashing into the hall, and Victor was in the grip of the stranger, who hauled him toward the dumbwaiter. Numb with shock and disbelief, Victor offered no resistance as the big man lifted him into the elevator.

"Climb out at the bottom and wait for me to join you," the man directed. He pressed the button, and frowned.

It took a few seconds for Victor to comprehend that the dumbwaiter wasn't working as it should. There was a low whine from down below, but the car didn't move.

The stranger seized Victor's wrist and raced to the doorway. "Stay close to me," he cautioned, hurtling both of them from the bedroom and bearing to the right.

Victor, still in a daze, gazed down the hall. His father was down there. Butch Ricco and Louie Pesini, also. And a few more who were in the same export business as his dad. They were crouched in doorways or flat on the floor, firing at men Victor had never laid eyes on before. As the child looked on, Louie Pesini clutched at his throat and fell, his legs pumping as if he were the bullfrog Victor had caught.

The man holding Victor moved amazingly fast now, faster than Victor thought any person could move, speeding down the hall to the end, into a spare bedroom his grandmother used when she visited on the holidays. The whole time the walls and the floor thumped as if being pounded by an unseen hammer.

Victor didn't protest when the stranger shoved him into a chair. He observed the big man wrench open a window and lean out.

"It will have to do."

"What?" Victor said blankly, struggling to think clearly. A gigantic blast rocked the hallway. More harrowing shrieks were cut short by the metallic chatter of automatic weapons.

The stranger lifted him to his feet. "Ever played piggyback?"

"What?" Victor repeated. What did riding on his father's back have to do with anything? He wondered if maybe he was still dreaming.

"I'm going to hang from the sill," the stranger was saying. "I want you to climb out on top of me, then hang from my neck." He peered into Victor's eyes. "Do you understand?"

Victor was too bewildered to do more than nod. He watched the stranger slip a leg over the bottom of the window. In the hall the loudest explosion yet shook the house to its foundation.

Victor thought he heard his father call his name. He turned.

One of the men who had attacked the house was in the doorway. He held a machine gun of some kind, and he pointed it right at Victor.

## CHAPTER SEVEN

The Executioner had one leg over the windowsill when the gunner filled the doorway. His instant reaction was to swivel the submachine gun at the figure and fire.

Bolan was holding the Model 12 in his right hand. As compact as it was, the SMG bucked like a mule if not grasped securely. His rounds caught the gunner in the crotch, then drilled a path up across the man's torso and head as the weapon's muzzle climbed.

The soldier motioned to the boy to hurry. The youngster, though, moved as if his mind were stuck in neutral and he couldn't get his limbs to shift into gear.

The firing in the hall had attained a crescendo. Another grenade detonated. A man screeched, his death cry chopped off by a gurgling whine.

"Come on!" Bolan urged, wedging the submachine gun under the front of his belt. The boy stepped close enough to grab, and Bolan did so, roughly pulling him to the window. Being gentle was a luxury neither of them could afford. In moments more Camorran hit men might appear, and they would be sitting ducks.

"Climb on my back," Bolan said as he dangled both legs over the side and hung by his hands from the sill. "Hurry."

The boy complied, but sluggishly, crawling at a snail's pace onto the sill and fearfully lowering himself past the Executioner's broad shoulders.

"Clamp tight," Bolan ordered. He raised his chin so the child could slip an arm around his neck, coughing when the boy nearly crushed his windpipe. "Not so tight," he said.

"Sorry," the youngster mumbled.

"What's your name?" Bolan asked, thinking that it might calm the boy if they were on friendlier terms.

"Victor. My friends all call me Vic."

"Well, Vic, you can call me Mike." Bolan used a cover name he frequently employed. "We're about to reach the ground the hard way. Whatever you do, don't let go."

"What will happen to my dad, mister?"

Bolan hesitated. It was hardly the right time or place to discuss the Don's impending fate. "We'll talk about it later," was all he would say.

Without warning, another figure appeared. This one tottered, covered with blood from several wounds. Leo Tinelli had to grip a dresser for support as he crossed toward them. His eyes found the boy. "Take care of him, mister," he said. "He's the only worthwhile legacy I'm leaving behind."

"Dad!" Victor shouted, and tried to claw his way back up onto the soldier's shoulders.

Bolan clamped his chin onto the boy's wrist. There was no time to lose. "Hold on!" he warned, but Victor resisted, tugging furiously until the mafioso scolded him.

"That will be enough, son! Do as the man says!"

Bolan wasn't quite sure why Tinelli had agreed to let him save the boy. They didn't know each other. Tinelli had no real reason to trust him. Maybe it was the last-ditch desperation of a father grasping at straws. Maybe Tinelli was operating on gut instinct and believed he was trustworthy. Whatever the case, it had taken more courage than Bolan would have credited the mobster with.

"Don't let them get him," Tinelli pleaded, then spun as shots roared close to the door.

Above the window was a rain gutter, to their left the downspout. Bolan began to swing from side to side. In three swings his feet were brushing the spout. At the apex of his next arc he pushed off from the sill and flew through space with the boy's fingers gouging into his flesh. A startled yip sounded almost in his ear.

Bolan grabbed the downspout as he began to drop. The metal was as slick as glass, his purchase as precarious as a mountain climber's on the north face of Mount Everest. He started to slide down, gaining momentum much too swiftly. Gripping the downspout with all his might, he pressed his knees against it to further arrest his descent. Friction warmed his palms, his legs. He lost skin when his palms were lacerated by a row of rivets.

A cross brace saved them. Bolan's right foot slammed onto it, jarring them to a stop. They had fallen over ten feet but they were in one piece. He climbed down rapidly, half expecting to be shot in the back.

At the bottom Bolan had to pry the boy's fingers apart before he could set the youngster down. "We're not out of danger yet," he emphasized, taking the child's hand and running toward a patch of woodland halfway down the hill. Victor ran like someone drunk or seasick, not once taking his eyes off the third-floor window.

Bolan felt sorry for the kid, but not the father. Leo Tinelli had been responsible for dozens of bloody murders. "A minor-league Al Capone," was how a federal prosecutor had once described him.

Nor was Tinelli's wife free from blame. Like most wives of Mafia, she had been well aware of her husband's illegal activities. And like most, she had been willing to turn her back on them. The money, the furs and expensive cars, the grand house and other properties had mattered more to her than the lives of those her husband routinely snuffed out.

The soldier reached the trees and sank to his knees behind a bush so the boy could catch his breath. No more shots rang out. The house was as quiet as a morgue.

"Who are those bad men, Mike?" Victor Tinelli

asked. "My dad and you mentioned something about the Camorra. What's that? I've never heard of it before." His lower lip quivered. He was close to tears. "Why would those men want to hurt my mom and dad?"

Bolan recalled his conversation with Brognola in Washington, D.C. Where should he begin? What would it benefit the boy to learn that the Camorra and the Mafia both got their starts in Italy centuries earlier, the Mafia in Sicily, the Camorra in Naples. What difference did it make that about the turn of the nineteenth century both gained a foothold in America and preyed on the growing Italian population, or that war had broken out over the lucrative new turf and the Mafia drove the Camorra from U.S. shores?

The boy was better off not knowing, Bolan decided. Let someone else fill him in.

A shout rose at the rear of the house. Three gunners dashed out, the leader pointing at the woods and yelling in Italian, "I saw them go that way, the son and one other. Talosi wants them found. There must be no witnesses."

"Geez!" Victor blurted. "Are those guys after us?"

"They sure are," Bolan said, hauling the youngster to his feet and angling deeper into the oaks and maples. Dawn was about an hour off, and already pale light bathed the countryside, enough for them to see by. Enough, too, for the gunmen to see them. Victor lagged, fatigue and turmoil taking their toll, so Bolan scooped him into his left arm and picked up the pace.

The Camorran killers crashed through the brush, making no attempt to use stealth, haste driving them to be reckless.

Bolan could guess why. The grenades and gunfire had been loud enough to be heard a long way off. Someone might have contacted the sheriff's department. The Camorrans wanted to be long gone when the officers got there.

So did Bolan. Being grilled by hostile lawmen until Brognola could be contacted and have him released wasn't his idea of a good time.

There was a steep gully at the base of the hill. Bolan would rather go around, but it ran for hundreds of feet in both directions. Holding Victor higher, he slid down the near slope, digging in his heels to keep from losing his balance. As it was, he nearly fell thanks to a fair-sized rock embedded in the earth. His left toe struck it, jarring it loose, and it swept out from under his sole, almost upending him.

Once safely at the bottom, Bolan bore to the left, westward, fleeing as fast as his burden allowed. The youngster offered no protest. Ahead a huge knob of dirt jutted into the gully on the left. Bolan was almost to it when, glancing back, he spied figures emerging from the trees. Flinging himself behind the knob, he lay with his back on the slope, Tinelli's son at his side.

"Don't make a peep," the soldier whispered.

The three hit men were close together, their SMGs sweeping back and forth. They looked every which way, plainly mystified by Bolan's disappearance. At a nod from one of them, the three separated. One went east, posing no immediate threat. But the second one hiked west along the gully rim, while the third stumbled down into the gully, then hesitated, unsure of which way to go. Finally he headed east.

Murky shadow mired the bottom of the gully. Bolan wasn't worried about being seen. The gunner needed to be almost on top of him. Letting go of the boy, he adopted a two-handed grip on the submachine gun.

As wary as a stalking wolf, the Camorran slowly advanced, pausing after each stride to look and listen. He stared into the gully several times. If he saw the earthen knob, it didn't alarm him.

Bolan let the man get within a few yards of his hiding place. Then he reared up and loosed a precise burst, aiming to chop the gunner in two at the waist. There was only one problem. The hit man had lightning reflexes. Even as Bolan rose, he spun and triggered a few rounds of his own before Bolan's slugs ripped into his midsection.

The Camorran was knocked backward, his Uzi tilting upward. The man twirled onto the grass, his legs hanging over the edge, and went into severe convulsions.

Bolan was spared injury, but the few rounds the gunner got off struck his submachine gun. The

Model 12 sailed from his stinging fingers, clattering to the earth at his feet. Bolan immediately picked it up, and just as promptly discarded it. The shots had damaged the bolt housing. The weapon was useless.

To the east one of the hitmen shouted, "Paolo, did you get them?"

"Come on," Bolan said to the boy, and they resumed their flight. Victor dragged his feet, shaking his head.

"Please, mister. Let me go. I need to rest."

The soldier realized that the horror of losing both parents and the stress of the running firefight were putting the youngster in ever deepening shock. Small wonder the child couldn't think clearly.

"We can't stop yet," Bolan whispered. "Not until I get you out of here, like your father wants."

"Dad! Mom!" the boy said bleakly. "They're dead!"

Bolan could hear the two members of the death squad in hot pursuit. Clasping Victor about the waist, he sped to the west. A bend loomed, and beyond it the gully ended. Fortunately the slope was gradual enough that Bolan could go up it without having to rely on his hands for support.

As he cleared the rim, a Camorran shouted, "There they are!"

To Bolan's right were more trees. He plunged into them as the pair unleashed a hornet's nest of buzzing lead that stung the vegetation all around him but didn't connect with him or the boy. The foliage closed around them. Bolan angled to the left. He wanted to find a spot to make a stand, to end it quickly, before more hit men showed up, but he had no such luck.

He rounded a cluster of trees, bypassed a thorn thicket and drew up short in baffled agitation. In front of him reared the electrified fence. On the other side was thick forest, but it might as well be on the surface of the moon. He had no means of getting over the barrier with the youngster.

Bolan raced eastward. His only hope now was to reach the gap in the fence the Camorrans had made earlier. The death squad on the hill would be busy mopping up for a few more minutes, or so he hoped. All he had to do was elude the pair dogging him.

The area near the fence had been cleared of brush, creating a narrow path. Bolan was able to run twice as fast, but he was handicapped by Victor Tinelli. The boy had gone as limp as a wet rag. All the life seemed to have drained out of him, and he gazed forlornly into the distance.

The two gunners had given chase. Bolan stayed closer to the tree line than the fence to make it harder for the Camorrans to get a bead on them. Sooner or later, though, the killers were bound to get a clear shot.

The fence looped by degrees around to the southeast. By pouring on a burst of speed, Bolan pulled far enough ahead that his pursuers briefly lost sight of him. The moment that happened, Bolan slanted into the vegetation, jumped over a log, and crouched. He released the child, then the Beretta. He removed the sound suppressor from a jacket pocket, but the triggermen appeared before he could thread it onto the pistol.

The pair were bounding like antelope, but wary antelope, their SMGs leveled, prepared to fire at the first hint of a threat.

Bolan sighted on the leader. It was an easy kill. They both would have been, had Victor Tinelli not picked that moment to burst into tears, uttering a gut-wrenching sob torn from the depths of his very soul. The two Camorrans snapped to a stop just as Bolan fired. His shot winged the lead man, who twisted to the impact but didn't go down.

The pair swung toward the woods, their SMGs rattling off a litany of death as they backpedaled and dived into the woods in the shelter of a giant willow tree.

Victor went on crying, his small shoulders quaking, his body heaving. His cries were a beacon that would guide the killers unerringly to the log.

Bolan did something he regretted having to do. He clamped a hand over the boy's mouth, yanked Victor upright and retreated into the woodland. Victor struggled fiercely, kicking and punching. His blows were too weak to do Bolan any harm, but the thrashing bundle slowed him, forced him to pay attention to the boy when he should be paying attention to their surroundings.

The soldier didn't intend to go very far from the

fence, but no suitable cover appeared. He traveled twenty yards, thirty. A twig crunched to his right, evidence the gunners were paralleling him, waiting for their chance.

Victor stopped resisting. Tears continued to flow, though, and he sobbed aloud every few seconds. Bolan's hand muffled them, but he couldn't hold on to the boy forever. The soldier needed both hands free to fight effectively.

Sprinting past a pine, Bolan saw a hollow about the size of a small car and about knee deep. He dropped into it, whispering into the boy's ear, "If I let go of you, do you promise not to make a sound?"

Victor nodded.

No sooner did Bolan ease his hand off than the youngster sniffled loudly. Bolan covered the boy's mouth and nose again, then tensed as a hint of movement to the northwest confirmed the gunmen had also heard.

Again Bolan tried. "You can't make any noise, Vic. None at all. Do you understand?"

Once more the child nodded.

Not wanting to make the same mistake twice, Bolan tried a new tack. "If you keep on sniffling, they'll pinpoint us. We might never get out of here alive. Is that what you want?"

The query provoked an odd response. Victor's face became icy. His once innocent eyes reflected simmering hatred for a few seconds, hatred so intense it was startling to behold in one so young. His answering nod was curt.

Dreading what might happen, Bolan raised his hand. The boy glared at the woods, making no sounds whatsoever. The soldier crawled to the rim and peered into the undergrowth. He took the time to attach the sound suppressor.

Nothing happened for long minutes. Then a squat shape appeared twenty feet away, crabbing forward, swiveling from side to side, the gunmetal sheen of an SMG visible in the dim but growing light.

The Camorran was scouring bushes and trees. It never occurred to him to look down. Bolan fixed his sights on the center of the man's forehead and cored it with a single well-placed shot. The gunner flopped about, making plenty of racket, advertising his death and forewarning his friend.

Bolan moved along the edge of the hollow, only exposing himself from the eyes up. He turned his back on Victor for just a moment and heard the boy scramble up the side. Whirling, he leaped, his fingers just missing the child's leg. He opened his mouth to order the youngster to come back but thought better of the idea.

With single-minded determination, Victor crawled toward the body, impervious to the branches that snatched at his pajamas or scratched his face.

Bolan hissed to get the boy's attention, then motioned for him to turn. Victor refused to obey, leaving the soldier no choice but to crawl out after him.

As Bolan did, the burp of an SMG punctured the predawn quiet. Geysers erupted next to him. He couldn't spot the shooter, so he flung himself forward to grab Victor, who pushed him back with surprising strength.

The concealed gunner let rip again. This time the shots were a trifle high. Bolan caught sight of a bulky form crouched on a low tree limb and emptied the Beretta into it. The man's SMG fell first, then the Camorran followed.

With speed born of long practice, Bolan replaced the spent magazine in his pistol. He rose to verify the kills. A click made him look around.

Victor Tinelli had picked up the first hit man's Uzi and was trying to work it. He fumbled at the selector switch, then pointed the SMG at the dead Camorran and squeezed the trigger. When it failed to fire, he sobbed and tried again. Another click sparked raw rage. He gripped the Uzi by its short barrel and raised it to strike the dead man.

"No!" Bolan said, reaching the boy in a bound. He tore the Uzi free and tossed it into the weeds. "You don't want to do that."

Victor's voice crackled with spite. "How do you know what I want or don't want, mister? This is one of the men who shot my mother and father! I want to see them all dead! Dead! Dead! Dead! Do you hear me?"

Bolan heard him, all right, and so could anyone within a hundred yards. Seizing the youngster's wrist, he hurried to the fence and continued to the southeast.

The boy kept up but sulked.

The Executioner glimpsed the house through a break in the trees. No hardmen were evident. Yet. He hastened on.

"I'll kill each and every one!" Victor suddenly snarled. "You'll see! One day I'll pay them back for what they've done! They'll suffer like no one has ever suffered before!"

"Vengeance never solves anything," Bolan whispered, and felt like a hypocrite for doing so. Who was he to lecture the boy on revenge? He had spent years waging a one-man war against the Mafia because it had destroyed those who meant the most in the world to him. Just like the Camorra had destroyed those who meant the most to Victor.

"I don't think you know what you're talking about," Victor snapped. "It may not solve much, but I will feel a lot better when the ones who are to blame are dead."

Bolan tried one more time. "There's more to life than killing, son. Don't waste yours hunting down men who will probably be dead by the time you're old enough to go after them."

"They're going to pay, mister. No matter how long it takes. No matter how many of them are alive. They're going to hurt like I hurt. Only worse."

They fell silent. Bolan saw the futility of trying to reason with the boy. The loss was too fresh, too agonizing. In a year or so Victor might change his tune. If not, then the violence spawned by Victor's father would come full circle and consume his offspring.

Due east of the hill the trees thinned. High grass extended hundreds of feet to an island of brush. Since there was no sign of Camorrans at any of the windows, Bolan broke into the open, the boy's hand in his. They made it without being spotted.

On hands and knees, Bolan crept to where he could see the spot where the hit team had penetrated the grounds. The moving van was still parked at the side of the road.

The murmur of low talk from high on the slope alerted the soldier to a quartet of hardmen winding down the drive toward the gate. Of the nine hit team members, these four were the only ones left. They slowed repeatedly to look back, evidently expecting their three friends to rejoin them. Soon trees hid them.

Bolan's mind went a mile a minute, calculating probabilities. "We have to reach the truck before they do," he told Victor. "Hold on tight." With that, he forked an arm around the boy and streaked toward the gap. If he could get there before the gunners came out of the trees, they were in for an unwelcome surprise.

Victor, for once, was as docile as a lamb.

A band of pale pink crowned the horizon when Bolan squatted at the opening, then slid through.

He turned to help the youngster, but Victor needed no assitance. Side by side they ran to the truck.

The door had been left open. Bolan slid into the driver's seat and reached for the ignition. He could strand the Camorrans if he got out of there before they showed, but the driver had taken the key.

Then the quartet tramped around a curve. Bolan ducked and went to jump from the cab. "Into those reeds," he directed, nodding at a strip of marshland bordering the road.

Victor Tinelli didn't obey. Stepping to the front of the truck, he cupped his mouth and hollered, "Here we are, you scum! Come and get us if you dare!"

## CHAPTER EIGHT

*Washington, D.C.*

There were nights when Hal Brognola would give anything for an hour of uninterrupted slumber. This was one of them.

Since early morning the dedicated Fed had been at the Justice Department building. Part of the time was spent at his desk going over the latest intel. Part of the time he was in conference with high-ranking agents, plotting strategy, or shuttling from office to office on various tasks. The few seconds he had to spare were spent helping himself to coffee or simply staring out his window and longing for the vacation he was never able to take.

By evening the day shift was gone, the swing shift on duty. But Brognola had to stay on to oversee the latest crisis. He'd hoped that later he could catch forty winks on his couch. Circumstances spoiled his plan.

When night spread over the country, reports of Mob warfare started coming in fast and furious.

First the Camorra hit the compound of a Mafia

leader in New Jersey. Then a *consigliere* to a top Los Angeles mafioso met his end in heavy traffic when a pair of sedans pulled up on either side of his limo and shooters pumped over a hundred rounds into it. A woman in another car, on an outing to treat her three small children to ice cream, was caught by flying lead, died instantly, crashed through a guardrail and flipped her compact. By some miracle the three kids survived without a scratch.

In Las Vegas the war raged full blown. A brothel owned by the leading Vegas mobster was bombed. Nineteen women perished and twenty-two were hurt, five critically.

The upper floors of a famous casino were given the same treatment as the Blackjack in Atlantic City. Seventeen members of the Mafia died, along with thirty-eight hapless civilians.

Hour by hour the toll mounted.

Brognola was under pressure from all quarters. The President put him in charge of the overall operation and demanded that the crimson tide be stemmed or there would be hell to pay. The heads of the FBI, the ATF and other agencies, under fire from the media and politicians eager to make points with their constituents, were giving the big Fed flack for failing to end the bloodbath.

There was nothing Brognola wanted more. The only problem was that he had no inkling of where to begin. The Camorrans were as slippery as greased snakes. No one could predict where they would strike next. They never stayed in any one place very long. Unlike the Mafia, they had no known associates who could be induced or coerced into betraying them.

Battling them was like battling a legion of ghosts who were flitting around the U.S. wreaking havoc at will.

Brognola rubbed his taut face, then stared at the clock on the wall. Soon it would be dawn, and another grueling day would begin. Another day, and more innocents would lose their lives.

That was the worst part. Brognola had grown accustomed to criminals offing one another. It was par for the course. He never batted an eye when an organized-crime honcho was the victim of an internal dispute, or when triggermen gunned down one another. They got what they deserved.

Civilians should be exempt from the carnage. The Mafia knew enough not to involve bystanders in their personal grudges. They were fully aware that killing outsiders generated more heat than they liked to bear.

Kill a mobster, and the law didn't care. Kill a housewife or a child, and the police wouldn't rest until the culprit was in custody.

Brognola had lost count of how many innocents had lost their lives in this latest clash. As much as he despised the Mafia, he had to admit that they weren't to blame this time. It was the Camorra who had started the war, the Camorra who slew its enemies and anyone else with savage abandon, and the Camorrans were the bloodiest butchers he had run up against in ages.

The big Fed glanced at a file on his desk. It contained the latest confidential information from Interpol and a report from the man in charge of the Italian equivalent of the Justice Department. He couldn't wait to relay the intel to Striker.

The Justice man glanced at his watch and scowled. Bolan should have checked in long ago.

Below, a pretty young woman was out walking her dog. She strolled along as if she didn't have a care in the world, playfully petting the Samoyed when it nuzzled her and tugged at its leash. She was happy, content with her life.

Brognola sipped his coffee and wondered if she would be willing to trade places.

*New Jersey*

IT WAS JUST another house in a middle-class section of Teaneck, New Jersey. The frame affair was two stories high and boasted a lawn the size of a pool table. The neighbors had heard a rumor that it was owned by a man who spent most of his time in Florida, a man no one who lived on that street had ever met. So many of them were more than a little curious when they emerged from their own homes to leave for work and saw four sedans parked at the curb in front of the mystery man's house and two more in the driveway.

No one thought the number of cars to be somewhat unusual. Their absent neighbor had returned, they reasoned, and his relatives had come to see him.

Such was the human capacity for rationalizing every odd incident that took place, that no one questioned why the relatives were there at so early an hour. Or why the mystery man had arrived in the middle of the night. Or even why all the shades were drawn and a husky man in a black suit and sunglasses sat in a lawn chair on the front porch reading a newspaper.

If anyone had got up the nerve to go pay their respects, they would have been rudely turned away. Joseph Castellano had given orders that he wasn't to be disturbed by anyone unless it was an emergency. He had too much to do.

For an hour after his casino had been blown to smithereens, Castellano had been too stunned to do much of anything. Gradually his shock had given way to anger, then to rage.

Not for nothing had he once been one of the most feared mafiosi on the East Coast. He had risen through the ranks the hard way, and he had learned his lessons well.

Castellano's top priority had been to spirit his wife and her mother to Bermuda for a surprise holiday. His grown children had been contacted next and given enough money for them to lose themselves anywhere on the planet for as long as Castellano deemed it prudent.

Then Castellano had put his two crews on a war

footing. His soldiers had gone to the trenches, converging at preselected hideouts where ample weapons and food were stockpiled.

The safehouse in Teaneck had never been used before. It was cramped and crummy by Castellano's standards, but he was safe. His enemies couldn't possibly find him, since he was the only one in his organization who had known about the house until the moment he got there.

Phone calls to peers had revealed that the Mafia was under attack on all fronts. Someone had the gall to declare open season on the most feared organization in America. That someone had to be insane, he'd concluded.

Then a call from New York had set Castellano straight. A source at the Justice Department, who routinely took money under the table for pertinent tips, claimed that the Feds knew who the lunatics were.

The Camorra.

The news had shocked Castellano almost as much as the loss of his cherished casino. He was aware, of course, of the early history of both organizations, of the power struggle that had taken place in America and given the Mafia supreme reign over all illegal rackets.

Few people outside the Mafia knew that La Cosa Nostra got its start in Italy in 1282, or that it originally was formed to protect oppressed Sicilians from the ruling French. Back in those days the Mafia had been the Italian version of England's Robin

Hood and his Merry Men. La Cosa Nostra had protected the poor, defended the weak and helped drive the oppressors from the country.

Only later did the Mafia turn to criminal activities to support its growing empire.

The Camorra, however, had been an outright criminal entity from the very outset. Based in Naples, it had lived in peace with the Mafia until the lucrative new fields in America sparked the war that saw the Camorra defeated and driven back to Naples.

Now it was back, with a vengeance.

There could be no denying that the Mafia was in for the fight of its life. In Italy the Camorra was just as powerful as the Mafia. And where the Mafia had spread westward to snare America in its iron grip, the Camorra had spread eastward across Turkey into Asia and now controlled a territory equally large.

Joseph Castellano would never admit as much to his underlings, but he was worried. Extremely worried. The Camorra had a war chest as deep as the Mafia's. Worse, the Camorra had as many soldiers, if not more. It was a worthy adversary, one of the few who could challenge the Mafia and actually win.

Castellano thought about his casino and had to bite his lip to keep from roaring in outrage. He asked himself why the Camorra had picked him as one of its first targets. Was it because of his reputation? No, he decided. That couldn't be it. There were mafiosi much more dangerous than he was, men who killed for the sheer thrill of it.

Was it because he had a high profile in the media? Castellano mused. He recalled that Giadone in Florida also made the news often, and that the Vegas mobsters were as open about their activities as mobsters could be and not get themselves thrown behind bars.

That had to be it.

Suddenly the phone jangled, startling Castellano. Angrily he snatched it to his ear and growled, "Yeah? Speak to me!"

"Joseph, it's Bruno. Is this line secure?"

Castellano was all attention. Don Gaito in New York was the only boss who knew the phone number to his secret retreat, and Gaito wouldn't call unless it was urgent. "Yes. Let me guess. More bad news."

"They nailed Fabiano and Vitale."

"The bastards!" Castellano snarled. Fabiano had been a fellow New Jersey mobster, Vitale a highly respected West Coast *consigliere*. "How much longer are we going to let this go on? When do we start striking back?"

"A sit-down has been called. All the bosses will be there. The Families need to work together on this or we don't stand a prayer."

"Where and when?"

"Midnight tonight. In Chicago. Don Fallini is personally guaranteeing everyone's safety. No personal grievances will be aired. The only business will be what to do about these vermin."

The news delighted Castellano. Fallini was a standup guy, one of the old school, a mustache pete who ran his crew as if he were a military commander and they were Marines. He always kept to his own territory and honored the territory of others. There was no one more highly respected.

It provoked a question. "Has the Camorra hit Fallini yet?" Castellano asked.

"No," Gaito replied. "As a matter of fact, Fallini is the only one they haven't hit. Everyone else in the whole damn country, but not his organization."

"They're scared of him," Castellano guessed. "Those Chicago boys are tough and the Camorrans know it."

"Maybe."

"Why else has he been spared?" Castellano quizzed, and since he knew Gaito so well, the answer popped full blown into his head. "Wait a minute. You're not saying what I think you're saying? That Fallini is somehow in league with the Camorra?" He couldn't help but laugh. "Really, Bruno. And I thought that *I* had a suspicious nature."

"Give me one good reason why it couldn't be true?"

"I can give you tons of reasons, but the main one is Fallini himself. You know as well as I do that he's not one of the new breed of punks who would sell out their own mother if the price was right. Fallini can trace his roots back to Sicily, back further than any of the rest of us. The Mafia is in his blood. He lives and breathes by the code. He would never turn on us."

"Maybe," Gaito said.

"You're still not convinced?" Castellano reminded himself that the New York Don had once been betrayed by a trusted lieutenant and nearly gone to prison. "Okay. How about this." He paused. "Do you remember the time some of Fallini's own men went into the drug business without consulting him? Do you remember what he did to them when he found out they were selling the stuff at elementary schools?"

Gaito's gruff laughter rumbled down the wire. "I remember, all right. He had them taken to a warehouse and his enforcer chopped them to pieces with a fire ax. They say that he stuffed what was left of them, and their drugs, into steel drums. The bastards wound up at the bottom of Lake Michigan."

"Exactly," Castellano said. "Would a man like that, a man who won't abide having the old ways abused, turn on the organization he loves so much?"

The New York boss sighed. "No. I suppose not. But it's still damn strange that the Camorrans haven't hit him yet."

"Maybe they're saving Fallini for last," Castellano speculated. "If so, they're making a big mistake. He won't stand still while the rest of us go under. I know him, Bruno. He'll come to our aid if we ask."

"If you're right, the meet should be safe enough. I've got all the details right here." Gaito hesitated. "Oh. Before I forget. Have you heard from Leo Tinelli, by any chance?"

"No. Why? Should I have?"

"Not necessarily. I was just hoping, is all." There was quiet at Gaito's end for a bit. "I've been trying to reach him at his place west of the city for half an hour, with no result."

"You don't think—"

Castellano didn't finish his question, and Gaito didn't volunteer a response. Neither had to. They both knew that they were thinking the same thing.

"The stinking Camorra," Castellano shortly huffed. "I hope they all rot in hell!"

"We have to kill them first, and so far we haven't laid a finger on the weasels," Gaito mentioned. "No one has."

"We will," Castellano vowed. "They bit off more than they can chew when they went up against us. They're all dead men, but they just don't know it yet."

"I hope you're right. I hate to be a pessimist, but if we don't get our act together soon, the days of the Mafia in America are numbered."

IT WAS HARD TO SAY who was more astounded by Victor Tinelli's outburst, the Camorrans or Mack

Bolan. The four gunmen halted in amazement, then charged toward the fence.

The soldier was out of the cab and at the boy's side before the echoes of the shout faded in the marshlands to their rear. He grabbed the youngster's arm and pulled him behind the cab as the truck resounded to the thud of heavy slugs.

"Let me at them!" Victor cried, striving to break loose. "They have to pay!"

Bolan had had enough. He gave the boy a shake that rattled Tinelli's teeth. "Listen up! Unless you quit acting this way, you'll never live long enough to pay any of them back."

The windshield abruptly splintered, then the glass in the window on their side rained on them in a shower of shards.

"Move!" Bolan said, pushing the boy across the road and into a belt of trees and growth that bordered the marsh. As soon as the vegetation closed around them, the soldier bore to the west, staying near the road rather than try to make it through the marsh with the boy at his side.

Shoes slapped the asphalt. The four Camorrans materialized next to the moving van. Talosi ran toward the trees, and two of his men followed but the last one balked.

"Why bother? We took care of all the rest. Now we have to get out of here before the police arrive."

Talosi barely slowed. "That kid is Tinelli's brat. Do you want to be the one to tell Scarlotti that we let him get away?"

The fourth man was convinced. Hefting his SMG, he trailed the others. He was armed with a Beretta in wide use in Italy, but it wasn't the Model 12 Bolan had appropriated when the firefight began. This one was the Model 4, an early SMG with a conventional blowback design but an unusual wooden stock. Most unique of all, the ejection port was on the left-hand side. The magazine held forty 9 mm rounds.

Bolan clamped on to Victor's shoulder, shoving the boy to the ground. "Not a sound," he whispered sternly, and was rewarded for wanting to save the child's life with a withering glare.

Talosi and the other Camorrans barreled through the underbrush to the edge of the marsh. There they stopped to survey the intimidating expanse of water, reeds and lilies.

The soldier was counting on them to go farther. When they did, he lingered until they were screened by a hummock, then he yanked Victor erect and bolted for the moving van. Climbing into the cab, he drew his ankle knife and bent under the dash.

"Keep watch while I hotwire this thing."

Victor's lower lip jutted out like that of a belligerent bulldog. "You shouldn't push me around the way you do, mister. I don't like it."

"Would you like it better if you were dead?"

Bolan ran a hand down the steering column to a cluster of wires. In all his travels he had rarely met a kid as hardheaded as Tinelli. A chip off the old block, as the saying went. Discarding the distracting thoughts, he traced the wires to find the two that would do the job. It took longer than he liked, for while the sky was growing lighter, the interior of the cab was still as gloomy as a crypt.

He found the wires in question, cut them, stripped the ends, and sat up. "Get ready," he advised the boy. He touched the bare leads. The engine growled to life, but it sputtered instead of roared, the carburetor coughing as if it had emphysema. He tried again and the sputtering was worse.

"What's wrong?" Victor wanted to know.

"When they shot at us, they hit the engine," Bolan deduced. Casting the wires aside, he slid from the cab. "We'll go up to your house and try to find a working phone."

Victor glanced at the crown of the hill, then blanched. "I'd rather not. I—" The boy choked off, fighting back more tears.

Bolan wished he could oblige, but leaving the youngster behind was a certain death warrant. "You can hide in the garden while I go in," he said, offering a hand.

Victor started to back away. The soldier leaned forward to grasp the boy's wrist, and as he did, lethal hail zipped through the space his chest had just occupied.

*"Get them!"*

It was Talosi and the death squad, splashing swiftly toward the road, the hardman with the old SMG in the lead. He was the one who had nearly terminated the Executioner. He tried again, firing as

Bolan threw himself and Victor behind the front tire. Asphalt churned, metal spanged, rubber thumped to multiple concussions.

Bolan rolled into the open, arms rigid, the Beretta tracking the quartet who were spreading out, all of them shooting now, their combined firepower making it sound as if a dozen men were beating on the cab with hammers. The soldier acquired a target and stroked off two rapid shots.

Slammed up short as if he had run into a brick wall, the Camorran placed a brawny hand over his sternum, gurgled blood, and toppled into the marsh with a loud splash.

The Executioner had to seek shelter again as the remaining three unleashed everything they had, their unified fire enough to fell a rampaging bull elephant. He reached down to his side, palming the Desert Eagle.

The shooting died. Bolan peered under the cab but couldn't find the gunners. It was cat and mouse now, and the cat had the added chore of safeguarding the cheese. Victor had squatted between the cab and the van. Bolan pointed at the latter's front tires and whispered, "Get behind there."

For once the boy wasn't disposed to argue. He began to crawl toward the van.

Suddenly weeds rustled, and the three Camorrans darted onto the road at three different points, two at the front of the truck and one at the rear.

Bolan swung around as the first shooter flashed past the bumper. The Desert Eagle boomed, the big

.44 slug smashing into the gunman's chest. The killer was flung to the earth, his pistol skittering under the cab.

Spinning, the soldier saw the Camorran with the old SMG sprint around the far corner of the van. They fired simultaneously. The hit man's rounds chipped the road next to Bolan. His own shots, one apiece from the Beretta and the Desert Eagle, chopped the gunner backward.

Bolan remembered Talosi. He pivoted, or tried to. The leader of the hit squad was only a few yards away, an Uzi held rock steady. There was no way Bolan could evade the lead that would spurt from the barrel. But as Talosi tensed to fire, a pistol blasted and his head was bashed sideways by a round that nailed him flush in the left eye.

The soldier straightened and took a step.

On his knees in front of the bumper, savage exultation lining his boyish features with sadistic glee, Victor Tinelli grinned and said, "See, mister? I told you I'm going to pay them back! I told you!"

# CHAPTER NINE

*Washington, D.C.*

The Executioner was treating himself to a full cup of black coffee when Hal Brognola entered the office and sank into the chair behind the desk. "Don't take this personally," Bolan quipped, "but you look like week-old roadkill."

The big Fed barely cracked a smile. "And don't take this personally, but I don't give a damn. Can I help it if I didn't get to shave this morning and my clothes look as if I've slept in them?"

"Did you?"

"What do you think?" Brognola smacked a sheaf of papers onto an already large pile, then stifled a yawn. "I can hardly leave with all that's going down."

"So what's the latest?" Bolan inquired, and took a sip of coffee.

"Where do I begin?" Brognola rejoined in exasperation. Tapping the pile, he said, "It will take me a year to process all these reports. More and more come in every hour."

"Any intel we can use?"

"Some." Brognola regarded a memo pad. "Before I get to it, you might be happy to learn that Victor Tinelli will probably be adopted by an uncle who has no links to the Mob. Social services has contacted him, and he's expressed an interest—" Brognola stopped, puzzled by his friend's expression. "What's wrong? I thought you would be glad for the kid after all you went through to save him."

"All I went through," Bolan repeated softly, reliving those awful moments when Talosi had been jarred by the shot and the boy had crowed like a rooster. "And for what? Ten years from now he might be in a position where I have to kill him."

Brognola digested the news. "Do tell. I had no idea." Clearing his throat, he said, "Let's talk about the Camorra, then. At least we've found out who is running the show."

"Scarlotti," Bolan said, recalling the name Talosi had mentioned.

"Antonio Scarlotti," Brognola elaborated. "He's been running the Camorra for about a year now, according to Interpol. He took over after his father was blown to kingdom come. And get this." Brognola leaned on an elbow. "Interpol believes Scarlotti was to blame."

"A sterling citizen," Bolan muttered.

Brognola snorted. "Not in the least. Italian police attribute over a dozen deaths to him, but they were never able to prove a single one. He's as slick as he is vicious, and as vicious as he is hungry for revenge.''

''No one had a clue what he was up to?''

''The Italian authorities were stumped. They knew that some of his top men were making frequent trips to the U.S., but not why. They also received tips that the Camorra was buying large shipments of weapons, enough to supply an army. But when they tried to find where the weapons were being stored, or if they had been resold on the black market, it was as if the crates had vanished off the face of the earth.''

''This Scarlotti has a knack for always staying one step ahead of the opposition.''

Brognola went on. ''About a month ago Scarlotti himself vanished. No one had any idea where he had gone until he launched his war against the Mafia. The Italians are sending over two of their best men to help us out, but I don't see what good they'll do unless they can gaze into a crystal ball and predict where Scarlotti will strike next.''

That brought up a point Bolan wanted to discuss. He had told Brognola about his run-in with the Camorrans in New York City, and about Scarlotti's mention of the Windy City. ''We know he plans to head for Chicago.''

''Thanks for reminding me.'' Brognola reached into the inside pocket of his jacket and produced an airline ticket. ''First-class. On the taxpayers.''

Bolan accepted it. He was booked on an evening flight out of Washington National Airport.

"A snitch in New York has relayed word that there is a big meeting of all the top mobsters slated for Chicago sometime tonight. We don't know where yet, but I'd like for you to be on the scene if something breaks."

"Scarlotti must know about it, too. But how did he find out so fast?"

Brognola laced his fingers and propped them behind his head. "I've been wondering the same thing. So far he's outfought the Mafia at every turn. He's raided hideouts even we didn't know exist. He's hit Mob businesses we had no idea were linked to organized crime."

There was only one possible explanation, in Bolan's view. "He must have someone in the Mafia on his payroll, someone who has been leaking information all along."

"Maybe several leaks," Brognola ventured. "Another possibility is that his own people have infiltrated the Mob. Evidently he's been planning this for quite some time. Years, in fact."

A gust of wind buffeted the window. Bolan rose and scanned the city. The Capitol, the White House, the many monuments—they were more than mere marble, mortar and stone. They were symbols of everything America stood for, symbols of the freedom Bolan had fought so hard to preserve, symbols that were being mocked by a brutal butcher who treated ordinary Americans as if they were so much cannon fodder.

"This business about Chicago is intriguing,"

Brognola stated. "Did you know that it's the only major city the Camorrans haven't hit yet?"

"On purpose, you think?"

"Why else would Scarlotti spare Fallini when every other Mob Family has been hit? My hunch is that he wants the Mafia to think Chicago is a safe haven. He planned it this way before the war even began."

Bolan glanced at his friend. "Do you realize what you're saying? You make him sound like Napoleon or Julius Caesar."

"Is it that farfetched? Think about what Scarlotti has done. Whatever else can be said about the man, there's no denying his genius. He's beating the Mafia at its game, on its own turf. Outnumbered ten to one, he's winning despite the odds. No real general could do any better."

The soldier had never heard the big Fed lavish so much praise on a common criminal before. "No real general would wage war on civilians. No real general would slaughter women and children." Fire danced in his eyes. "I hope to remind him of that, in person."

*Chicago, Illinois*

JOSEPH CASTELLANO FLEW into Chicago on his private aircraft, a Saberliner as richly furnished as *Air Force One*. The moment the jet pulled up to the hangar at O'Hare International Airport, it was ringed by men in dark suits. They were his own soldiers, sent ahead to make sure no unpleasant surprises greeted him.

Castellano bustled off the Saberliner into a limo. It was a custom job, complete with armored plating and shatterproof glass. The driver was also one of his men. "Head north up I-94," Castellano directed. "I'll tell you which exit to take."

By prior arrangement, only the bosses knew where the sit-down was to take place. None of their underlings was being told, thus reducing the risk of a leak.

Three sedans filled with hardmen flanked the limo as it wheeled from the airport and blended into the heavy flow of traffic.

For the first time since his casino had been destroyed, Castellano allowed himself to relax. The tension flowed away like water down a drain. As it did, a tidal wave of fatigue slammed into him, and he leaned back, closing his eyes.

Castellano had forgotten how much of a strain it could be to live on the raw edge for days at a time. The nervous system could only handle so much sustained tension, then the body began to break down, bit by bit. Mental clarity was shot all to hell; a person's stamina suffered; irritability was common.

In his early days, Castellano had been able to handle the stress with no problem. But he'd been in the prime of his life, not a man getting on in years. He made a note to force himself to get enough rest over the next several days or he would be no good to anyone, especially to those depending on him the most, his lieutenants and soldiers. They were the ones who would suffer the most if he made the wrong decision at a crucial moment. He owed it to them to stay sharp, to be ready for anything.

Which was a lost easier said than done, Castellano admitted. Never knowing where the Camorra would strike next, never knowing if the next door he opened might set off a bomb, or if a sniper or a carload of assassins might try to snuff him out, grated on Castellano like sandpaper on bare skin.

He was jittery. He hated it, but there was nothing he could do to combat the feeling. It was just there, every waking moment.

The ride northward helped to soothe Castellano's frayed nerves. They travelled past Des Plaines and Park Ridge, past Northbrook and Wheeling, past Deerfield, the urban sprawl gradually giving way to rural countryside, as he had been told it would.

Don Fallini had picked the site for the sit-down wisely. Rather than hold the meeting in downtown Chicago, where the Camorra could easily hit them and melt away into the throngs on the street before the law arrived, Fallini had picked a unique spot where security would be ideal.

Decades earlier, back in the heyday of Prohibition, back when Al Capone and his boys ruled the roost, the Chicago branch of the Mafia had obtained a number of properties out in the country for the express purpose of smuggling booze and guns and whatever else was hot at the time.

Among those properties was a hunting lodge that had been around since the turn of the century. Situated close to the Wisconsin border, on the shore of Lake Michigan, it was known as the Moose Head.

According to Don Gaito, the odds of the Camorra knowing about the lodge were remote to nil. No longer used for smuggling operations, Fallini had converted it into his private retreat. Three or four times a year he drove up and spent a few days fishing and hunting to recharge his batteries.

There was only one road in and out. Since the lodge backed onto the lake, no one could approach it from the east without being spotted. On the other side, the forest had been cleared for hundreds of yards and was mowed regularly, affording a clear field of fire.

It sounded perfect.

As an added precaution, Fallini had assured Gaito that nearly every soldier in his organization would be on hand to provide protection. Men with rifles and SMGs would be posted at ten-yard intervals around the perimeter. Nothing would be able to get in or out without his say-so.

Castellano gave directions as needed. When they turned onto the secondary road that paralleled the shoreline, he felt more at ease than ever. Lake Michigan was so immense it reminded him of the ocean, and Castellano had always loved the seashore. He was tempted to have the driver pull over so he could walk along the beach with his shoes off, as he had liked to do when he was a kid.

Common sense prevailed. Grown men didn't do such things, he told himself.

Ahead appeared a gas station and a small market. A sign proclaimed that they sold fresh sandwiches and cold beer. Castellano's stomach rumbled, reminding him that he hadn't eaten since the night before. Tapping the partition, he said, "Pull over up there."

"We have plenty of gas," the driver mentioned.

"I'm the one running on empty," Castellano said. "Get me a couple of sandwiches. Pastrami on rye if they have it. If not, then ham and cheese. And a root beer."

As the driver slowed, Castellano spied a white stretch limo and a sedan parked near the store. Standing next to the limo was a man built like a balloon. Dressed in a garish pin-striped suit and green felt hat, the man looked exactly like the pimp he was. "Fat Sal," Castellano muttered. Then, louder, he said, "Pull up next to that poor excuse for a blimp. Tell the boys not to get nervous. I know that clown."

Walkie-talkies enabled the driver to keep in touch with the soldiers in the three sedans. The word was relayed, but five gunners still popped out of the foremost sedan when their little caravan coasted to a stop, and they came forward to surround Castellano.

Fat Sal was slurping on a chocolate milkshake.

His own hardmen closed to protect him, but he waved them off with a flick of a thickset hand. "Don't sweat it, fellas," he said jovially. "Hello there, Joe. Long time no see."

Castellano was glad of that, but he didn't let his feelings show. He despised Sal Nordeli, a leech who made his living exclusively off of prostitutes and showgirls. It surprised him that Nordeli had been invited to the sit-down. It only showed how desperate the situation had grown. "How are things in Vegas?"

"Need you ask?" Fat Sal rejoined, and burped. "If this stupid war keeps up, I'll be broke within a month. A lot of my girls are too scared to work." He slurped noisily on his straw. "I keep telling them that they have nothing to worry about, but they won't listen. They know about the brothel that was blown up."

Castellano credited them with more brains than their boss. "Let's hope that all goes well at the sit-down."

"What can go wrong?" Fat Sal said. "Those Camorra geeks are scared of Don Fallini. They won't dare invade his territory."

Castellano made small talk until his driver came out. "Well, it's been nice seeing you again," he lied. "Watch yourself."

"Not to worry," Fat Sal said, patting the white limo. "I just got this baby a month ago. It has a bar, a TV, even a satellite hookup, although I haven't quite figured out how to work the damn thing. Plus armor plating and glass a bazooka couldn't dent.'' He beamed proudly. ''Worth every penny, don't you think?''

Castellano wondered how many hours Sal's girls had to work to come up with enough pennies to pay for it. Absently nodding, he slid into his own limo and slammed the door. ''Get me out of here,'' he told the driver. ''The stench is spoiling my appetite.''

MACK BOLAN HAD no sooner set down his duffel bag in his hotel room than the phone buzzed.

''Perfect timing, Striker,'' Brognola said. ''I just received word that something is in the wind at Fallini's residence in Evanston.'' The big Fed paused. ''Do you mind working with our local people on this one, or do you want to go solo?''

Normally the Executioner preferred to ply his trade alone. It wasn't so much that he was a loner at heart, although that was part of the reason. Simply put, he'd learned the hard way time and again that he was vastly more effective when he operated alone. The only back he had to protect was his own, and he didn't have to pay for mistakes made by others.

But the firefight at the Tinelli estate had taught Bolan a lesson. This time operating alone had its drawbacks. It was one thing to go up against the Mafia or the Camorra separately, quite another to be caught in the middle and have to take on both at once. ''I have no objections,'' he said.

"Good. Agents Lassiter and Rafferty will be there to pick you up in ten minutes. Meet them out front."

"My cover?"

"The usual. I'll make it clear to them that they're to do whatever you say. They'll give you a free rein."

"Any other news?" Bolan asked.

"Word from Detroit that a boss was gunned down while visiting his tailor's. The tailor bought the farm, too. And three capos in the Gambini Family in Atlanta were rubbed out by a car bomb that killed four bystanders. Business as usual."

"Don't worry. We'll get Scarlotti sooner or later."

"It's the 'later' that worries me."

The big Fed hung up. Bolan changed from a sports jacket into a lightweight coat with enough pockets to store half a dozen spare clips and assorted lethal items. He was out on the curb at the appointed time.

A brown unmarked four-door pulled up. Out poked a mane of red hair and a face that should have been in makeup commercials. "Agent Belasko? I'm Agent Rafferty. I believe you're expecting us?"

Bolan slid into the back seat. The redhead studied him, unasked questions lurking at the back of her eyes: Who was he? How is it that he had so much clout? Why was he being forced on the Chicago field office whether they wanted his help or not?

"This is Agent Lassiter," Rafferty introduced her partner, an older man with gray hair at the temples and no latent curiosity. Experience, as the old saying went, was always the best teacher.

"My pleasure, Mr. Belasko," Lassiter said while wheeling into the avenue. "I trust Mr. Brognola has filled you in?"

Bolan repeated Brognola's exact words.

"All day cars have been coming and going at Fallini's," Lassiter said. "Within the past hour, five showed up and have been parked out front, just waiting. We figure that he'll be leaving soon and taking a lot of muscle along."

"He's heading for the sit-down," Bolan said.

Rafferty bobbed her head. "That's our guess. And we'll be with him all the way."

"You're planning to tail him?" Bolan asked skeptically. Fallini would spot a tail right away and do whatever it took to shake it.

Lassiter smiled. "Give us more credit than that, Mr. Belasko. We planted a wireless VHF transmitter in his private limo the last time it went into the shop to be serviced. The transmitter has a range of twenty miles, so we can hang back and shadow him without Fallini being the wiser."

Rafferty took up the account. "At the time, we had him under surveillance in connection with an extortion racket. No one foresaw this Camorra mess."

"Who could?" Bolan said. He was amused by the probing glances she bestowed on him when she thought he wouldn't notice. "Has there been any hint at all that Scarlotti is in Chicago?"

"None so far as we know," Lassiter said. "We've put the heat on our street snitches, but none of them have heard so much as a peep. If you ask me, the Camorrans made a mistake by not hitting Fallini sooner. He's ready for them now. If they do show, he'll make them wish they had stayed in Naples."

"Will he?" Bolan mused aloud, recalling his talk with Brognola.

The redhead's flashing blue eyes narrowed. "Pardon my asking, Mr. Belasko, but do you know something that the rest of us don't?"

"Only that some words of wisdom have been around for ages for a reason."

"Sir? I'm not sure I follow you."

Bolan made it as plain as he could. "Never count your chickens until they're hatched, Agent Rafferty, or you might wind up with egg on your face."

SALVATORE NORDELI—"Fat Sal" to those who knew him best—bit off a thick piece of greasy sausage and chomped heartily. The back seat of his limo was covered with snacks he had bought at the market, including a bag of jumbo candy bars he couldn't wait to tear into.

Nordeli had always had a weakness for food, just as he'd always had a weakness for women. Thanks to the first craving, he weighed 304 pounds, buck naked. Thanks to the second, he had a nice house in Vegas and a healthy bank account. To say nothing of his new wheels.

Scores of pretty babes hustled their tails for Nordeli seven days a week from dusk until dawn. It was safe to say that he had more whores on the hook than anyone else in Nevada, and he was proud of the fact, too.

He knew that some of his associates sneered at him behind his back. He didn't care. Let them work five times as hard as he did to make their money. He'd rather earn his the easy way. Life was too short to spend it in a sweat.

"Say, boss," the driver unexpectedly remarked, "looks as if there's a line down."

Nordeli glanced up.

A mile back they had turned onto a winding highway that would bring them to Lake Michigan and the Moose Head. A few hundred feet ahead, on the left, was a dirt road. Just before it, a cable of some sort lay across the highway. Parked on the shoulder was a utility company truck bearing the words, Illinois Power and Light. A barrier had been erected in front of the cable, and three men in hard hats were huddled next to a power pole.

"Just great," Nordeli groused.

One of the hard hats saw the approaching limo and rose, motioning for it to stop. Acting rather sheepish, he sidled around to the driver's side and leaned down to see in the open window. "Sorry, sir, but the wind has downed a power line."

"How long before we can go on?" Nordeli asked.

"Let me check with my supervisor." The hard hat straightened and nodded at the two men by the pole, then reached under his jacket and pulled out a mini-Uzi. At a range of less than six inches, he shot the driver to shreds.

Nordeli sat as rigid as stone, too stupefied to move. Only vaguely was he aware that the two hard hats by the pole had also produced SMGs and were firing at his men in the sedan behind the limo. Only vaguely did he realize that four more gunners had spilled from the back of the bogus utility truck and added their firepower to the slaughter.

The phony repairman smirked at Nordeli as he extended the Uzi. "Antonio Scarlotti sends his regards, pig."

The Uzi burped.

## CHAPTER TEN

By Mafia standards Vincenzo Fallini lived modestly. His three-story house was no more extravagant than those of his neighbors. He didn't have a swimming pool, a hot tub, tennis courts or any of the many perks men in his position indulged in. Quaint flower gardens bordered his circular driveway, and the front gate hung open.

Agent Lassiter nodded at the residence, saying, "You'd never guess that the boss of Chicago's underworld lives there, would you?"

Bolan had to admit that he wouldn't have. Their car was parked on the other side of the street, nearly a full block from the brownstone. There had been very little activity since they arrived.

The sun crowned the western horizon. Pink fingers clawed across Lake Michigan. Ships were coming in, others leaving. The scene was idyllic.

Lassiter's cellular phone chirped. He was only on it a minute, saying "Uh-huh" a lot. "That was our office," he reported. "We've been keeping tabs on the airlines, the bus terminals and the trains. No unusual influx of Mediterranean types has been noted. I doubt the Camorrans are going to show.''

"What about moving vans?'' Bolan asked.

The agents looked at him as if he were from another planet. "Sir?'' the redhead said.

"They used rented trucks to hit a boss in New York,'' the soldier divulged. "Maybe that's how their hit teams travel from city to city. No lawman is going to think twice about a moving van that pulls off an interstate highway.''

Lassiter and Rafferty exchanged glances. "Why didn't anyone let us know?'' the older agent grumbled, snatching up his phone. He put in a call, then told Bolan, "Two of our men are going to contact every rental outlet in the city. It could be midnight before they're done, though.''

Ten minutes of uncomfortable silence ensued. Rafferty broke it by turning to the back seat and saying as sweetly as a little girl trying to cajole her parents, "It was quite a surprise to get a phone call from Hal Brognola personally. We've all heard of him, of course, but it isn't often that a field agent is contacted directly by one of the head honchos.'' Her pause was masterful. "Known him long, have you?''

Bolan kept a straight face. "We were conjoined twins separated at birth.''

Lassiter cackled.

Agent Rafferty flushed as scarlet as her hair but maintained her sweet disposition. "Touché. I suppose I deserve that for snooping. But you can't blame me for being inquisitive.''

"I'd be, if I were in your shoes,'' Bolan admitted to put her at ease.

Just then the front door to Fallini's house opened, disgorging a steady file of hardmen in suits who piled into the waiting vehicles. One of the last to emerge was a white-haired man as straight as a rod, his every movement brisk and precise.

"Don Vincenzo Fallini,'' Lassiter declared.

The Mob boss ducked into his limousine. In single file the procession wheeled along the driveway and turned left, heading in the opposite direction.

"Time for fun and games,'' Rafferty said. From the glove compartment she removed a gadget the size of a large portable radio and placed it flat on her lap. "I love the S-930,'' she remarked. "It's easier to use than my VCR remote.'' Fingers flying, she turned the unit on, adjusted the gain on the grid display, then fiddled with a knob until a small dot resolved into a bright pinpoint moving toward the top of the grid. "Bingo. We're in business, people.''

Lassiter cranked the engine and pulled out. He got on the phone to other agents who would also be trailing the limo. Three separate tracer cars were being used to guarantee that Fallini wouldn't give the Feds the slip. In addition six cars containing extra agents had been assigned to trail the tracers.

Bolan felt like the proverbial fifth wheel. Until

they learned where the Mafia meet was being held, he had to let the FBI do all the work.

The Mob convoy made straight for I-94 and bore to the north. Lassiter stayed about five miles behind. When the limo slowed, he slowed. When it sped up, he did the same. The outskirts of the city faded to the rear, and still the mafiosi didn't deviate from their course.

"Where the hell can they be going?" Lassiter wondered. "At this rate we'll wind up in the boonies before too long."

"Does Fallini own any property in the country?" Bolan inquired. The Camorra had already shown that it liked to hit its targets where the Mafia would least expect, as was the case at Tinelli's sanctuary in the marshlands.

"West of here is an old brewery he bought years ago," Rafferty revealed, "but no one has used it in ages."

"He also owns some prime real estate northwest of the city," Lassiter said. "Undeveloped acreage, though."

The agents stayed in contact with the other tracer cars and the backup agents. They were upbeat, confident that their quarry wouldn't elude them. Bolan reserved judgment. When dealing with the likes of Fallini and Scarlotti, there was no such animal as a "sure thing."

"We're over twenty miles from Chicago and still going strong," Lassiter presently commented, and chuckled. "Maybe Fallini plans to swing up through Wisconsin and Minnesota to the border. Wouldn't it be a hell of a note if the sit-down is in Canada?''

"Don't even joke like that," Rafferty chided. "You know we can't leave the States without authorization.''

"I can," Bolan said.

The redhead appraised him carefully. "Why am I not surprised? Something tells me that there isn't much you can't do, Mr. Belasko. What's that military expression—'rank has its privileges,' eh?''

"Something like that.''

More miles went by. At last the blip on the receiver moved to the right. Rafferty gave a gleeful if unladylike snort and declared, "They've taken an exit.''

By then the sun had set. Homes were few and far between, streetlights even rarer. For a while they followed a secondary road that flanked the lakeshore.

"He's stopped," Rafferty suddenly announced.

Lassiter reduced his speed by half. "Relay the news to the backups. All vehicles are to pull over and wait until they hear from us. We'll check it out.''

The distance narrowed to four miles. To three. Then two.

"We're under a mile from the limo," Rafferty soon informed them. She began to lift her head, then stiffened. "Wait a minute! Fallini is on the move again! He's continuing north.''

Bolan saw a smattering of lights in the distance, the brightest a neon sign. "It's a gas station," he said.

"But they haven't gone far enough to need gas," Rafferty said. "So why did they stop?"

The soldier had no ready answer. It disturbed him, though. "Pull into the parking lot. We don't want to get too close to Fallini. He might spot our headlights."

Two cars were at the pumps, two more parked in front of a market. A woman was carrying a toddler from a rest room.

There was no sign of the mobsters.

"Want me to top off the tank or something?" Lassiter asked.

"Why not?" Bolan said. It would allow Fallini to get farther ahead. He wasn't worried about losing the convoy, not as long as the transmitter continued to function properly. Once the sedan braked, he put a hand on the door handle. "I'll be right back. I'm going to check things out."

Bolan hadn't taken five steps when a slender figure materialized at his elbow.

"I'd like to stretch my legs, too," Rafferty said. "If it's all right with you, sir, that is?"

"Suit yourself," Bolan responded. She was entitled to do as she pleased, but he couldn't help wonder if she was tagging along because she didn't quite trust him. At the market he held the door. For some reason the redhead smirked as she entered.

An elderly man sat behind the checkout reading

a newspaper. The sole customer was a middle-aged woman with her hair up in curlers.

Bolan bought a pack of gum and offered a stick to Rafferty as they crossed the lot to the pumps.

"Thank you, sir."

"Quit calling me that. 'Mike' will do fine."

"Whatever you say, si—" She smiled sheepishly. "Sorry. It's hard to treat a superior like one of the boys, if you know what I mean."

"My official capacity is that of a liaison. I'm not here to act as your boss," Bolan clarified.

"I beg to differ," Rafferty said. "Mr. Brognola was quite clear. In no uncertain terms he told us that we are to do what you want, when you want, no questions asked. If that doesn't make you my superior, I don't know what does."

They were at the car. Bolan pulled on the door, then happened to glance at the rear of the market. The snout of a dark sedan poked past the corner. Leaning against the front fender was a black-haired man in a black suit and shoes. The man was studying them closely.

Acting as if he hadn't noticed, Bolan slid in. "Pull out slowly," he told Lassiter. "Don't exceed the speed limit unless I tell you to."

The older Fed dutifully complied. Rafferty shot Bolan a quizzical look.

Shifting so he could drape an arm over the top of the back seat, Bolan saw headlights flare to life behind the market. The sedan lost no time in wheeling onto the highway, heading in the same direction they were going. "We've picked up a tail," he announced.

Lassiter stared into the rearview mirror. "Want me to shake them?"

"And confirm their suspicions?" Bolan shook his head. "No. They might be in radio contact with Fallini. For the time being we don't do anything."

Rafferty had been consulting the tracking device. "The Don is about two miles ahead of us."

"Contact your backups. Tell them to move on out."

A few quick calls on the radio, and Rafferty reported, "They're on their way. The nearest backup is about five miles behind us. Want me to have them speed up and overtake the sedan?"

"No." Bolan was emphatic. The Mafia gunners were bound to spot it, and a running firefight would take place. Since he had no idea how close they were to the sit-down site, it was best to keep a low profile for now.

"Fallini has turned east," Rafferty suddenly said, and swiftly pulled a map from a briefcase on the seat beside her. She had to rely on a pencil flashlight to see. "It's a secondary road in the middle of nowhere." She ran a red fingernail across the map. "It connects to another highway that parallels the lakeshore."

Bolan had a decision to make. Should they take the secondary road, too, or go past it to fool the gunners behind them into thinking that they were not stalking the Don? "How far ahead is Fallini now?"

"Over a mile and a half," Rafferty said. "He's taking his sweet time. I doubt he's doing fifty."

The soldier performed a few calculations. Since the S-930 had a range of twenty miles, he figured they had ten to fifteen minutes to spare. "When we get to the secondary road, go on by."

Lassiter's unflappable composure showed a crack. "Are you sure, sir? What if we lose Fallini?"

"It's my head that will be on the chopping block," Bolan said, giving Rafferty a meaningful look. "You're just following my orders."

The junction shortly appeared out of the darkness. Lassiter gave it a wistful look as they passed. "I just hope whatever you have in mind works."

Bolan felt the same way. He gazed out the back window, looking to see Fallini's soldiers turn right at the intersection. They should follow their boss once they were convinced Fallini was in no danger.

The gunners kept on coming.

"Uh-oh," Rafferty said.

The soldier drew the Beretta and added the sound suppressor. Tapping Lassiter on the shoulder, he directed, "When I give the word, I want you to slow enough for me to jump out without breaking every bone in my body."

"You'll need help," Rafferty volunteered.

Bolan double-checked that the sound suppressor was on tight. To Lassiter, he said, "Keep going for a mile or so, then turn around and pick me up. It should be over by then.''

Rafferty refused to take the hint. ''Didn't you hear me, Mike? Two can get it done better than one.''

''Do you have a sound suppressor?'' Bolan asked.

''No, but—''

''I go it alone.'' The Executioner gauged the distance between the two vehicles at four hundred yards. A curve loomed approximately two hundred yards to the north. ''See that?'' he asked, again tapping Lassiter. ''Be ready.''

''Good luck, sir,'' the older Fed said.

''I wish you'd let me lend a hand,'' Rafferty persisted.

Bolan faced the door and tugged on the handle. Wind whistled as he opened it a few inches and propped his feet against the rocker panel. The car took the turn doing close to sixty. As soon as they were screened from the gunners, Lassiter slammed on the brakes and counted down the miles per hour.

''Forty! Thirty! Twenty!''

Shoving the door, Bolan launched himself into the cool air. For a moment he seemed to hang motionless. At the spot he had jumped, the shoulder of the road was narrow and fringed by high weeds and brush. His right shoulder smashed onto the gravel hard enough to scrape the skin raw but not enough to snap his collarbone. He tucked and rolled, hurtling into the weeds like a human battering ram, flattening them as he tumbled, going much too fast to suit him but unable to stop until he came up against a tree stump. Jarred, he heaved upright and sprinted to the highway. He almost failed to make it in time.

The hardmen had sped up. Traveling at close to seventy, they screeched around the turn. There were four or five, Bolan couldn't tell exactly. He did see the driver clearly enough. Whipping up the Beretta as he dropped into a combat crouch, he stroked off two parabellum sizzlers.

The windshield laced with cracks. The driver threw his hands to his head and screamed. The other gunner in the front seat lunged at the steering wheel and tried to bring the vehicle under control, a doomed effort. Roaring along at more than fifty miles per hour, the car slanted to the far side of the highway, jumped a ditch and went airborne. Tires spinning, engine revving, it plowed into a row of saplings and splintered them as if they were so much kindling.

Bolan lost sight of the car as it slewed into denser woods. A resounding crash signaled it had come to a stop. He leaped over a series of broken saplings, wound among tall pines and spied the vehicle lying on its side, the crumpled front end lodged against a tree half as wide as the car. Steam spewed from the ruptured radiator, while smoke rose from the engine.

The rear door flew open. A hardman pushed up from within, coughing and sputtering. He hung half over the side, swatting at the smoke. Suddenly he spotted the Executioner and clawed under his jacket.

Bolan had the man dead to rights. At his shot the gunner twisted sharply and dropped into the car. Someone cursed. The body was hiked back up until it slid partway through the window and slumped back onto the roof.

The Executioner circled. As he stepped past the grille, he saw a mobster scrambling over the dashboard to climb out through the shattered windshield.

"Bastard!" the man raged, extending a revolver.

It would have been smarter to shoot rather than yell. Bolan beat him to the punch, his slug adding a new nostril. The gunner slumped onto jagged glass, but he was in no condition to care.

Cautiously Bolan stepped closer. The driver lay crumpled on the front door. So he had accounted for three of the four or five occupants. Where were the others?

The rustle of leaves gave him a split-second forewarning. Flattening as rounds pinged off the hood, he caught sight of the shooter thirty feet to the northwest. The man ducked behind a tree before Bolan could fire. Making like an eel, he wormed into a band of thick grass that in turn brought him to a large oak. Hugging the bole, he stood.

Other than the death rasp of the radiator, the woods were quiet. Bolan tried to locate his quarry, but the hissing was as loud as a whole nest of riled vipers sounding off at the same time. Not worried about the noise he made, he dashed to another trunk. If he couldn't hear the gunner, the gunner couldn't hear him.

Bolan wanted to end it quickly and get back to the road. Every minute was vital. He hunkered next to a thicket and automatically glanced over a shoulder.

Something moved near the broken saplings.

The soldier realized that while he had been seeking to outflank Fallini's soldier, the mobster had outflanked him. Pivoting, he ran to catch the wily gunner before the man got out of sight. A couple of rapid shots drove him onto his belly, but only long enough to return fire. A shadow he took to be the mobster turned out to be a dead tree.

The real mafioso was moving again, hobbling as if he had a bad leg.

Bolan's eyes narrowed. As dark as it was, he could tell there was something wrong about the man's silhouette. In a few seconds it came to him. There were two men. One was hurt and was being helped by his companion.

That both were fit enough to fight back became clear when Bolan rose to follow and two pistols cracked simultaneously. The slugs zinged near enough to give him pause. He headed to the northeast, his tread as silent as a seasoned hunter's.

If either of the gunmen got away, they would contact their boss, and Fallini might see fit to call off the sit-down. They had to be stopped.

Bolan saw the highway. He was north of the spot where he had plunged into the forest. As yet there was no sign of the Feds but they would be along shortly. Slowing, he moved to the edge of the asphalt.

Fifty feet distant, the pair of hardmen emerged. The hurt one was doubled over, staggering every few steps. They came to the ditch and he stumbled, his groan barely loud enough for the soldier to hear.

Crabbing onto the highway, Bolan took his time taking aim. He wanted to be sure. But at that very moment a car engine growled, and the FBI agents sped around a bend to the north. Their headlights caught him smack in the harsh glare.

The mobsters saw him. The one who wasn't hurt let go of his injured partner and adopted a two-handed grip. His friend fell onto a knee and brought up a Smith & Wesson.

Bolan fired, dived to the left, rose into a crouch and fired again. It was a technique he had honed to perfection, and it served him in good stead. His first shot spiked the gunner who posed the greater threat, the man who had survived the crash unscathed. His second shot ended the suffering of the gunner who had been hurt.

The screech of locked brakes made Bolan whirl. The car was canted across the highway, its tires squealing. Bolan could see Lassiter frantically spinning the steering wheel, but it had no effect. The car knifed toward him, so close already that it appeared he didn't have a chance of living out the night.

But Bolan hadn't lasted as long as he had by having slow reflexes. As he whirled, he leaped straight into the air, tucking his knees to his chest. The car's front end swept under him, brushing the heels of his shoes. The radio antenna clipped him on the knee, tearing his pants but doing no real damage. He alighted in the middle of the highway as the vehicle slid to a lurching halt.

Rafferty jumped out of the vehicle and ran around the front of the car, calling, "Are you all right, Mr. Belasko? I thought you were a goner!" She took his arm as if expecting him to keel over.

Bolan, touched by her genuine concern, slowly straightened. "I'm okay."

Lassiter stared meekly out his window. "Sorry, sir. I didn't see you until the last second." He was so rattled, he was shaking.

"No harm done," Bolan said.

Rafferty shook her head in amazement. "You must be part kangaroo. How you managed to jump so high, I'll never know."

"Adrenaline," the soldier replied. Ushering her around to the passenger's side, he told her to climb in. "I'll hide the bodies." It only took a minute. He left them next to the saplings, covered by branches and brush. As he jogged back to the car, the redhead turned a worried expression his way.

"What is it now?" Bolan asked.

"The signal from Fallini's limo." Rafferty gave the tracking device an angry shake. "I've lost it."

## CHAPTER ELEVEN

Agent Leslie Rafferty kept saying the same thing over and over as their car hurtled eastward along the secondary road. "It can't be. It just can't be."

"Maybe your unit is on the fritz," Lassiter broke in at one point. Then he gave a little jump in his seat, as if he'd had a brainstorm. "Say, did you remember to put in new batteries before we left the office?"

The redhead gave her partner the sort of look that could wither a plant at ten paces. Grumbling to herself, she went on fiddling with the gain and resolution controls. "The transmitter must have crapped out," she guessed aloud. "Microchip circuitry isn't indestructible, you know."

Bolan had borrowed the map and her flashlight and was taking note of their location. "The highway that borders Lake Michigan is only a quarter of a mile ahead of us," he noted. "When we get there, take a left."

"How do you know Fallini didn't go south instead?" Lassiter asked.

"He's been heading north since he left Chicago.

There must be a reason.'' Bolan scrutinized the map between the intersection they were nearing and the Wisconsin border. There was only one small town, known as Winthrop Harbor, which had a population of six to seven thousand. He mentioned the fact to the agents. ''Has it turned up in any local field reports pertaining to organized crime?''

Lassiter answered. ''I've been assigned to the Chicago office for over five years, and I've never heard the name mentioned. If Fallini owns property there, he's kept it a closely guarded secret.''

Rafferty gave a start of her own. ''There are his regular disappearances—'' she said lamely.

''His what?'' Bolan probed.

''Two or three times a year he vanishes, never longer than a week, usually for no more than two or three days. Several times our people have tried to tail him, without success.''

Lassiter beamed. ''We could be on to something here. Ever since I can remember, a rumor has been floating around that the Don has a special retreat in the north part of the state.'' He made a smacking sound with his lips. ''We never have been able to pin the damn place down.''

It gave Bolan food for thought. ''Let's assume the transmitter is still working. What would keep the signal from reaching us?''

Rafferty shrugged. ''Oh, I suppose if it were in a vault or ten stories underground we wouldn't pick it up.'' She scanned the country on either side of the road. "For that matter power lines and radio towers could interfere with reception."

The soldier had seen neither in a long time. He set the map down when they came to the junction. Lassiter did as he had been told. To the east the surface of the huge lake sparkled with the reflection of countless stars. Otherwise the water was as dark as the grave.

They had proceeded a short distance when the phone beeped. Rafferty did the honors, disappointment creeping into her voice. On hanging up, she sighed and shifted. "So much for your hunch about moving vans, Mr. Belasko. Our people have contacted over half the rental companies in the city and haven't turned up anything suspicious."

"Too bad," Bolan said. But he was still certain the Camorra planned to hit the Mafia sometime during the big meet. So some Camorran hit men had to already be in the city. Maybe Scarlotti himself would show up. Although that just might be wishful thinking.

IT WAS A rambling farmhouse built around the turn of the century. Long neglected, the farmhouse suffered a leaky roof, the paint had largely peeled and several of the windows were cracked.

Antonio Scarlotti had no cause to complain, though. He was more interested in the big barn behind the farmhouse than in the house itself.

At that moment the barn was a whirlwind of activity centered around the stripped-down frame of the white limousine that had formerly belonged to Fat Sal Nordeli from Las Vegas. The body men were lining the frame with plastic explosive. Others were attaching packets to the inside of the fender wells. Still more were cramming explosives into the rocker panels, to the inside of the bumpers—in short, into every nook and cranny on the vehicle. A sinister smile curled Scarlotti's mouth. By the time his men were done, the limo would be a mobile bomb capable of mass destruction on a staggering scale.

Guilo Falcone strutted over, declaring, "It's going well, boss. Andreotti tells me that they'll be done by one."

Scarlotti's smile contorted into a frown. "Is he hard of hearing? Are you hard of hearing? When I told you that I want the work completed by midnight, that's exactly what I meant." Bending so he was nose to nose with his lieutenant, he growled, "Have I made myself perfectly clear?"

Falcone's smug attitude evaporated. "We heard you, boss. But it's a lot to ask." He gestured at the workers. "See for yourself. They're going as fast as they can, but there's only so much they can do—"

Like a striking cobra, Scarlotti's right hand lashed out and fastened on to the young killer's neck. Falcone proved his courage by not flinching, although his throat bobbed.

"I don't want to hear your pitiful excuses, Guilo," Scarlotti said in the manner of a teacher scolding a prized pupil. "The car must be done by midnight so it can arrive at the Moose Head by quarter past twelve. If it's not, it will not be of any use to me. We will lose perhaps the best and only chance we will have of eliminating the top Mafia dogs in one blow."

Scarlotti's grip grew noticeably stronger. "That will make me very, very angry. And you really don't want to see me angry, do you?"

"No, sir."

"Then be so kind as to relay my displeasure to Andreotti. I trust that will spur him to greater speed."

Falcone hurried off. Scarlotti inwardly laughed and turned toward the wide double doors just as a car horn sounded outside. Checking his watch, he stalked to the front of the barn and stepped outdoors. Four of his men had a portly specimen surrounded and were covering him with their *luparas*.

"Ah, Milano!" Scarlotti said. "You are forty-five minutes late."

The heavyset man mopped his perspiring brow with a monogrammed handkerchief. He was nattily dressed, including gold cuff links, a gold tie clip and a gold watch that had to have cost a small fortune. "I did the best I could, Mr. Scarlotti," he responded. "But my boss isn't letting anyone out without his personal say-so. I'm lucky that I could get away at all."

Scarlotti smiled. "Haven't you learned yet that

fortune is a most fickle mistress? One man's luck can be another man's downfall, or vice versa.''

''Spare me your bumpkin homilies. You know why I'm here.''

''Yes, you've come for your money. But before you get what is due you, I have a few questions.''

Milano grew defensive. ''Questions? What the hell are you trying to pull? Our deal was plain and simple. Information in exchange for money. So where is my two million?''

Scarlotti wagged a finger at his visitor. ''Where are your manners? Can it be that the once high and mighty Mafia is composed of common thugs and ruffians nowadays?''

''Quit trying to bait me,'' Milano retorted. ''If I cared about La Cosa Nostra, would I have agreed to sell out my own Don?''

''You sold out Fallini because you are a greedy bastard,'' Scarlotti said. ''You have always lived well beyond your means. That is why you are so deeply in debt, why you were so eager to accept my offer.'' He clasped his hands behind his back. ''We knew that we could turn you from the outset.''

''Okay. Okay. So I've got a few character flaws. Who doesn't?'' Milano leaned against his car. ''Besides, you can hardly blame me for abandoning a sinking ship. At the rate you're going, in another month there won't be anything left of the Mafia in America.''

''Such is my fondest wish,'' Scarlotti conceded.

"Now to business. Does your boss suspect the trap we have laid for him?"

"Are you kidding? Not on your life." Milano chortled. "He thinks that coming to the lodge was the brightest idea he's ever had. The idiot! He doesn't even remember that I was the one who suggested it to him."

"Has Nordeli's absence been noticed?"

Milano chortled louder. "Who in their right mind would miss that slob? If Fat Sal were never to show up, no one would give a damn."

Scarlotti glanced into the barn at the flurry of tasks being performed. "Oh, Nordeli will arrive soon enough."

"I don't want to hear about your plan," Milano said. "The less I know, the better. All I want is my two mil so I can get back before Fallini wonders what took me so long."

"Be patient," Scarlotti said, and raised a hand when the Mafia turncoat went to object. "First things first. I need to know exactly how many Dons are attending the meeting. The last time we talked, you told me that you were uncertain."

Milano scowled. "And I still am. Fallini is playing this one close to the vest. I think nine are supposed to show up, plus about a dozen lesser bosses like Fat Sal."

"How many soldiers?"

The capo impatiently tapped his foot. "Every last member of my regime has been called in, and so have two other regimes. That makes over sixty. Plus

Fallini's own men. I'd say about eighty from Chicago alone. Then you have to factor in the soldiers the Dons and other bosses will bring. Make it 100, 120 tops.''

Scarlotti gazed at the stars a moment. He strolled to his right as if deep in thought. When he stopped, he no longer stood between his four men and the mafioso. "Maybe 100? Maybe 120? I can't help but think that you are being much too vague."

"I'm telling you all I know," Milano declared indignantly.

"As one of Fallini's top lieutenants, you should know the exact number. Could it be that you are holding out on me? That you intend to take my money, then turn on me and inform your boss that we are going to hit the lodge?"

The portly man licked his thick lips. "What kind of a fool do you take me for? I'd never be stupid enough to double-cross you." He mopped his forehead again. "As for the rest, I can't say exactly how many soldiers will be there because the Dons who are coming haven't let us know how many they're bringing. Each boss can bring as many as he wants."

"Such inefficiency. I would never tolerate it in my own organization. No wonder the Mafia has proved so easy to destroy." Scarlotti sighed. "All right. Call me foolish, but I will take you at your word."

"Any more questions?" Milano demanded.

"No. I believe that covers everything of importance."

The Chicago gangster held out his pudgy right hand. "Finally. Hand over the money. If I don't get back soon, I'm in big trouble."

The corners of Antonio Scarlotti's mouth quirked upward. "I am afraid you are already in big trouble."

Milano went as rigid as a broomstick. "What?"

"I have made no secret of my hatred of the Mafia," the Camorra's leader declared matter-of-factly. "But there is one thing I hate even more. Can you guess what that is?"

The mobster glanced at the four gunners, at the shotguns they held, his face becoming as white as a bedsheet. He didn't reply.

"No?" Scarlotti said. "Well, I'll tell you. The one thing I hate more than the Mafia is a traitor to his own people. Of all the virtues, I value loyalty the highest."

Milano forgot himself. "This from a man who murdered his own father? Is that your idea of being loyal?"

The Neapolitan's eyes danced with inner flames. "So you have heard that vicious rumor, eh? Well, let's assume, for the sake of argument, that it happens to be true. Do you think that makes me a hypocrite?"

"The worst kind."

"But what if I were to tell you that my father had to be removed for the good of the Camorra?

That there is a higher allegiance than simple blood ties? That our oaths to our organizations must be put before all else, including family? Surely you can understand?''

"Family is just as important. You'd never catch anyone in the Mafia murdering his own father. It's as low as a man can sink."

The flames brightened. "Yet another Mafia weakness. It explains a lot." Scarlotti consulted his watch. "Time to end this charade, I'm afraid."

Milano recoiled. "Now hold on, mister! We had a deal!"

"A deal with a turncoat is no deal at all."

Grasping at straws, the capo blurted, "You're making a mistake! If I don't make it back, my boss will be suspicious. Security will be tightened. He'll double the guards. You'll never be able to pull it off."

Scarlotti chuckled. "I suspect that you overrate your importance in the scheme of things. Fallini will be so busy entertaining his guests that it will be many hours before he wonders where you have gotten to. And even if I'm wrong, there is nothing the Mafia can do to stop me. I have laid my plans too well."

Sweating more than ever, Milano started to back toward the rear of his car. "Look, forget about the two million. Just let me leave in peace, and I'll disappear off the face of the earth. You'll never see or hear of me again."

Like a cat toying with a mouse, Scarlotti watched

the mafioso intently. "At least have the dignity to accept your fate like a man."

Milano's reservoir of courage was only skin deep. He broke, bleating, "Damn you! I don't want to die!"

Scarlotti looked at his four triggermen. "Do it."

The mafioso swooped a hand under his jacket. It was his last earthly act. Four shotguns discharged buckshot into him from less than ten feet, blowing him apart. His head, his chest and his stomach exploded in a grisly shower of pulped flesh and blood. Milano tottered, but somehow his body stayed on its feet. Half his face was gone, his chest was a smoking cavity and his intestines were oozing from his ruptured abdomen, yet he stood there, swaying, like a horrible caricature of a movie monster.

"Remarkable," Scarlotti commented. Walking over, he poked the fat man's left shoulder with a single finger. The body pitched backward, making an audible squish.

"Want us to bury him, boss?" a gunner asked.

"Traitors do not deserve such an honor," Scarlotti answered, turning to the barn. "Drag him off into the woods. We'll let the animals dispose of his remains."

Rubbing his hands in satisfaction, Antonio Scarlotti squared his broad shoulders and inhaled the crisp air. All his years of plotting and preparation were about to pay off. The vast amount of money and resources he had committed to the Camorra's quest for vengeance would shortly reap a glorious harvest.

"WE'RE PICKING UP the signal again!" Rafferty stated, smacking the dash in her excitement. "Don't ask me how or why, but we are!"

Mack Bolan had been staring out over Lake Michigan. Their car was just cresting a hill and before them stretched a narrow valley that sloped down to a small cove. On a spear-shaped peninsula that jutted into the lake, a cluster of lights had appeared.

"What the devil is that, sir?" Lassiter asked. "We're nowhere near that town you mentioned."

Bolan leaned over the front seat. From the number of lights there had to be a lot of buildings. "Maybe we've hit the jackpot."

The redhead contacted the other FBI agents as Lassiter wound down a grade to a straight stretch of highway that would take them right past the peninsula. A sign reared on the right, an old sign, chipped and weather-beaten, the words so faded that Bolan could barely make them out.

"The Moose Head Lodge," Lassiter read aloud. "Luxury Accommodations At Reasonable Rates. The Finest Hunting And Fishing For Your Money."

A board had been nailed across the sign, announcing that the resort was closed. The board seemed to be nearly as old as the sign itself.

"Strange," Lassiter said. "The place doesn't look closed to me."

Bolan rolled down his window. Most of the lights were clustered in the center of the peninsula. The exceptions were two rows that stretched to the right and the left, almost to the water's edge.

The road curved away from the lake. A line of tall trees blocked their view, but only for a short while. Soon the road curved back again. They were nearing the peninsula. Bolan spotted a high fence.

"This has to be it," Lassiter stated.

As if to confirm his statement, they came to a turnoff. Beside it a large sign informed one and all that it was a private drive. Entry was barred by a sturdy gate. Four men in dark suits stood inside the gate, a couple of them smoking cigarettes.

Rafferty flashed a smile at Bolan. "There is a Santa Claus after all! Just think! If we only had probable cause to bust these guys, we'd have the haul of the century."

Bolan was noting the height of the fence. Thanks to a lamppost next to the gate, a sign mounted on it was plain to see: Warning: High Voltage. A little farther on he spied a pair of Mafia hardmen patrolling the perimeter. They made no effort to hide the rifles they carried.

Lassiter whistled softly. "We'd need a tank and a small army to get in there, and all we have are a dozen agents." He glanced around. "How do you want to play this, sir?"

"Keep on going," Bolan instructed. "The mobsters will assume we're heading for Winthrop Harbor.'' He nodded at Rafferty. ''Have the other agents pull over before they get to the valley. Too many cars going past at this time of night will make the guards wonder.'' He pondered a moment. ''Make it clear that they are to hide their vehicles. We don't want any late arrivals to spot them, and have them be ready to back us up at a moment's notice.''

The redhead grinned. ''Just a liaison, huh? You give orders as if you were born to command.''

Bolan wasn't surprised to learn that the fence completely cut off the peninsula from the mainland. The only way on or off from the landward side was by the well-guarded private driveway. He waited until a curve hid their taillights, then told the Feds to pull over.

''What are you up to?'' Rafferty queried as he opened his door.

''Do you have a spare radio?''

It was Lassiter who responded. ''Here. You can take mine.'' He unclipped his from his belt. ''We only need one anyway.''

The soldier thanked him. ''Kill your engine and sit tight. I don't know how soon I'll be back.'' He went a few steps. ''If you haven't heard from me in a hour, you're on your own. Do what you think is best.''

''Wait—'' Rafferty said.

But Bolan was gone, sprinting into the pines and across a grassy strip to a rocky beach. To his left

Lake Michigan blended into the background of the night. To his right the peninsula poked six or seven hundred yards into the lake. He prowled the shoreline until he found where the fence barred anyone from setting foot on the Mafia's sanctuary.

Bolan moved to the water and started to strip off his jacket. He was in for a long, cold swim. A collection of driftwood, including a few logs, gave him pause. He examined one almost as long as he was and as thick around as an oil barrel. Dragging it into the water, he shoved it in until it bobbed gently, then he climbed on, lying flat on his stomach, and paddled vigorously.

The lake was tranquil. The log cleaved the surface neatly, becoming easier to propel as it gained speed. Bolan stayed forty yards out from the north shore of the peninsula, far enough that any gunners roving the shoreline wouldn't hear the faint splash his hands made every time he dipped them in.

Far out on the lake a ship appeared, a tanker on its way to Chicago. No other vessels plied the waterway. Nor was there much action on land. Another pair of hardmen were visible on a bank, but both men faced south and didn't spot him. He stroked onward, toward the tip of the peninsula.

A boulder-strewed spur offered the concealment he needed. Bolan had to push against the end of the log to get it to angle into shore. When the log grated against the bottom, he slid off, sinking in up to his knees, and pulled the log far enough onto the beach to prevent it from floating off. He might need it again.

The Executioner turned to the boulders and promptly drew up short.

Someone had coughed.

Two gunners materialized from out of the pines that lined the shore.

## CHAPTER TWELVE

Joseph Castellano was impressed, and it took a lot to impress him.

The New Jersey mobster had always prided himself on running a tight ship, as it were. His men always did as they were told when they were told to do it. No excuses were tolerated; no complaints were allowed. Any soldier who didn't pull his own weight was ousted without a qualm. If the offender happened to know information Castellano didn't want made public, then a concrete cocoon and a dip in the Atlantic Ocean were in order.

But Castellano had never seen any operation that meshed as smoothly as Don Fallini's. The Chicago boss ran things with military precision. His soldiers were the next-best thing to a platoon of Marines, no-nonsense types proficient at dispensing death in a variety of ways.

Fallini had given Castellano and a few others a grand tour shortly after Castellano arrived. He'd seen for himself the dozens of guards roaming the grounds and those posted at strategic points in the main cluster of buildings.

At long last Castellano felt safe. Since the bombing of his casino, he had been a bundle of nerves, jumping at loud noises and suspicious of everyone and everything. Even at his safehouse in Teaneck, he had been plagued by gnawing doubts that he wasn't one hundred percent secure.

Now he could relax and enjoy himself.

Forty-five minutes before the sit-down, Castellano was at the bar in the lodge, a Scotch whiskey tipped to his lips. Around him milled twenty of the top bosses in the country. About half he had met before. The rest he knew by reputation.

Out of the mix stalked a bulldog of a man who gave off an air of scarcely controlled violence. Men much taller and broader than he was instinctively got out of his way. He was like a pit bull in the midst of terriers. "Joseph!" he said warmly, offering a callused hand. "It has been too long."

"That it has, Don Gaito," Castellano said. By using the title, he tacitly acknowledged that the New York boss was his superior.

"Please," Gaito said, shaking hands, "between friends, first names only." He encompassed the spacious room with a sweep of his arm. "What is your assessment of our Chicago friend's organization?"

"They aren't the barbarians everyone claims they are," Castellano said. "The Chicago Families have come a long way since the days of Capone and his crew. They were animals."

"True enough." Gaito leaned closer so only the

Jersey boss could hear. "Just between the two of us, do you think we can trust Fallini?"

Castellano was reminded once again of his friend's paranoid nature. "I would stake my life on it," he said.

"That's good. Because you are."

Whatever retort Castellano might have uttered was snipped off by the arrival of their host. Don Fallini whisked into the room, greeting those he hadn't yet met, renewing old acquaintances. As always, he conducted himself with the stately dignity of an ancient Roman senator. When at length he reached the bar, he ordered a drink, then faced the pair from the East Coast.

"Gentlemen. I trust you have found my arrangements to your liking?"

Castellano nodded. "I couldn't have done better myself. I can only hope that when this awful business is over with, you will do me the honor of being my guest at my home on the south Jersey shore. It's only a fourteen-room house, but the fishing is great and there is plenty of peace and quiet."

"I may just take you up on your gracious offer."

Fallini's drink came. Castellano saw Bruno Gaito study their host closely and was taken aback when his friend gruffly demanded, "Something is wrong, Fallini. I can see it in your eyes. What gives?"

The Chicago boss was as surprised as Castellano. "What they say about you is true, Mr. Gaito. You don't miss a thing." He lowered his voice. "Since you have asked, I will be frank. I am somewhat concerned by the absence of one of my capos. He claimed that he had to go meet someone who had news of the Camorra, and he never returned.''

"Maybe the scumbags nailed him," Gaito said.

"Perhaps. Although, as far as I know, Scarlotti and his bunch are nowhere near Illinois." Fallini took another sip. "In any event we cannot let it disrupt the meeting. Not with what is at stake."

Castellano scanned the room. "Is everyone else present and accounted for?"

"All except Salvatore Nordeli from Las Vegas. I invited him at the last minute, so perhaps he was unable to tear himself away from his women."

An electric charge seemed to ripple down Castellano's spine. "But he's here. I saw him earlier."

"At the lodge?"

"No. At that market halfway between I-94 and here. He should have arrived hours ago."

Don Fallini set down his unfinished drink. "This is most distressing. Two disappearances in so short a time?" He adjusted his tie and smoothed his jacket. "I will have my men investigate. In the meantime, my friends, it might be best if we kept this information to ourselves. Some of the others might see fit to cut and run if they got wind of it."

Gaito grunted. "Fine by me. Just don't keep any more secrets from us. Sink or swim, we're all in this mess together."

Castellano was profoundly upset. Just when he thought that he was safe, his world threatened to come crashing down around him again. He barely heard their host inform them that the sit-down would begin in twenty minutes whether Nordeli and the missing capo showed up or not. He nodded absently when Fallini excused himself. A hard squeeze on his wrist brought him back to reality.

"Snap out of it, Joseph," Gaito said harshly. "The two of us have to work together or neither of us will leave here alive."

"What are you saying?"

The New York Don sniffed. "I should think it would be obvious. Fallini is a stand-up guy, but he doesn't have everything under control like I figured he did. We have to take steps, just in case."

Castellano tried to follow his friend's train of thought, but his brain was stuck in neutral. "What steps?"

"Think, man. Think." Gaito drew him to one side of the bar. "If the Camorra attack this joint, I don't intend to stay boxed in with all the rest. It'll be every man for himself. I'm going to have my boys bring my car around to the side of the lodge and keep it there. I'd advise you to do the same."

It was sound advice, Castellano admitted. Most of the vehicles were in a garage southeast of the lodge. He hadn't minded pooling his with the rest because the garage was guarded day and night by Fallini's men. But now that he thought about it, having the limo handy for a quick getaway was more important. "I will."

"While you're at it, have some of your boys mingle with Fallini's soldiers. Tell your men to keep their eyes and ears peeled. If they overhear anything unusual, anything at all, they should pass it on to you right away.''

More sage wisdom. Castellano had a whole new appreciation for why Gaito was the top New York boss and one of the most respected men in the Mafia. ''Anything else?''

''That should do it for now,'' Gaito said. Cracking a grin, he gave Castellano's shoulder a friendly poke. ''You might want to lighten up a little. Walk around with a sour puss like that, and everyone will know something is wrong.''

''I'll try.''

Gaito arched an eyebrow. ''Trying is for losers, Joseph. Winners go out and *do*.'' He headed for the lodge entrance, chatting amiably with others along the way.

Castellano marveled at his mentor's self-control. Adopting a poker face, he walked toward a side door that opened onto a hallway. No one paid him any attention. Once out of the building, he surveyed the lake and the forest to the west. Where before the scenery had seemed so serene and inviting, the brooding waters and gloomy woodland now seemed rife with menace.

He could only pray that Gaito was wrong.

CROUCHED BEHIND BOULDERS on the north shore of the peninsula, Mack Bolan watched the pair of gunners walk slowly toward him. They talked in low tones. It was evident that they hadn't seen him, that they didn't know anyone else was within a hundred yards. When they were close to the boulders, they halted. One pulled out a pack of cigarettes.

Bolan drew the Beretta. He had removed the sound suppressor in order for it to fit into his shoulder holster. Now he quietly took out the attachment.

"—hate it when the boss comes up here," the gunner partial to a smoke was saying. "This place bores me to tears. All these trees and rocks and nothing else. Hell, how can anyone stand to live in the country?"

The other man laughed. "Ask someone who was raised on a farm. Me, I'm city bred, just like you, Vinnie. But I don't see things the same way." He took a deep breath. "I sort of like it up here. It's real peaceful."

"It used to be, Moe," Vinnie grumbled. "But now, with those Camorran bastards whacking us every chance they get, we can't take anything for granted."

Moe nodded. "The boss seems to think we're safe enough, though. He said as much."

"Bull."

"Huh?"

"If he really believes we're so safe, why is practically every soldier in the Family here? And don't give me that garbage about security for the sitdown. The boss could provide security with a third of the men he has here."

Bolan extended his pistol but held his fire when

the two triggermen hiked westward, their backs to him.

"You might have a point," Moe conceded. "Still, I doubt we have much to worry about. Even those Neapolitan morons wouldn't be dumb enough to attack us when we're ready for them. They like to catch us when we're off guard."

"Says you. Me, I'm not letting down my guard for a minute. No, sir. No one is getting the drop on me."

The Executioner lowered the pistol. When the gunners melted into the night, he jogged across the beach and into a cluster of pines. Almost immediately he caught sight of another pair of guards to the south, tramping eastward. He swung wide of them, alert for more.

The peninsula was essentially flat except for a sawtooth earthen spine thrust upward by a geologic upheaval ages past. Not quite twelve feet high, it was easily scaled.

Bolan went prone and surveyed the buildings. At the center of the peninsula stood the main lodge, an enormous log edifice that had to have cost a fortune to build. Three smaller, newer buildings flanked it. To the east and west of the lodge were a dozen large cabins. Beyond it was the driveway that linked the hideaway to the highway. Lights blazed all over the place, illuminating every nook and cranny. No one could get close to the buildings without being seen. Guards were everywhere.

The soldier memorized the layout to relay to the

Feds. He began to back down the spine, stopping when footsteps crunched to the south. Yet another pair of hardmen was coming toward him. These two had SMGs leveled and were scanning the knobs of earth at the top of the spine. There could only be one reason. They had caught a glimpse of him, perhaps the silhouette of his head and shoulders when he rose above the crest. But they had misjudged his exact position. Halting fifteen feet off, they concentrated on a spot above them.

The soldier cored their brains, a single shot apiece. As they crumpled, he slid down, dirt rattling, pebbles clattering. The noise wasn't very loud but apparently it was loud enough because suddenly someone in the woods to the east called out, "What was that?"

Bolan darted to the north and ran for all he was worth. Once the bodies were discovered, the alarm would be sounded. That section of the peninsula would be crawling with hardmen. He had to get to his log quickly.

No other mobsters appeared, and Bolan reached the tree line without mishap. About to venture onto the open beach, he paused on seeing something strange out in the water. It was a series of dark bumps strung out in a ragged line. Whatever they were, they hadn't been there before.

His hesitation saved his life.

For down the shoreline rushed Vinnie and Moe, drawn by the outcry Bolan had heard. They were staring into the trees, their backs to the lake. It was a fatal mistake.

As the Executioner looked on, two of the "bumps" rose up and aimed spear guns at the unsuspecting gunners. Metal glinted in swift flight. Vinnie and Moe were pierced between the shoulder blades, the points of the spears bursting through their sternums. Both gunners died on their feet, dumbfounded looks on their faces.

At a signal from one of the scuba divers, twenty frogmen waded to shore. They lost no time stripping off their scuba gear. Tanks, wet suits, flippers, belts, all were piled neatly at their feet. They pulled dark pants, shirts and shoes from waterproof packs, as well as small SMGs, pistols, knives and daggers and assorted hardware.

The Camorrans had arrived.

Exhibiting military precision, they separated into four squads and were about to plunge inland when the underbrush crackled and two mafiosi blundered onto the scene. They no sooner stepped from concealment than a dozen Uzis fitted with suppressors burped simultaneously. To say the doomed twosome resembled Swiss cheese when the firing stopped would be a gross understatement. The withering spray of lead had chewed them to ribbons.

Again one of the Camorrans gestured. The squads peeled apart and glided into the vegetation. Four of them passed within twenty feet of the soldier. He had a downed limb to thank for his deliverance. Partially covered by it, he was impossible to see.

Open warfare was about to begin. Bolan wondered if more frogmen had landed at other points on the peninsula. Probably. Once again Antonio Scarlotti had demonstrated a flair for tactics that went far beyond anything Bolan had come to expect from most criminals. Maybe Brognola was right, after all. Maybe Scarlotti did have a streak of genius.

The Camorrans were gone. Bolan ran to the boulders that ringed the log and squatted. Unclipping the radio, he switched it on. A red power light was supposed to glare, indicating the batteries were charged. Instead, it flickered feebly. He gave the radio a shake, then pressed the transmit button and said just above a whisper, "Rafferty, do you copy?"

Static crackled, breaking off every few seconds. Bolan tried again with the same result. The radio was designed to be waterproof, so he doubted that he had damaged it when he paddled from the mainland. Especially since he had taken extra care not to get it wet.

Bolan recalled Lassiter asking the redhead if she had remembered to charge the batteries to the tracer unit. Maybe the FBI agent had failed to take his own advice with regard to his own radio.

Mildly exasperated, Bolan tried again. The Feds had to be appraised of the new development. It was the moment they had been waiting for. They could bust on in with their sirens wailing and arrest everyone.

Realizing the radio was useless, Bolan debated his next step. It would take fifteen to twenty minutes for him to return to where he had found the log and alert Rafferty and Lassiter, time that could be better spent doing what he did best.

Once the battle raged in earnest, the Feds were bound to hear and come on in anyway.

Bolan ran to the bodies of Vinnie and Moe. The Camorrans hadn't bothered to take their weapons, so Bolan helped himself to an Ingram M-10 fitted with a web strap attached to a swivel mounted on the barrel. It had no suppressor, but it would have to do. Two extra magazines were in Moe's pockets. Vinnie had carried a Colt AR-15 with a collapsible stock.

The soldier slung the subgun over his left forearm for the time being. He ran westward, following the contours of the shore until he was due north of the northernmost cabin. Lights were on inside. He came as close as he dared to the circle of light cast by a lamppost.

Yelling broke out toward the middle of the peninsula. So did automatic gunfire. The *crump* of an explosion lit up a corner of the lodge.

A grenade, Bolan knew. He saw the cabin door open, and out spilled five gunners. Hardmen rushed out of the other cabins along the row. Confusion reigned for a few seconds as they shouted back and forth. When another grenade went off, they awakened to the danger their bosses were in and charged toward the lodge.

A group of six or seven men appeared east of the cabins. They unleashed a volley that shriveled the ranks of the onrushing Mafia soldiers. The mafiosi sought cover and gave as good as they got, slaying several of the Camorrans and driving the rest back into the pines.

All across the peninsula, gunfire had now broken out. Men were bellowing, screaming, cursing, dying. Bolan had seen more than his share of Mob warfare, but nothing like this, nothing to match the numbers involved. Certainly nothing to match the sheer savagery and bloodlust of the two sides involved. Mutual hatred fueled the bloodbath. No quarter would be given until one side or the other prevailed.

It was next to impossible for Bolan to tell the players without a scorecard. Camorrans and Mafia gunners dressed virtually alike. The Camorrans, being native Italians, had the characteristic features and hair coloring of their countrymen, but in the dark it was hard to tell a black-haired Camorran from a dark-haired mafioso.

Bolan did notice that the Camorrans favored Uzis over other SMGs, just as they had in New York and New Jersey. Since they had never shown any such preference in their native Italy, he suspected that Scarlotti had smuggled crate loads of the popular Israeli SMG into the U.S. specifically for the war.

It was another shrewd tactical decision. Uzis were more compact than most SMGs. The minis and the micros were two of the smallest on the market. Even so, they boasted impressive cyclic rates that were more than enough for any gunner to hold his own in pitched combat with a similarly armed enemy. Best of all, the minis and micros had about the same muzzle velocity as the full-size Uzis, 1310 feet per second.

The Executioner sprinted to the rear of the first cabin, jogging along the back wall where the shadows were deepest. Almost instantly two men raced out of the trees. Whether they were Camorrans or Mafia gunners was of no consequence. Bolan had no favorites. He was there to put both out of business. The slaying field was wide open.

As far as he was concerned, it was him against everyone else.

Bolan relied on the Colt AR-15. Similar to the M-16 in size and caliber, it molded to his hands like an old friend. The major drawback to this version was its 5-round magazine. He emptied it drilling the two soldiers.

Casting the rifle aside, Bolan cradled the M-10 and bolted forward. The swirl of combat centered on the lodge and the buildings nearest it, but all along the row of cabins individual clashes were taking place. Bodies dotted the landscape. From the woods to the east and the direction of the mainland came the blasts of shotguns, pistols and subguns.

The Camorrans had attacked on all fronts at once.

Judging by the din, the Mafia was putting up stiff resistance. It wouldn't be long before the FBI joined the fray.

A hedge brought Bolan to a halt. Slanting to the right, he was almost to the end when a hardman hustled out of the night not ten feet away. They spied each other at the same moment, and the gunner brought up a Browning autorifle.

A tap on the trigger was all Bolan needed to crank out a 9 mm hailstorm. Rounds stitched the man's chest, knocking him back into the murk.

Bolan ran on, his goal the lodge. Ahead a fierce conflict between a large group of Mafia soldiers and Camorran hit men was raging. The soldiers had the same goal as Bolan. The hit men were determined to keep them from getting there. Lead flew thick and furious.

The risk of taking a stray slug was enough to cause Bolan to head for the forest. Explosions buffeted the air. Mafiosi at the upper windows in the lodge were firing down into encircling Camorrans. Speeding up the driveway was a white limousine. Miraculously no one was shooting at it.

The Executioner took it all in at a glance, a glance that would have been better directed in front of him. Because just as he came to the trees, a hulking shape reared out of nowhere and a pistol boomed.

## CHAPTER THIRTEEN

The sit-down had been under way for more than ten minutes when the shooting began. Joseph Castellano was seated next to Bruno Gaito at an enormous oval table on the second floor. Don Fallini had just given a short speech in which he thanked everyone for showing up and was pouring himself a glass of water. The other bosses were either conversing in low tones or waiting for the Don from Detroit to speak. Each one of them was to take a turn, in rotation.

"What's with the gunfire?" the boss from New Orleans demanded.

Fallini was already in motion. Hastening to the door, he briskly snapped, "Find out who is firing and why!" to a waiting lieutenant. The man dashed off, gunners in tow. Other soldiers entered and moved to the wide windows.

Some of the bosses rose and made as if to leave. Fallini stopped them with a disarming smile. "Gentlemen! Gentlemen! I'm sure we have nothing to worry about. Let's continue, shall we? This meeting is too important to be put off."

They had hardly settled down when more shooting broke out. This time it didn't taper off, but grew louder. Raised voices rent the night.

Stunned silence fell over the room. Each of them knew what it meant. Secretly all of them had hoped that it wouldn't come to pass, and now that it had, their minds balked at accepting the reality. All except for Bruno Gaito. He was on his feet first and at the door before anyone else moved.

"I'm out of here, people. If you're smart, you'll do the same." The New York boss opened the door. "If any of you make it out alive, meet me in two days in L.A. at the place where we had the West Coast sit-down last year. I believe everyone knows where it is." With that, he was gone.

Castellano roused himself to follow, his *consigliere* at his heels. He heard Fallini assuring the others they need not worry, that his men could handle the Camorrans.

"Says you," the boss from Houston stated, rising. "You also claimed those curs would never find this place." His comment sparked a general exodus, with bosses shoving one another to get to the door.

Thankfully Castellano beat all of them. He ran to a spiral staircase and raced down it to the ground floor. By prior agreement, he had only brought his *consigliere* and one capo to the meeting. The rest of his men were in a cabin to the south. Turning to the capo, he barked, "Get the rest of the boys and meet me at the front gate."

"We'll be there."

The noise outside indicated a major battle was taking place. Slugs splattered against the building and zinged through windows as Castellano sprinted toward the north side of the lodge. He was halfway across the dining room when the building was jarred by an explosion.

"Grenade, boss!" the *consigliere* cried.

Castellano didn't let it slow him down. The side door was open, manned by two of Fallini's soldiers who were firing at targets near the cabins. "Step aside!" he commanded.

The thinnest of the gunners looked around. "I wouldn't go out there if I were you, sir. The Camorrans are all over the place. We can't guarantee you'll be safe."

"Your boss promised us protection," Castellano reminded them. "I expect you to do your best to see that I reach my vehicle."

The two hardmen swapped looks.

"We'll do what we can, sir," the thin one said.

"Lead the way."

The Jersey boss was only three steps behind them when they charged outside, but it was enough to save his life. The instant the two soldiers appeared, they were riddled, sinking lifeless in crumpled heaps. Castellano dived for the turf, bumping into his *consigliere*.

An engine roared. Bruno Gaito's black limo rocketed down the circle driveway to the straightaway to the gate and zoomed off doing over seventy. Bullets spanged off the armor plating and the windshield, doing no real damage. Four sedans flashed from the garage to fall into place behind the limo.

Castellano realized that Gaito had to have told his soldiers to stay close to their cars and be ready to leave on short notice. He wished that he had exercised the same foresight. His own boys might not make it out because of his lapse.

A momentary lull brought Castellano to his feet. His limo was only twenty feet off but it seemed like a mile, seemed as if he were running in slow motion. His driver leaped out to open the rear door for him. "No!" he roared. "Get back inside before you—"

The crown of the driver's head flew into the air. Spewing a scarlet trajectory, the swatch of hair and flesh smacked Castellano in the face. Some of the blood flew in his eyes and mouth. He gagged, swatting the scalp aside. Blinded, he stumbled and would have gone down if not for his *consigliere,* who caught hold of him and forcefully threw him into the back seat.

"Hang on, Joe!"

The *consigliere* leaped behind the wheel and revved the engine. Slamming the gear into Drive, he tromped on the gas.

Castellano made a mental note to give the guy a hefty hike in salary if they lived long enough. Swiping blood from his face, he almost cheered as they zoomed toward the straight stretch to the gate.

To Castellano's astonishment, Nordeli had finally

arrived. The white limousine was hurtling toward the garage and cover. The poor slob had gotten there at the worst time possible and didn't have the brains to get the hell out while he still could.

Incredibly no bullets struck Nordeli's vehicle. The Camorran hit men were too busy eliminating their Mafia opposition.

The white limo entered the parking garage without so much as a scratch.

"Some people have all the luck," Castellano muttered.

IN THE HULKING GUNNER'S haste to shoot Mack Bolan, he brought up his pistol too fast, with no regard for a low limb at his elbow. His arm smacked against it just as he squeezed the trigger. The premature shot missed the Executioner by a hair. Bolan had only to jab the muzzle of the Ingram into the man's gut and stroke the trigger.

The Executioner ran on into the trees and turned to the south. A trio of hit men, framed by saplings, was pouring fire at mafiosi pinned down beside a cabin. He did the mobsters a favor and disposed of the trio with a short burst. Not a minute later he gave two Mafia hardmen the same treatment.

Bolan was close to the lodge now, close enough to witness furious hand-to-hand at a side entrance already littered with corpses. Stilettos and daggers flashed. A man screeched, his neck slit from ear to ear.

Up on the third floor, gunners were still firing

down, but not as many. Bolan waited for his chance, then streaked to the rear corner. The area in back of the lodge was a slaughterground of blasted forms. The combat, though, had passed on to other points. Bolan gained the next corner without anyone taking a potshot at him.

He was in time to see Don Fallini step from the lodge. Gunners had spread out in two rows, forming a human shield for their boss, and for others who rushed out at a word from the Chicago boss. A few of them Bolan recognized from file photos and his days spent infiltrating the Mafia. They were fellow bigwigs, bosses from other cities.

Most of them made it to the garage. The Don from New Orleans wasn't so fortunate. A wild round caught him in the left ear and blew his brains out all over the boss from Seattle, who stopped in horror and took a round in the shoulder for his carelessness.

Fallini was the last to go in. He didn't race madly, as the others did. He walked, taking his sweet time, as if he were out for a stroll in a park and not in the middle of the mother of all firestorms. The man had style, if nothing else.

At long last sirens wailed. Flashing lights converged on the peninsula. Whether the gunners at the gate would let the Feds enter was problematic at that point. At any rate the agents were on their own.

Bolan needed to stop the bosses from getting away. He started to jog toward the rear of the garage, but a shout from a sharp-eyed gunner provoked a blistering fusillade of lead that drove him back. He replied with the Ingram and was driven back again. From the garage issued the snarls of engines turning over. In another few moments the bosses would make their break and he was powerless to stop them.

After ejecting the magazine from the SMG, Bolan slapped in a new one. He was going for broke. All or nothing. He coiled to make his bid when suddenly the soil under his feet shook so violently that he pitched against the lodge. He had the illusion that the wall sprang to meet him, that the logs buffeted him to the earth when actually it was a shock wave that would have registered off the Richter scale if a seismometer had been nearby.

The sound of the explosion was another split second in coming. It was Armageddon made audible. It was Hiroshima at ground zero. It was without exception the loudest blast that the warrior had heard in his long career. Or so he imagined. Perhaps it was his proximity to the target that made him think so. Perhaps it was how close his eardrums came to being ruptured.

Flat on his back, he felt the ground under him heave upward as if it were a bucking bronco and he a rodeo rider. He saw the rear wall of the lodge tilt toward him. Impossibly it appeared that the building was going to crash down on top of him. He flung himself to the left, rolling out into the open, not caring if the gunners spotted him because they could no more get off a shot than he could.

Instantly hot wind blasted him, heat scorched him, as if he had somehow rolled from Illinois into the Sahara Desert. He blinked, then blinked again, riveted by a sight few men ever get to see and live to tell of it.

The huge garage was no longer there. Where the garage had been, a towering column of debris, dust and flame heaved upward. With the devastating force of a volcanic eruption, an explosion had quite literally blown the structure sky-high. The crown of the billowing cloud seemed to touch the stars. For a few moments the image was frozen. The expansion of gas and matter had attained its apex.

Then, like a punctured hot-air balloon, the firecloud began to fold in on itself. The force of the explosion had been expended. Gravity reclaimed its own.

Debris began to rain to the ground, small bits and pieces at first, growing larger swiftly. A jagged chunk of concrete bigger than a car smashed to earth six feet from Bolan. Had it struck him, he would have been pulverized. Stinging slivers tore his cheek.

Covering his face with his arms, Bolan rolled back behind the lodge. It offered some protection but not enough. The night rained debris. Busted wood and mangled steel beat a steady staccato all around him. There was a rending crash. Glass shattered. Something thumped him on the shoulder blade, then his left shin was seared by pain.

There were times when seconds could seem to

span ages. This was one of them. Bolan knew that from the moment he first felt the shock wave to when the debris stopped falling, no more than fifteen seconds had elapsed. Yet, to him, it was an eternity.

When the crashing, rattling and pounding ended, Bolan lifted his head. Dust choked the air. What was left of the garage covered the immediate vicinity with rubble a foot high or higher. He slowly stood.

Above him the lodge wall had been marred by a wide crack that threatened to split it in two. A portion of the roof had caved in. Bolan stepped past the corner and discovered the south side was much worse. Half of it had been blown inward, nearly all the rest had collapsed.

Of the garage, not a standing shred remained. Even the concrete foundation had been torn loose and reduced to fragments the size of gravel. Here and there among the rubble lay the grotesquely twisted bodies of automobiles, limousines mangled beyond all recognition. Engine blocks that normally could withstand incalculable pressure had been squeezed and bent and carved into sections.

Bolan's ears were ringing. It was several seconds before he realized that either the night had gone deathly silent or he had gone deaf. He gave his head a shake and heard the piercing scream of sirens. But that was all. No gunshots, no grenades, no shouting. The battle had ceased, as if on signal. And maybe the explosion had been a signal of sorts, letting the attackers know that they had done what they came to do.

The Camorra had accomplished something no one else had ever been able to accomplish. It had destroyed the upper echelon of the Mafia in one fell swoop.

The Feds arrived in a blaze of lights and burning tires. Weapons out, they rushed groups of Mafia gunners who made no effort to resist. Stunned by the debacle, the majority of hardmen stood with their arms limps, their mouths slack.

Agents Rafferty and Lassiter ran toward Bolan. "Where's Fallini and the other bosses?" Rafferty asked. "We'll whisk them behind bars so fast, their heads will spin!"

Bolan watched tendrils of smoke rise from the ruin.

"Mr. Belasko? Mike? Didn't you hear me?" Rafferty urged. She nudged him. "Are you all right, sir?"

"Fine," Bolan said, but someone who knew him better would have known differently.

"Please, sir, where can we find Don Fallini and the rest?"

His mouth a thin line, Bolan pointed at the spot where the garage had been. "Do you have a sieve?"

"WHAT'S WRONG, Striker?"

Mack Bolan stood on the windswept east shore of the peninsula, his hands in his pockets, gazing out across Lake Michigan. It was past five in the morning, and a blush of pink tinged the horizon. "What makes you think anything is the matter?" he responded without looking around.

Hal Brognola frowned. He had flown in from Washington the minute he heard about the outcome. To be exact, he had ordered a jet readied after talking to Agent Rafferty. He had asked about his friend, and her answer had deeply disturbed him.

"Mr. Belasko is fine, sir," she had said. "I think he is, at least. He won't say much."

"He wasn't wounded?" Brognola had immediately asked.

"No, sir. He just keeps to himself. He only talks when someone talks to him." She had paused. "I don't know quite how to describe it. You'd have to see for yourself. The look on his face when he held those ashes in his hands—"

"What ashes?" Brognola had broken in.

Rafferty had coughed as if embarrassed. "Over where the garage had been. He was squatting there with a handful of ashes trickling through his fingers. And he had the strangest expression. So I went over to ask if he was okay."

"What did he say?"

"That's even stranger. He told me, 'It shouldn't be this way.' Then he got up and walked off without a word of explanation."

That had clinched it. Brognola had whisked to Chicago and from there to the Moose Head. The agents on the scene acted as if the President himself had shown up. He had approached Bolan twice, and both times been interrupted before he could say what was on his mind. Now they were alone.

"It isn't like you to mope," Brognola commented.

"Who's moping?"

The big Fed halted next to the man who was more like a brother to him than he would ever openly admit. "What would you call it? Come on. What gives? Something is eating you. If you'd like, I'm willing to listen."

Bolan was a long time replying. Sighing, he said, "It's the war, Hal. We win battle after battle, but there's always another to be fought. It never ends. It's the price free men pay for their freedom."

"'Eternal vigilance is the price of liberty,'" Brognola quoted. "Yes. I know. So? What does that have to do with what transpired here?"

"On the surface of things, this was just another battle in the unending war," Bolan said. "But it was more than that, much more. The Mafia is crippled. The Camorra stands to wipe it out before too long."

"I should think that would make you glad. No one has fought longer or harder against the Mafia than you have."

"The Mafia is a cancer eating at America from within. If it had its way, it would corrupt our society from top to bottom, from the politicians and judges it buys off to the kids on the street who peddle and buy its drugs."

Brognola mulled it over. "I know I'm not getting enough sleep. Or maybe I'm just dense. But I honestly don't see your point."

"As vile as the Mafia is, it pales in comparison with the Camorra. The Mafia doesn't make a habit of blowing up hundreds of innocent people. It doesn't routinely gun down mothers or wantonly murder children. As much as I hate to admit it, even the Mafia has its limits." Bolan paused. "Antonio Scarlotti has none whatsoever. He'll kill anyone, anywhere, if it suits his purpose. He's a butcher."

"You won't get an argument from me." A light bulb flashed on in Brognola's brain. He studied his friend before saying, "Is that what this is about? A case of the devil we know being better than the new devil in town?"

"More or less." Bolan stepped to the water's edge and let it lap at his toes. "As bad as the Mafia is, as much hurt and heartache as it's caused, that's nothing compared to what Scarlotti and the Camorra will do. Think of it."

Brognola had. Every waking moment since the crisis began. "And you're letting it get you down?"

"No. Not down. I'm not about to throw in the towel." Bolan looked at him. "Knowing the war is endless is one thing. Knowing that it will get worse before it gets better is a given." He took his hands from his pockets, picked up a rock and chucked it into the lake. "Living the truth, having it jump up and kick you in the gut, having your nose rubbed in it, well—" He said no more.

"It sounds to me as if you need to climb back in the saddle as soon as you can."

About to throw another stone, Bolan glanced at the big Fed. "Have anything for me?"

"Not yet. Most of the Mafia riffraff are being shuttled to Chicago and will be interrogated over the next several days. Maybe we'll learn something important."

"Did your people take any of the Camorrans alive?"

"I wish. The only Camorrans we've found are dead ones." Swiveling, he saw the damaged roof of the lodge above the trees. "Lassiter is making a sweep of the peninsula to see if there are any we've missed."

From out of undergrowth a few yards away a gruff voice snarled, "There are, pig!" The snout of a pistol poked out, followed by the bruiser who held it. His dark suit was rumpled, his left hand pressed to an even darker stain on his right shoulder.

Brognola made no sudden moves. Out of the corner of an eye he saw Bolan inch a hand toward his jacket.

"Do that, mister, and your pal here buys the farm," the gunner warned, pointing his pistol at Brognola's head.

Reluctantly Bolan hiked his arms.

"That's a good boy," the gunner said. He sidled to the left to better cover the two of them. His Heckler & Koch P-7 was iron steady. "I don't know who the two of you are, but it's plain you're high-muck-a-muck Feds of some kind. Especially you.'' He wagged the pistol at Brognola. "That makes you just what I need.''

Brognola wanted to distract the man, to give Bolan a chance to go for one of his guns. "Are you a Camorran?" he asked.

The hardman spit. "Don't insult me, mister. I'm one of Fallini's boys. Frank and me were patrolling the beach when a bunch of geeks in skin diving suits took us by surprise. They figured I was dead, but I was only playing possum.'' He laughed bitterly. "I crawled into the brush there and hid until it was over.'' He laughed louder. "I thought my luck had run out, but I was wrong.''

"Meaning?" Brognola said.

"It should be obvious, Fed.'' The man stepped in close and jammed the P-7 against Brognola's neck. "The two of you are my ticket out of here.''

"It'll never work.''

The gunner snorted. "Hell it won't! I heard what you said. This place is crawling with badges. It would only have been a matter of time before they found me. Now I get to waltz out without a hitch.''

Bolan took a half step forward. "Take me instead of him. I promise to go along quietly.''

"And you expect me to believe you?" For someone who was wounded and hemmed in by federal agents, the mafioso was in remarkably fine spirits. He cackled, then sobered, grabbing Brognola by the collar and sliding behind him. "Okay, chumps. No more fun and games. Lose your hardware or lose your lives. It's that simple.''

# CHAPTER FOURTEEN

The Executioner had no choice other than to comply. Gingerly, applying only two fingers, he eased the Beretta from its holster and set it at his feet. The Desert Eagle went next to it. Left untouched were his ankle knife and a few deadly items stashed in his pockets, items he dared not resort to unless Brognola was in the clear.

"Hoist your arms and don't twitch, pal," the mafioso ordered. After the Executioner complied, the mobster frisked Brognola, helping himself to the big Fed's pistol, which he tucked under his belt.

"So far, so good." The gunner smirked. "Now comes the tricky part. The two of you are going to head for the garage. I'll be right behind with my gun pointed at the back of this chump's head." He rapped Brognola on the skull hard enough to make him flinch. "One wrong move, any slipups at all, and I'll splatter your brains from here to kingdom come."

"It won't work," the big Fed told him.

"So you claimed before. Just let me be the

judge." The gunner beckoned at Bolan, motioning for him to go around and precede them westward.

"No, you don't understand," Brognola elaborated. "The garage isn't there. It's totally destroyed. Your boss and the other bosses went up with it."

Fallini's underling reacted as if he had been slapped. "You're serious? That was the explosion I heard? Damn!" His brow furrowed. "If what you say is true, then we're done for. The Mafia won't last out the year. It's every man for himself from here on out."

Brognola saw his chance. "In that case give yourself up now and I can guarantee that you'll serve a light sentence in exchange for testimony we can use in court against others."

"Rat on my own?" The gunner shook his head. "No way, Fed. I took an oath. We call it the *omèrta*."

Bolan knew it all too well, and knew that Brognola was wasting his time. The *omèrta* was the Mafia's notorious code of silence. Soldiers would rather have their tongues cut out than turn against their Families. With his own eyes he had seen mafiosi who had endured torture that would have brought most people to the brink of insanity, yet they never gave up their own.

"Your oath was to Fallini, wasn't it?" Brognola was saying. "With him gone, you have no reason to hold back information."

The man gave the Fed a push. "Shows how much you know, chump. Just keep walking. And I don't want another peep out of either of you unless I tell you to talk. Got that?''

"You're making a mistake," Hal said.

"Who died and appointed you as my mother? Shut up and walk."

The Executioner was a yard or so in front of his friend. He tried to keep an eye on the hardman by tilting his head, but the man growled at him to lower his arms, face front and act as if nothing were wrong, or else. Since Brognola would take the first slug, Bolan squared his shoulders and walked on until they were in sight of the devastated buildings.

In addition to the structural damage sustained by the lodge and the loss of the garage, several cabins had taken hits from grenades. One had caught fire and burned to the ground. It smoldered yet, embers glowing red.

"Damn those Camorrans all to hell!" the hardman cursed, half in shock at the extent of the destruction. He went on without thinking. "Another few days, and the boys from Sicily would have been here! Then we would have shown them! The boss was going to spring the news on the—" Catching himself, he scowled at his own blunder, then gouged Brognola with the pistol.

"What do you want us to do?" the big Fed asked, stalling in the hope one of the FBI agents would notice their plight and pick the gunner off. It was still too dark, though. Unless an agent passed within a few feet of them, it wouldn't be apparent.

"Do exactly as I tell you," the gunner said, and

extended his free hand past Brognola's shoulder to indicate where four sedans were parked. "We're going to stroll on over there as if we're the best of friends. And you had better pray that your buddies don't get wise to us or there will be two more funerals in a few days. Get my drift?" He smacked Brognola on the head.

Brognola had to clench his teeth to keep from losing his temper and doing something he would regret. "We understand perfectly."

"Good. Then get moving, chump. You too, tough guy." He nodded at Bolan and slid the pistol under his jacket.

The Executioner headed for the cars. Off to the right several Feds were dragging bodies out of the woods and lining them up in tidy rows. To the left a pair of agents was entering the pines. Not one gave the trio a second glance.

They had to pass the lodge, go down a walk and cross a narrow strip of driveway to reach the vehicles. That entailed going past three lampposts. Bolan mentally crossed his fingers that an observant Fed would catch on, but the lodge was soon behind them and they were halfway along the walk.

"Mr. Brognola! Mr. Belasko!"

It was Agent Rafferty, running to intercept them, a clipboard in her right hand.

Bolan halted. So did Brognola. The gunner stopped, too, nervously licking his lips and sidling behind Brognola. "Give me away, and you're history," he whispered.

Rafferty hardly showed any interest in the mafioso. "Are you leaving, sir?" she asked Brognola. "There are couple of things I wanted to go over with you before you do. If you'd be so kind."

Brognola struggled to keep his voice calm, his face worry free. "I'd like to oblige you, Agent Lassiter," he said, "but I have to get back to Washington right away. Please give my regards to Agent Rafferty, will you? Tell him that he can give me a call tomorrow, and we'll go over those preliminary reports."

Bolan had to hand it to the redhead. She never batted an eye.

"Very well, sir," she replied, casually transferring the clipboard from her right hand to her left. "I'll let him know. Any specific time you'd like him to phone you?" And with that, she went for her gun.

Somehow the man sensed what they were up to. Even as Rafferty exploded into action, so did he, the Heckler & Koch sweeping out from under his jacket and swinging toward her. She almost beat him. Even though he already had his pistol in his hand and didn't need to clear leather, she was starting to level her service weapon when he pointed his at her face. She was a dead woman.

Or would have been, if not for the Executioner. A single bound brought Bolan next to the gunner. His right hand gripped the man's wrist, his left the man's elbow. Wrenching downward, he smashed the gunner's forearm onto his knee. The P-7 went off harmlessly into the ground. Pivoting, Bolan twisted the arm with all his might, and there was a loud crack.

The mobster cursed and punched at Bolan's neck. Ducking, the Executioner executed a flawless foot sweep, upending the soldier onto his back. Still game, the hardman aimed a vicious snap kick at Bolan's knee. Again the big man pivoted. His right foot caught the gunner in the mouth, crunching teeth. The gunner snarled and made a desperate lunge for his fallen pistol.

Bolan lunged also, his hand as stiff as a board and as hard as a brick. He slashed the mobster across the throat, dropped into a forward stance and poised his hands to close in again, if need be.

There was no need.

The mafioso convulsed wildly, limbs flailing, sputtering and wheezing in a vain bid to suck air into his lungs. His throat was crushed. Blood gurgled from his parted lips. Eyes wide, he attempted to rise, jerked in severe spasms and sank back, lifeless.

Rafferty gaped at Bolan. "Sweet Jesus! Where did you learn moves like that?"

The Executioner didn't see fit to tell her. He stepped back as agents rushed toward them from all directions. Brognola took charge, explaining and giving instructions. Left to his own devices, Bolan walked toward the cars. Ironically the hardman had the right idea. He had done all he could there. It was time to go.

"Mr. Belasko?"

Rafferty was holstering her weapon. She caught up, her visage sour, as if she had just sucked on a lemon. "Is it me? Or is it my breath?"

"Pardon?"

"Don't play games with me. You've been treating me as if I had the plague from the moment we met. I'd like to know why. Is it a clash of personalities? Or are you one of those meatheads who thinks that women have no business being in law enforcement?"

Bolan ventured a friendly smile. "None of the above. If you'll remember, I haven't treated you any differently than I treated Lassiter."

"I suppose you didn't. But it's still no excuse. I'd like us to be friends."

"I thought we were." Bolan surprised her by taking her hand and squeezing. "Take care of yourself." He began to turn, but she snagged his sleeve.

"You, too, Mike." She hesitated. "I hope we meet again some day under better circumstances."

"You never know. It's a small world."

Rafferty ruefully surveyed the battleground. "Not small enough. I can think of more than a few people it would be better off without."

Bolan had never agreed with anyone more.

*New York*

IT WAS EIGHT in the morning when the jet arrived at La Guardia International Airport from overseas.

It had been a long flight, from Ankara to Istanbul to Athens to Rome, and from there to Paris and then on to the U.S.

Among the passengers were six men who had boarded in the capital of Italy. Tourists, supposedly. Their passports were in order, and they had no problem with customs. To a man they wore neatly pressed dark suits, had short black hair and features tanned by the Sicilian sun. Each carried a single suitcase.

A van met them at La Guardia and whisked them to downtown Manhattan, to a business front for the New York Family of Don Bruno Gaito. It was a modest firm that distributed vending machines to the Tri-State region. It also distributed drugs, smuggled in the vending machines.

The six men were treated like royalty. Gaito's capo who met them ensured that their every need was met. They were wined and dined in a back room, the food and drink courtesy of a restaurant around the corner, a restaurant Gaito also owned.

At eleven, as prearranged, a call came through from the West Coast. The capo spoke briefly before passing the phone to the stockiest of the six men. His name was Angelo Cardoni. He had been born and raised in Sicily, starting life as a simple shepherd. In his late teens an incident took place that changed everything.

Cardoni's father was also a shepherd. One night three drunken rowdies from the city took it into their heads to scatter the flock. When Cardoni's father tried to stop them, they stabbed him. The younger Cardoni went berserk. He attacked the rowdies with his bare hands, wrested the knife from the man who had murdered his father and slew all three. He was arrested, tried and convicted. He faced the prospect of life in prison.

Then the unforeseen occurred. The Don of that section of Sicily had heard of his case and saw to it that a judge freed him on a contrived technicality. Cardoni was invited to the Don's mansion, treated grandly, shown that the Don valued a man who could do what Cardoni had done. Before long Cardoni became the Don's chief enforcer.

The Don had ties to Don Fallini in Chicago. When Fallini asked for help in dealing with the Camorra, the Sicilian Don had volunteered the services of Cardoni and five of his best men.

Fallini told only one other Don, Bruno Gaito, about the hit men he was importing. Gaito's influence was such that he could guarantee the men entered the country without a hitch. He also offered to see to their every need and get them safely to Chicago.

With Fallini's death, little had changed. Don Gaito was now their patron as long as they remained in the States. So when Angelo Cardoni took the phone, he spoke with proper deference, as he would to his own Don. "It is an honor to speak to you in person, Don Gaito. My Don sends his warmest regards. We await your orders."

No one would have guessed it to look at him,

but Bruno Gaito spoke four languages. His grasp of the Sicilian dialect was flawless. "My lieutenant knows what has to be done. He has all the information you need. The items you requested have all been obtained. If there is anything else you require, you have only to say the word."

"We look forward to serving you and our other American brothers."

"Get them, Angelo. You are our last hope."

Cardoni was flattered. "I have never failed yet. You know my little secret."

"Yes. Your Don is to be commended for his brilliance."

Actually it had been Cardoni's idea. Two years after he became chief enforcer, common hoods had foolishly tried to muscle in on his Don's territory. They were stupid, but they had automatic weapons. For a while they held their own since they outgunned the Don's soldiers, who relied on their traditional *luparas*. Shotguns were just no match for SMGs.

Cardoni had been sent in. He used his wits and found an informer who let him know where the hoods were to hold a meeting. An ambush wiped them out. But the conflict had taught him a valuable lesson.

Cardoni had gone to his Don. "We must have the kind of weapons that our enemies have," he had said. "The old ways are fine, but we must adapt or face the same situation again."

His Don had agreed. Within the month a young

army sergeant by the name of Denaro, who hailed from their province, was wooed and won over. He refused a second enlistment and joined the Family.

Automatic arms were purchased. So were grenades, plastic explosives, nerve gas and more. Denaro instructed Cardoni and four others in their proper use. In no time the Don had a unique, highly skilled hit team at his disposal.

Now that hit team was going to do what a legion of Mafia gunners had been unable to achieve. They were going to take the Camorra down.

After the phone call, Cardoni, Denaro and the others were ushered into a back room. There they found the items Don Gaito had gone to great expense to procure. Everything was loaded into the trunk of a car.

Soon two vehicles pulled out from the rear of the vending-machines business. In the front car rode four of Gaito's most trusted men. In the other were the imported killers. Traffic was heavy. So heavy, none of them had any idea that they were being followed.

MACK BOLAN HAD LATCHED on to the Sicilians at the airport. He had trailed them into Manhattan, parked a block away and pretended to read a newspaper until they pulled out from an alley and headed south. Beside him on the seat was a radio. On the back seat lay his duffel.

It hadn't been difficult for the Feds to learn when the hit team was entering the country. After the gunner in Illinois had let it slip about "the boys from Sicily" who were due in, Hal Brognola had put the resources of the federal government to work.

Through contacts in the Italian government, Brognola had discovered that six Sicilians had booked a flight and were due to arrive two mornings after the battle at the Moose Head.

Ideally it would have been best for the Feds to be on hand when the Sicilians stepped off the jet, pack them onto a return flight and send them on their way without a lick of bloodshed. There was only one problem. The Feds had no legal justification for booting the Sicilians out as undesirable. None of the hit men was wanted, not even in Italy, where they had slain dozens. Their Don had seen to that.

Brognola had weighed his limited options and decided there was nothing he could do until they showed their hand. He had discussed it with Bolan. The Executioner had agreed to shadow them and take appropriate action as soon as it was warranted.

Also on the seat next to him was a file containing the scanty intel Brognola had gleaned from Italian authorities. It included a mug shot of Cardoni taken at the time of his arrest for killing the men who murdered his father. It also revealed that one of the hit men was a former military man. Other than that, the Feds knew very little. As far as Bolan was aware, he was up against a pack of ordinary triggermen.

The mafiosi crossed to Jersey City and from there into Newark. They continued south on the New Jersey Turnpike until they came to Highway 195, which they took east. Bolan hung well back. A tractor trailer that fell into place behind the mobsters helped immensely. The big rig screened him for almost twenty-five miles.

Eventually the two sedans turned south once more, taking secondary roads, driving steadily deeper into a part of New Jersey Bolan had been to on several occasions.

It was known as the Pine Barrens. Stretching from Camden to about Cape May, from Asbury Park to near Trenton, was a sprawling wilderness of pitch pine choked with brush. Unpaved roads crisscrossed the region. The few locals were known as Pineys, and they kept pretty much to themselves.

The Mafia knew about the Barrens. Often bodies were dumped there, at spots so remote there was no risk of them ever being discovered.

Bolan was puzzled as to why the hit team had gone there. He speculated that they were on their way to a hideout where they would wait for word from Gaito. It was a logical spot to hide out.

Although there was virtually no traffic, shadowing them was easy. The rural roads were so dusty that the mafiosi raised thick clouds as they sped along well over the speed limit. Bolan had only to follow the dust trail, and he couldn't lose them.

It was the middle of the afternoon when Bolan spotted a flash of sunlight off of the mobsters' vehicles. They had pulled over and parked. He promptly veered across the shoulder and into the brush, no mean feat since in many places the road sank half a foot below the surrounding terrain and both sides were hemmed in by a solid phalanx of trees that reached thirty feet in height.

Killing the engine, Bolan removed his sports jacket, leaned over the seat, opened the duffel and pulled out a fatigue jacket. Out came his M-16, which he had broken down into the upper and lower receiver groups. He now reassembled the rifle by placing the two sections together and reseating the receiver pivot pin.

The Executioner withdrew three magazines and verified they were fully loaded. Placing the selector lever on safe, he inserted one into the magazine feedway, pushing up until he heard a distinct click. Next he pulled the charging handle to the rear and let go.

A sheathed Ka-bar combat knife went on his right leg. He debated taking grenades and opted not to. A handful of gunners didn't merit resorting to explosives.

Cranking the window down, Bolan slid out rather than make noise opening and closing the door. He jogged westward until he was fifty yards from the two parked cars.

The four soldiers from New York lounged against the first vehicle. There was no sign of the six from Sicily.

Bolan circled deeper into the woods, confident

he would find their trail. Mobsters had never impressed him as being adept at woodcraft and wilderness survival. Most were city boys, only at home with concrete and asphalt under their feet.

The undergrowth grew thicker. Bolan could appreciate why every year two or three people wandered into the Pine Barrens and were never seen again. He was abreast of the cars when he saw his first track, a smudged print where a Sicilian had jumped over a log. It told him two things. One, the Sicilian was remarkably light on his feet. Two, the man had changed into combat boots.

Bolan soon found other tracks, leading northward. All of them were boot prints. Mystified, he sought to catch up, but it soon was clear that they were moving much more swiftly than he'd expect of typical triggermen. He thought that he would hear the crack of twigs, the crackle of brush. But they proved him wrong again. They were as silent as he was.

He came to a game trail. The Sicilians had taken it to the northeast to make better time, just as experienced woodsmen would do. A kernel of insight flared, but it was too late for Bolan to turn around and go back. He had to see it through.

For over a mile and a half the Executioner wound through the Pine Barrens. The woods were alive with birds and squirrels. Once a rabbit bounded across his path.

The ground began to slope. The game trail led to the crest of a hill choked with pines. Bolan left it and padded to a point where he could peer through a thicket at whatever lay below.

On a shelf partway down were the six Sicilians. They no longer wore business suits. To a man they were dressed in combat fatigues. To a man they packed enough hardware to take on a full platoon.

Bolan hadn't counted on that. He wasn't up against a bunch of inept triggermen this time. Single-handedly he had to take on a Mafia commando squad.

# CHAPTER FIFTEEN

Killing was hard work.

Young Guilo Falcone was a tired man when he arrived at the Camorra's secret base of operations north of Toms River in the Pine Barrens. The site had been selected eight months before the war began and stocked during the intervening months with enough arms and ammunition to last a full battalion a lifetime.

Falcone's boss, Antonio Scarlotti, thought of everything.

It had been Scarlotti, almost a year earlier, who sent some of his men to visit relatives in America. The relatives in some cases had lived in the U.S. for several generations. They were innocent dupes, unaware that their kinsmen were members of the Camorra.

Scarlotti had coached his soldiers well. They acquired critical information that would aid him in his quest to destroy the Mafia.

One, in particular, had an uncle who had settled on the outskirts of Hog Wallow. From the uncle the Camorran heard about the vastness of the Pine Barrens. He discovered that there were portions of the Barrens where humans had never set foot. And of course he had relayed the fact to his boss.

Scarlotti was quick to see the benefit. He ordered his underling to inquire around, to buy maps, to look for cheap real estate that would fit their needs.

The Camorrans stumbled on an abandoned nursery. Back in the thirties someone had the idea that he could build the biggest nursery the world had ever seen in a remote corner of the wilderness and make a fortune selling plants, shrubs and trees to residents of the metro areas. The overhead had been low, the growing conditions ideal. How could he lose out?

Enter Mother Nature. A hurricane had drifted north along the coast and spawned a flood that wiped out the nursery. The man with the brainstorm had decided that enough was enough and gone back to being an accountant.

The buildings still stood, though, in the center of an overgrown field fifteen miles from the nearest habitation. They reeked of must and mold and had been caked thick with dust when the Camorrans first arrived, but they were adequate to house a mountain of crates.

Seven gunners had been left to baby-sit the weaponry while Scarlotti led the rest in their landmark assault on the Moose Head. Now Scarlotti had gone on to the next target, sending Falcone to tidy up loose ends and bring every last soldier to the scene of what promised to be the final conflict between their organization and the Mafia.

"But what about the Uzis and the other things?" asked one of the men, indicating a stack of crates.

"Trucks will be here the day after tomorrow to pick everything up," Falcone explained. "All we have to do is take inventory and lock up on our way out." He offered his trademark smirk. "Or, rather, you seven will finish the count while I treat myself to a smoke."

None of the men resented his arrogance. They were Camorran soldiers, trained to do as their superiors wanted without question. To a man they were fiercely loyal to Antonio Scarlotti. And Falcone was one of their leader's right-hand men. They would follow him into the maw of Hell if that was what he wanted.

Falcone drifted to the rear of the main building. To the south was a low hill as heavily forested as the rest of the Pine Barrens. He leaned against the wall, lit his Italian-brand cigarette and puffed heartily.

There had been all too few moments to relax since the Mafia campaign began, and there would be fewer yet before it was over.

Falcone had harbored doubts when his boss first proposed the idea. Fight the Mafia? On its own territory? And wrest it away? If he hadn't known Scarlotti so well, he would have branded the man a lunatic.

As it was, Antonio Scarlotti would now go down

in the annals of Camorran history as the man who had redeemed the Camorra, who had erased old slights, righted ancient wrongs. Scarlotti was general, savior and warrior all rolled into one. He was the stuff of which legends were made.

Falcone was proud to work for such a man, proud to be part of the Camorra, to be there as history was in the making. He looked forward to the total destruction of the Mafia, to the accolades that would be theirs when they returned to Naples, to the—

What was that?

The young Camorran had glimpsed movement low on the hill. Somehow he had gotten the impression that a man had been staring at him from behind a bush and dived for cover when he happened to look up. But that was preposterous. There wasn't another living soul within miles of the nursery other than his own men.

Then there was an odd sound, and a spherical object sailed out of the pines toward the building, looping in a high arc. For a few moments the sun gleamed so brightly off the metallic casing that Falcone didn't realize what it was. When he did, he yelped and barreled for the door, roaring at the top of his lungs in Italian, *"We are under attack!"*

Seconds later the grenade went off.

HALF A MINUTE EARLIER, the Executioner had ducked below the rim and girded himself. He planned to move in fast and hard. The safest bet was to dispose of the Mafia commandos before they knew what hit them. To that end he flicked the selector lever to auto. A sustained burst would mow them down like weeds before a scythe if he did it just right. There was no margin for error. Miss one, and he would be chopped to ribbons.

He regretted not bringing his grenade launcher along. The M-203 could do with one grenade what it would take the M-16 an entire clip or more to accomplish.

The Sicilians had grenade launchers. Bolan had seen at least three, mounted under the barrels of what appeared to be BM-59 paratroop rifles.

Bolan had only laid eyes on a BM-59 once before. Manufactured by Pietro Beretta in Italy, it boasted semi- and full-auto fire, 20-round magazines and a grenade launcher tricompensator that cut down on recoil when a grenade was fired. The compensator also reduced muzzle climb when the rifle was on full-auto and even served as a flash suppressor.

The paratroop model was limited to elite Italian forces. It wasn't supposed to be available on the civilian market. But apparently anyone with enough power—and money—could get his hands on all they wanted.

He tucked the M-16 to his right shoulder and shoved onto his knees to open fire. But there was no one to shoot at. The ersatz commandos had vanished.

Thwarted, Bolan saw two of them slanting down the hill. The squad had broken into pairs, as a real army squad would have done, and was employing standard military procedure for engaging an enemy. Whoever these guys were, Bolan mused, they were extremely well trained.

But discipline was no match for experience, and in that regard Bolan felt he had the edge. He started down after the pair, only to halt when they pulled a disappearing act that would have made a Navy SEAL green with envy.

A man came out of one of the buildings below. He lit a cigarette and leaned back. As he moved his right arm, the flap of his jacket parted, revealing a shoulder holster.

Bolan didn't need to be told who the man was. A Camorran. The place had to be one of their hideouts, he reasoned, and the Mafia was about to indulge in some major-league payback. The imported assassins were wasting no time.

The Executioner started down the hill, stopping cold when he heard a familiar sound. Having used a grenade launcher countless times, he knew the noise one made. He saw the bomb arc up out of the brush, saw the man by the building stiffen, whirl and scream a warning to those inside. The man barely made it back in when the grenade went off, the blast rumbling like thunder across the Pine Barrens.

It was the cue for the six Mafia commandos to burst from concealment and rush the buildings. Two more grenades exploded, blowing holes in the rear wall of the largest structure. The six killers were three-fourths of the way across the weed-choked field that served as a buffer between the buildings and the woods when the Camorrans galvanized into action. SMGs opened up, shattering several windows from within. The mafiosi hit the dirt, blending into the weeds so well that Bolan couldn't spot a single one.

The Executioner was almost to the bottom. Lead suddenly clipped leaves on both sides, driving him onto his belly. It hadn't been deliberate. The Camorrans hadn't seen him. Some of their rounds had simply been fired high. Nevertheless, a wild shot was every bit as deadly as an aimed one.

Once again Bolan was caught in the middle of a raging firefight. It was broad daylight this time, but that didn't reduce the danger. In fact it increased it, for now the Mafia soldiers and the Camorran gunners could spot him that much easier. He had to be doubly careful, doubly alert.

A withering volley from the six BM-59 paratroop rifles drove the Camorrans from the windows long enough for the mafiosi to rise and rush the building. They fanned out, pincer fashion, half to a prong, sweeping on around the corners of the building.

Bolan intended to pick one or two off. But as he rose, figures appeared at the windows, Camorrans seeking the same quarry. He had to flatten, then crawled forward. For over a minute the woodland was deceptively tranquil, the only sound the rustling of the weeds and grass.

Then Uzis snarled and BM-59s barked in defiance. A man screamed and went on screaming, a wavering, gurgling cry, on and on and on, even after the firing ceased. Eventually it strangled off to pathetic whimpering mixed with choked pleas in Italian. "Help me, brothers! For God's sake, help me, I beg of you!"

Apparently no one was disposed to do so because the mewing was still going on when Bolan came close enough to fling a pebble through one of the windows if he wanted to. There were five buildings, all told, the big one and four much smaller, two qualifying as oversize sheds. Atop one of the latter was a small, faded sign that told Bolan the place had once been known as Baxter's Nursery, where If It Grows, We Have It! had been the motto.

Autofire broke out to the northeast. Figuring that both sides would be preoccupied awhile, Bolan sprinted to the corner and braced a shoulder against it. The clash was short, punctuated by sporadic firing afterward. As near as he could tell, the Mafia commandos were content to stay outside taking potshots at the Camorrans, while the Camorrans, for their part, were in no great rush to charge out and engage their bitter enemies head-on.

It told him a few things.

There couldn't be that many Camorrans inside. If there were, they wouldn't hesitate to take the fight to their attackers. And since the Sicilians weren't blowing the hell out of the nursery, either they wanted to take some of the Camorrans alive or there was something else that kept them from cutting loose with all their grenade launchers at once.

Bolan had to get inside. He stalked toward one of the ragged openings made by a grenade. It was just wide enough for him to squeeze through, but he reconnoitered first. Smoke swirled; shadows flitted about. Stacks of crates and boxes lined the opposite wall—nursery implements, he assumed, until he looked closer and read the stenciled legend.

The Executioner abruptly understood perfectly. The building was piled high with arms and ammunition. If both sides weren't exceedingly careful, they would blow one another sky-high.

Shoulders low, Bolan slid inside. He moved to the right, wreathed in shadows and acrid tendrils. Narrow aisles crisscrossed the building, rendering the nursery an enormous maze. From the front of the building came sporadic fire. A man shouted for another to get back. Bullets spanged off metal.

Bolan crept deeper into the lion's den. The aisle he took turned twice. Each time he noticed that the mewing of the wounded man grew louder. At the next bend, near the north wall, he heard soft sniffling and incoherent muttering. The Camorran was just around the corner.

As Bolan read it, the triggerman had been perched on a crate, firing out a high window. A round had caught the man in the left cheek, knocking him from his roost. He was on his back in the center of a wide scarlet pool, both hands clasped to his face, his lips working, his whole body trembling. The one eye that Bolan could see was closed.

The Executioner advanced, pausing when another grenade detonated. This one had been outside. He looked down at the hurt Camorran and discovered the man's eye had opened and fastened on him. Automatically the man lowered an arm to a holster at his waist, his draw awkward and sluggish. Bolan took a step, slamming his foot down on the Camorran's wrist, pinning it.

The shooter didn't resist. He was a gory sight, with the upper half of his cheek and part of his eye blown away. It was an exit hole, not an entry wound. The slug had nailed him in the back of the head, not in the front, maybe as he had been about to jump from the crate. In the shape he was in, he wouldn't last long.

The man stared at Bolan. "Please," he croaked in Italian. "For the love of God. I cannot take the pain."

A convenient renewal of hostilities provided the background noise Bolan needed. He touched the M-16's muzzle to the gunner's temple. The triggerman swallowed hard, closed his eyes and said hardly loud enough to hear, "Do it."

Bolan did.

He went on, listening to commotion ahead. The commandos were making a determined effort to break in, and the Camorrans were equally determined to keep them out. The firing rose to a feverish pitch. One more grenade, outside again, buffeted the wall.

In the lull that ensued, Bolan heard a loud creak to his right. A hand appeared above a stack of crates. It was tugging on a rope, and the next moment folding stairs swung down from the ceiling. A Camorran dashed up them, a rifle tucked at his side, a sly smile animating his swarthy face.

Bolan changed direction. He had to backtrack twice when he was stymied by dead ends. At length he came to the stairs. Above, the rifle boomed several times. He slowly climbed, scouring the building. Near the entrance several Camorrans were crouched behind a counter. There was no trace of the rest.

Aware that he was a perfect target, Bolan ascended the final ten steps and squatted just below a square opening. The rifle thundered again, letting him know that the Camorran was to his left. Poking his head out, he found that a huge rust-covered metal housing hid him from the gunner. It was one of nine or ten that ran the length of the building. All held giant fans that hadn't been used since the nursery closed down. They were caked with rust, just like their housings.

Bolan crept to the nearest. Forty feet beyond, on his knees close to the roof's edge, was the Camorran. He would pop up, snap off a shot and duck again before the commandos below could peg him. The rifle was an old Lee Enfield Mark I, once in widespread use in the British Empire and in Europe.

Converted to 7.62 mm for NATO use, it had a 10-round charger-loaded magazine. In the hands of a professional sniper, it was effective at ranges of over five hundred yards. That was rather paltry by modern standards but still good enough for most combat situations an infantryman might find himself in.

The Camorran was far from a pro. He demonstrated his lack of skill by the manner in which he twice fumbled with the bolt. He seemed to have a hard time adjusting to the bolt-locking system. Unlike many rifles, the action had to be worked to the very rear of the receiver, not just to the end of the breech.

Bolan inched past the fan. The instant he did, the gunner glimpsed him and spun, bringing the Enfield to bear. Bolan closed his finger on the trigger. A 3-round burst was all it took.

Chopped off at the waist, the Camorran was catapulted backward, his arms flung wide. The rifle clattered onto the roof as he sailed out over the brink and fell like a sack of cement.

Bolan ran close to the edge and spread out. The Mafia's hit men were pouring fire into the front of the building. Two were behind a shed, another firing from the window of a building to the north. Three were unaccounted for.

The Executioner swapped the M-16 for the Enfield. It was a lot heavier than the M-16 but nestled snugly against his shoulder. He aligned the front blade sight with one of the mafiosi beside the shed, then aligned the rear aperture battle sight with the front blade. The next time the man leaned forward to shoot, Bolan pegged him squarely, through the chest.

The Sicilian was slammed against the wall, did an ungainly twist and melted where he stood.

Bolan shifted to try for the second man. He fixed a bead at a point on a corner of the shed where the mobster's camouflage-painted face had appeared several times. Almost as an afterthought, he glanced at the gunner he had just shot—and blinked in surprise.

The Sicilian was rising. Slowly, hands propped on the shed, he marshaled his legs under him. He touched his chest where the round had drilled him, smiled half in disbelief and lurched from sight before the Executioner could fire again.

Body armor, Bolan realized. All of them had to be wearing vests. He should have noticed it sooner. Their fatigues were much too bulky for their frames.

Rounds suddenly peppered the edge of the roof, driving Bolan back. He claimed the M-16 and moved to the left to get a better shot at the commando firing through the window. It was then that the roof around him burst into splintered fragments. For a few harrowing moments he had no idea where the autofire had come from. Pivoting, he spied a pair of Sicilians at the west end of the roof, near a grappling hook.

Bolan ran for the closest fan. Slugs whined off

the metal as he dodged around the housing. The pair advanced, firing in turns, one opening up when the other went dry, never slackening, a tactic real commandos would use. Bolan dared not lean out to fire.

Discretion was the better part of valor. The Executioner retreated to the stairs and zipped down them on the fly. He was almost to the bottom when a Camorran hove up behind a pile of boxes. It was hard to say which of them was the more surprised but not hard to prove which one controlled his surprise better. The Camorran crashed lifeless to the floor as Bolan jumped down, his M-16 blazing.

He was tempted to try to pick the pair of Sicilians off as they descended, but an impulse goaded him into seeking shelter twenty feet away behind a barrier of sturdy crates. His prudence paid off.

A grenade bounced down the stairs. Bolan braced himself, but it was not a frag grenade. It was the illuminating variety, and it lit up the interior like a Fourth of July fireworks display. Fifty or sixty thousand candlepower blazed brilliantly for half a minute.

Bolan had turned away at the last moment. Sparkling dots pinwheeled before his eyes, and he covered them to spare the retinas from permanent damage.

Boots thudded. A flurry of movement confirmed the Sicilians had made it safely down.

Tense seconds ticked by. It was a full minute before Bolan could see again. A pair of ropes dangling through the opening showed that the Sicilians hadn't bothered to use the stairs. There was no denying the truth. Whoever had trained them had done an outstanding job.

Bolan moved toward the entrance. He guessed that the mobsters would do likewise since that was where the remaining Camorrans were concentrated.

Outside, other mafiosi were keeping up a steady fire, no doubt to keep the defenders occupied until it was too late. At the rear a pistol cracked twice. It was answered once by a BM-59.

The Executioner came within sight of the front counter. Only two Camorrans were there. As he looked on, the two camouflage-clad Mafia hit men rose head and shoulders above a crate. One shouted, "Drop your weapons and you will live!"

Evidently the word "surrender" wasn't in the Camorran vocabulary. Both gunners wheeled. Both were taught the folly of their resistance. But neither was slain outright. They were each shot in the shoulder, the bullets so precisely placed that they suffered broken collarbones and were forced to drop their weapons.

The bogus commandos glided into the open, covering the hurt Camorrans every step.

"Make no sudden moves!" one Sicilian warned. "We will spare you if you cooperate!" stated the other.

Bolan rested the M-16 across the crate in front of him to steady it. He would dispose of these two, then deal with the rest. As he lowered his cheek to the stock, a hard object scraped his cheek and a menacing voice hissed almost in his ear.

"Do that, mister, and you will be scraping your brains off the floor with a putty knife."

## CHAPTER SIXTEEN

*Washington, D.C.*

Hal Brognola stared at the sheet of paper in his hand and stated bluntly, "I don't believe it."

Agent Timothy Ferguson, a mousy man whose thick black-framed glasses were precariously balanced on the tip of his angular nose, fidgeted. "What is it that you can't accept, sir? I assure you that we went over those figures several times, verifying where possible and extrapolating where appropriate."

Brognola looked at the man and shook his head. "No. You misunderstand. I don't doubt your statistics. It's the shock of seeing the totals in black and white." He shook the paper. "This is deplorable, Agent Ferguson. This kind of thing can never be permitted to happen again."

"I heartily agree, sir," Ferguson said in his billygoat voice. "Can I get back to my office now? Preparing the hourly updates takes every spare minute I have." He nodded at the sheet. "That comprehensive assessment of the current status taxed my department to the breaking point.''

"Fine. Go right ahead," Brognola said, wondering why it was that some people were more comfortable around computers and books and pens and paper than they were with other people. "Keep me posted as the situation warrants."

"Most certainly, sir," Ferguson said, sounding offended, as if he took the directive as an inference that he might fail to do his duty. "When have we ever let you down?"

"Never," Brognola conceded.

"And we never will," the little man said stiffly. Without another word he marched from the office, closing the door in his wake.

Brognola scanned the sheet, tallying the staggering totals. Some he read aloud.

"Total number of known incidents to date stemming from Mafia-Camorra war, 168. Total number of known Mafia fatalities, 312. Additional suspected casualties, 41. Total number of confirmed Camorran fatalities, 21."

Brognola came to the last section of the report, the section detailing the cost to innocent citizens in terms of lives lost and property damage. "'Total number of civilians slain since start of war, 579.'

"I don't believe it!" Brognola said again. He could readily imagine what would happen when the President read that report. The Chief Executive would go through the roof, and Brognola couldn't blame him. The Justice Department was supposed to nip catastrophes like this in the bud before they could bear seed. When the press got wind of the full scope of the war, they would crucify every elected official in the city.

Worst of all, there was no end in sight. Even after the Camorra won—as it surely would, barring a miracle—the violence and bloodshed would continue for many months to come as the Camorra consolidated its power. Pockets of Mafia resistance would need quashing. The Triads, the cartels, the Jamaican posses, they all had to be taught that the Camorra was a force to be reckoned with.

America's streets would run red with blood.

Bolan had been right, the big Fed mused. Better the devil they knew than the one they didn't.

Which reminded him.

It had been too long since the last time Bolan reported in. Brognola decided to call communications to see if his friend had left any messages. On learning that there was none, he leaned back in his chair and massaged a kink at his nape.

Where could Bolan be?

More to the point, was he still alive?

*New Jersey*

THE EXECUTIONER TEETERED at the edge of eternity, a hair-trigger away from becoming another statistic in the next report.

He froze when the muzzle of a paratroop rifle was shoved against his cheek. There were two of them, one right behind him, the other covering him. Nearby stood a Camorran with a shoulder wound. Bolan offered no resistance when the man behind him snatched the M-16 and threw it to the floor. A hand seized the back of his shirt, and he was propelled into the open. A foot lashed out, snared an ankle and he fell onto his knees.

"Here is another Camorran dog!" snapped the man who had tripped him.

The two Camorrans by the counter looked at each other, then at Bolan. "What trick is this you play, Mafia pigs?" one demanded. "He is one of yours. We have never set eyes on him before."

Now the bogus commandos were perplexed. The bruiser who had manhandled Bolan walked up and prodded the Executioner with his BM-59. "Who are you?" he quizzed in Italian. "How is it that you are here?"

Just then two more Mafia soldiers entered through the front door. One was the gunner Bolan had shot. They came around the counter, and a hurried conversation took place in Italian. All eyes turned to Bolan.

The man spared by the body armor stepped up close, bent and examined the Executioner's face as if it were a sculpture by Michelangelo. He plucked the Beretta free, tossed the Desert Eagle aside and rummaged through Bolan's pockets, discarding everything. A pack of matches gave him pause. His busy brows met, and he regarded Bolan with renewed interest. In thickly accented English, he announced, "Our friend here is an American."

"What? Are you sure?"

"As sure as I can be about a man who does not carry any identification," the first man answered.

"But what is he doing here, Cardoni? Was he spying on them?" The man drew a wicked knife from a boot sheath. "I will make him tell us."

Another soldier chimed in. "Is that wise? If he is an American, maybe he has alerted his superiors. We must get out of here while we still can. Time enough to question him when we are safe."

Bolan coiled his leg muscles, waiting for an opening, but the rifle of the man covering him never wavered. Suddenly one of the Camorrans by the counter made a break for it, leaping onto the top and sliding across. As he slid off the other side, one of the commandos snapped off a single shot. The man pitched forward.

"That reminds me," the bruiser addressed Cardoni. "What about these other two?" He jabbed a thumb at the other Camorran near the counter and the wounded man by the crates.

"Need you ask, Luigi?"

As coldly as if he were exterminating cockroaches, the husky specimen drew a pistol, a Mauser-Renato Gamba Model 80, and shot the man by the counter through the right eye. The wounded Camorran squawked and turned to flee. Smirking, Luigi let his target take a few steps. The report of the shot echoed off the walls. The sound of the body falling didn't.

Cardoni, the apparent leader, crisply dispensed orders, and three of the commandos dispersed.

Luigi grasped Bolan's arm and shoved him toward the rear. "Move it!" he snarled.

Bolan complied. Soon he passed a commando shrugging out of a backpack. He looked back and saw the man remove a detonator, a timing device and a packet of explosives.

Luigi was also watching. "Wait until Scarlotti hears about this!" he gloated. "The bastard will have a fit!"

Cardoni didn't share his companion's glee. "The war is far from over. We have a long way to go yet. This is just the first round."

"Always the pessimist," Luigi snorted. "These Camorrans have no chance against us. They lack our training, our skill. The outcome is never in doubt. Within six months we will have driven them back to Naples with their tails tucked between their legs."

Again Cardoni disputed the man. "Training and skill count for much, yes, but so do sheer numbers. There are only six of us and many dozens of our enemy. We must be as sly as the fox, as fierce as the wolf."

Luigi liked to get in the last word. "That is all well and good, but you know as well as I do that the key to winning this war is Antonio Scarlotti. Kill him, and it does not matter how many dozens the enemy has. He is the brains of their operation.'' He made a mock slash across his throat. ''Just as with any viper, chop off the head and the body is useless.''

They were almost to the rear door when someone down an aisle to the left groaned.

''There is where I left him,'' Luigi announced, and darted into the aisle. He was gone no time at all. When he reappeared, he was shoving the young Camorran who had been enjoying a cigarette out back when the firefight began. The man had a nasty bruise on his right temple, and a bullet wound in his thigh. His wrists were bound behind his back. ''Here is our friend Falcone. We would not want to forget so important a person, would we?''

The man called Falcone glared defiantly at his captors as he stumbled into step with them. ''Mafia pigs! Antonio will make you regret this day.'' His gaze fell on Bolan. ''Who is this one?''

''That is what we would like to know,'' Cardoni said. ''We understand that he is not one of yours.''

''I never saw him before in my life,'' Falcone answered. ''He is certainly not a Piney. I bet he followed you here, you idiots.''

Luigi smacked the Camorran on the back so hard that Falcone nearly fell. ''It would not be wise to insult us again. We need you alive, but that does not necessarily mean that you must be in one piece when we question you.''

''I will not tell you anything!'' the young Camorran tough blustered.

"Ah, but you will," Cardoni said. "Before we are done, you will gladly tell us your whole life's story in the most exacting detail."

Falcone lapsed into sullen silence, which prompted a curt laugh from Luigi. "Capturing you is proof that the tide has turned. Our first attack, and we bag one of Scarlotti's most trusted lieutenants!"

Bolan wondered how the Sicilian knew of Falcone. So did the young Camorran, who came right out and asked them.

"That is our little secret," Luigi declared. "Suffice it to say that Scarlotti is not the only one who can buy information. Offer enough money to the right Camorran, and—"

"Enough!" Cardoni snapped. "You have said too much already. Do you want him to know all our secrets?"

Luigi was unfazed. "He knows nothing. You worry too much, as usual."

Falcone couldn't resist getting in a lick. "I'm not dumb, like you, mister. I know that there must be a traitor in our organization. Antonio will ferret him out and make him pay dearly for his treachery."

Flushing scarlet, Luigi clamped an apelike paw on the young Camorran's chin and shook it so violently that Falcone grimaced in pain. "And how exactly will your precious Scarlotti learn of our secret? Do you expect to tell him?" He hauled off and slapped the Camorran in pure spite. "I am not the dumb one here, jackass."

The third Sicilian, the one who hadn't uttered a word, went through the door first and turned so he could cover Bolan and Falcone as they stepped out. They were ushered to the center of the field. There, they were ordered to stop and wait. In approximately five minutes the three Sicilians who had remained behind to set charges showed up.

"All done?" Cardoni asked.

"It will be a sight to see," one of them replied, grinning.

At rifle point Bolan was marched to the top of the hill. He played along, giving his captors no excuse to inflict punishment. He also had an ulterior motive. As yet they hadn't thought to bind him, and he didn't want to remind them of their oversight by acting up.

The party halted. One of the commandos who had set the charges consulted his wristwatch. "In seventeen seconds," he announced.

Luigi poked Falcone with a finger as thick as a sausage. "How does it feel, Camorran filth, to have the shoe on the other foot? What you are about to witness is but a taste of things to come."

"Dream on," Falcone countered.

"Scarlotti is the dreamer, if he thinks that La Cosa Nostra will go quietly into the sunset. Those of us in Italy and those of us in America share common roots. We are Family in more ways than—"

Whatever else the burly Sicilian was going to say was lost to posterity thanks to a tremendous blast.

To Bolan's trained ear, it sounded as if half a dozen charges went off within milliseconds of one another. They were the catalyst that set off the cache of weapons and ammunition in a thunderous chain reaction of roiling clouds of debris and swirling smoke.

Everyone looked. Even the Sicilian who had been covering the Executioner and Falcone shifted to see the pyrotechnic display. There was an irresistible quality to an explosion, whether large or small, that drew human interest like flames drew moths. The reaction was automatic. It was also exactly what Bolan had hoped would occur.

The Sicilians had made another mistake. When they stopped, they had done so several yards below the Executioner, strung out in a row on the game trail. Bolan was above all of them, and he used the terrain to his advantage.

The instant the man covering him glanced at the nursery, the warrior pivoted, delivering a snap kick that caught the commando in the chest. To the Sicilian's credit, he tried to turn, but he was knocked off his feet, his finger tightening on the trigger of the paratroop rifle, which blistered thin air as the man crashed into Luigi and they both toppled, slamming into Cardoni and then into yet a fourth commando. It was like watching camouflage-clad bowling pins being bowled over.

Bolan didn't linger to see if the rest shared their fate. He plunged into the dense growth and headed north at a furious sprint, threading through the trees to make himself harder to hit in case the commandos recovered sooner than he anticipated. Heavy breathing and the drum of feet warned him that had to be the case, and he glanced over a shoulder to find the Camorran lieutenant hard on his heels despite the leg wound.

The Executioner had nearly forgotten about him. Bolan's first thought was to deck the Camorran and get out of there. Eluding the Sicilians would be difficult enough on his own. Then it hit him. Here was just the person Hal Brognola would like to have a long chat with. The Feds had wanted to take a Camorran alive since the war began.

So Bolan made no objection as the young tough followed him northward into the Pine Barrens. Several times Falcone tripped, but he was always able to right himself. He made a lot more noise than Bolan did, but the big American let it go for the moment. Speed was the important thing, speed and putting as much distance between them and the Sicilians as they could.

Bolan ran until he was caked with sweat. Pausing, he listened, but he could hear nothing above the wheezing of the Camorran. "Quiet down," he directed.

Falcone twisted, extending his bound wrists. "Untie me and we'll go our separate ways."

"Not a chance. Where I go, you go." To accent his point, Bolan grasped the killer and shoved him northward. "Keep on going. Don't slow down unless I tell you to."

"Like hell I will!" Falcone bristled, raising his voice.

Bolan didn't mince words. A fist to the gut jack-knifed the Camorran in two. Gouging a thumb and forefinger into Falcone's throat, he hoisted the man erect and said, "I won't tell you twice. Consider yourself in federal custody. It beats the alternative."

A shout to the south bore the point home. The commandos were tracking them.

The Executioner pushed Falcone into motion, then trailed him, tensed for treachery. It was all well and good, he mused, to want to take the Camorran back for the Feds to interrogate. But living long enough to do so was another matter. He had to face facts. He was outnumbered six to one. The men after him were exceptionally well trained and well armed, while he had no weapons at all. Even his ankle knife had been taken. And to compound a bad situation, he had a prisoner to safeguard.

There wasn't a bookie anywhere who would lay odds on his chances of still being alive at sunset.

Only one element was in Bolan's favor. He had honed his survival skills in the killing fields of Vietnam, polished them in combat in practically every jungle on the globe. As a guerrilla fighter, he had few peers. Unarmed he might be, but the Executioner was never defenseless.

Bolan allowed the Camorran to run until the point of exhaustion. When the man began to lurch and gasp, Bolan drew up, saying, "Far enough, for the moment."

Falcone sagged against a tree. The exertion had set his leg wound to bleeding freely. He pulled a handkerchief from his jacket and wadded it to staunch the flow. "I must rest," he panted. "Give me fifteen minutes and I'll be as good as new."

"You have half a minute," Bolan said, assessing how much of a lead they had. Five minutes, probably. No more than ten, tops. They had left a trail a simpleton could follow, and the commandos were bound to be fair hands at tracking. Hopefully they would pace themselves to avoid blundering into an ambush.

The Camorran bestowed a look of raw hatred on Bolan. "Who are you, mister? If you're a law officer, I demand to see some identification. I know my rights."

"Do you now?" Bolan responded dryly.

"That's right. All of us were briefed on our legal rights before we came to your country." He perked up. "It was my boss's idea, in case any of us were arrested. That way we could not be made to confess against our will. Very clever of him, yes?"

"He's a bright one," Bolan conceded.

"Oh, he is much more than that," Falcone said proudly. "There has not been anyone like him since the days of your infamous Al Capone. He takes what he wants and never lets anyone or anything stand in his way."

"Including his own father."

Falcone missed a beat. "You have heard, eh? Is that not proof of his devotion to the Camorra, that he would slay his own flesh and blood for the greater good?"

Bolan recognized a rabid case of hero worship when he saw one. Nothing he could say would persuade the young killer to change his opinion of Scarlotti. "Move out," he said, pointing to the northwest.

The Camorran balked until Bolan gave him a push. Reluctantly Falcone hastened on, his limp worse than ever. Half under his breath he indulged in a lusty string of oaths in Italian.

The lay of the land was essentially flat at that point, the pines as thick as ever. They came to a pond rife with lily pads and bullfrogs, and Bolan skirted it to the border of a lowland swamp.

Falcone scrunched his nose as if they had stumbled on a sewer. "You're not thinking of venturing in *there*, are you, American?"

"I am," Bolan admitted.

"Are you insane? There must be deadly snakes, and God knows what else. We should stick to solid ground and keep wandering until we strike a road."

Bolan edged into the water, which rose as high as his hips. The Camorran had a point. There were bound to be cottonmouths and copperheads in the vicinity, maybe a few timber rattlesnakes, too. But it was a risk worth taking. "Your friends back there can't follow us if they can't find any tracks," he remarked.

"Damn them!" Falcone said. "Damn you, as well!" The whites of his eyes shone as he stepped down the short incline. Fumbling at the buttons of his shirt, he tugged on something underneath. Of all things, it was an elaborate crucifix. "I hate snakes!" he complained, fondling it. "I hate them more than anything in this whole world!"

Bolan wasn't surprised. Even the most hardened of killers often had a pet fear, a private dread that instilled in them the same terror they instilled in others.

"Keep your eyes peeled and splash as you walk," Bolan suggested. "It should keep the snakes away from us."

"Tell that to the one looking at us."

Bolan swiveled and saw the head and neck of a dark, heavy-bodied serpent, close enough to strike either of them.

It was a cottonmouth.

# CHAPTER SEVENTEEN

Drab olive in color, with a broad head noticeably wider than its neck, the cottonmouth rated a reputation as one of the most deadly snakes in North America. Its venom wasn't as toxic as a rattler's, but it still claimed the lives of unwary hikers and swimmers every year.

Bolan had tangled with the belligerent reptiles before. He knew that when one opened its maw wide, exposing the cotton-hued lining of its mouth, it was preparing to bite. And that was exactly what this one did. Mouth agape, fangs bared, it turned first toward him, then toward the Camorran. The creature couldn't seem to make up its mind which one of them it should attack.

The Executioner froze. Sometimes a snake would lose interest if it wasn't openly threatened. He was glad that Falcone had the sense to stand still, too. His main worry now was that the commandos would burst on the scene before the viper slithered away.

The seconds became minutes, and the minutes were nerve-racking. Falcone squirmed, his face glistening. His eyes held a wild gleam. It was taking every iota of self-control the man possessed to root him in place.

The cottonmouth swam a few inches closer. It was facing Bolan, but suddenly Falcone's wounded leg started to buckle. The Camorran caught himself, although not before the snake swung toward him and hissed like a teapot gone amok. Falcone resembled a block of ice, his face a petrified mask.

Off in the pines a twig cracked.

Bolan didn't spot anyone, but it was only a matter of time. A very short amount, unless he missed his guess. He cast about for something he could use as a weapon but no dead limbs or high reeds were in reach. Relying on bare hands invited a bite. Nor would kicking at it be any better. As quick as the snake was, it would evade his foot and sink those lethal fangs into his leg before he could draw it back.

Falcone had a frenzied air about him. He was close to the breaking point, his lower lip quivering as if they were standing there in the frigid dead of winter. When the cottonmouth reared a little higher, he gulped and clenched his fists as if he were thinking of taking a swing at it, even with his arms bound.

Salvation came in an unlikely form. A pair of crows chose that moment to wing their way across the swamp. The shadow of one of the big black birds passed directly over the cottonmouth. As quick as thought, the snake turned and raced off into a belt of cattails.

Exhaling in relief, Falcone sagged and swore. "What was that all about? Why did it run off?"

"It mistook the crow's shadow for a hawk's," Bolan guessed.

"Really?" The Camorran uttered a nervous laugh. "For a minute there I figured that I was a dead man."

"You still may be," Bolan warned, nodding at the woodland they had passed through. Beyond the pond something had moved. He pushed into the swamp, the water inching higher until he was soaked to the waist.

Falcone struggled to keep pace, his bound hands handicapping him. He smacked them on the surface every few steps, his fearful gaze raking right and left in search of more snakes.

A small group of sparrows rose chirping from the brush southwest of the pond. Bolan zeroed in on a cluster of reeds to his left. The risk of encountering the cottonmouth's relatives was higher there, but it couldn't be helped. He parted the front ranks and slipped in among them, hunkering so the water rose to his shoulders.

The Camorran was no fool. "Now I know you are trying to get me killed, American! If I step in there, a snake will bite me for sure."

"If you don't, those Mafia hit men will get to snip your fingers down to the knuckles and yank your teeth out one by one,'' Bolan countered. ''Your choice.''

Falcone fumed. ''I hate this! I hate them! I hate you! I hate your disgusting country and everything it stands for!''

So far the Sicilians hadn't appeared, but Bolan felt in his bones that they would at any second. He had to calm the Camorran fast. ''Scarlotti is the one you should blame. He's the one responsible for your being here.''

The young tough sobered as if cold water had been dashed in his face. ''That shows how much you know. I would follow him anywhere. He is the heart and soul of the Camorra.''

''Stand out there in the open much longer and you'll never get to see him again.''

Falcone hesitated a few seconds longer, then gnashed his teeth and stalked into the reeds, shouldering them aside as if he were a raging bull, his legs flicking to either side to shake those around him. The water a few feet away rippled to the passage of an unseen creature, putting a stop to his antics. He gaped breathlessly as the ripples moved slowly away.

The Executioner felt something else brush his left shin, but he said nothing to the Camorran. It wouldn't take much to induce panic, and that could get them both killed.

A figure materialized from out of the foliage across the pond. His camouflage fatigues blended superbly into the background. If not for the movement of his reflection on the water's surface, Bolan wouldn't have spotted the man when he did.

Seconds elapsed. Two more soldiers appeared, Cardoni and Luigi, then the rest of the special hit team, spaced out at four-foot intervals. The man in the lead was their tracker, and he was competent at it. He followed the exact route Bolan had taken around the pond to the edge of the swamp.

Cardoni was anxious to go on. When the tracker delayed, scouring the grass, he said something that provoked a shake of the head. Luigi frowned and gestured. A dispute ensued. They had lost the scent and couldn't make up their minds which way to go.

Cardoni solved the problem by sending two men straight into the swamp, two slanting into it to the northwest, and two to the northeast. Luigi and one other commando waded straight toward the high reeds, the husky Sicilian in front.

Bolan slowly backed farther from the open water. He arched his brows to signal the Camorran to do the same and was answered with a shake of the head. Falcone stared at the green wall of reeds, paralyzed by his fear of the deadly serpents that might be lurking in there.

The two Mafia cutthroats were thirty feet from the reeds. Suddenly the second man gave a start and slapped at the water. Luigi stopped and seemed to be hunting for whatever his fellow commando had seen.

Bracing his feet on the slick bottom, Bolan lunged and grabbed Falcone's arm. The Camorran tried to pull back, to break free. Without hesitation Bolan kneed him in the groin. Falcone folded and would have gone under had Bolan not caught hold and dragged the feebly struggling killer into heavier cover. They were none too soon.

Luigi and the other Sicilian reached the reeds. Making no attempt to use stealth, they barged in, swatting stems aside with their rifles.

Twelve feet distant, Bolan firmed his grip on the Camorran to prevent Falcone from thrashing. Covering the man's mouth, Bolan whispered in his ear, "Make another sound and it will be your last."

Falcone began to quake. Every stray ripple, every rustle of the reeds, compounded his fright. He was a helpless wreck, a child terrified by a bogeyman of his own making.

Bolan could retreat no farther without being spotted. He dipped lower, until the water was just below his nose. A tadpole, or perhaps a minnow, wriggled across his left hand.

The Sicilian with Luigi wasn't happy. "I do not like this place," he griped. "Surely they would not have been foolish enough to go this way."

"The Camorran would not do it if he were on his own," Luigi responded while poking in the reeds. "He is nothing but hot air, Philio." The husky hit man paused. "But that other one, the American, he is made of fire and steel. I could see it in his eyes." Luigi straightened and moved on. "He would come this way to throw us off the scent."

Philio was gazing to the north. "At least this swamp is not very big. I can see the tree line a hundred meters off."

The Executioner prepared to launch himself at them. They were now only six feet away. Another step or two, and they couldn't possibly fail to spot the petrified Camorran. Then Luigi veered to the right, into a tangle of reeds that he felt had to be a better hiding place. Philio followed. Within moments they were gone, swallowed by the reeds except for the tops of their heads.

Bolan checked on the others. Cardoni and the man with him were crossing the open water and had already passed the reeds. Farther east, the last pair was plowing through weeds that grew close to shore.

"Stay here," Bolan told Falcone. Not that he expected the Camorran to go anywhere in the condition he was in.

Turning, the Executioner stalked Luigi and Philio. As well trained as they were, they made the same mistake so many of their breed did. They hardly ever glanced back. Since they had covered that ground, they took it for granted no one was behind them.

Bolan moved slowly, careful not to splash or create a wake. The reeds were soft and pliant enough that he need not worry about them snapping when he applied pressure, but they would rustle if he pushed too hard so he had to be vigilant.

Past the reeds were broad lily pads that formed

a rubbery green mat covering dozens of yards. Frogs scattered at Luigi's approach. Dragonflies flitted every which way.

Philio accidentally dipped the muzzle of his rifle into the water. He jerked it up, frowning at wisps of mossy vegetation that clung to the flash suppressor. Halting, he reached out to remove it.

Like an alligator closing on prey, Bolan neared the unsuspecting Sicilian. When he made his bid, he had to move swiftly or Luigi would cut him in two. Legs braced, he surged up out of the water, his left arm hooking Philio's jawbone and clamping tight even as his right arm constricted in an unbreakable vise around Philio's temples. Belatedly Philio reacted by throwing himself forward.

Bolan wrenched brutally to the left, then the right. There was a clean snap, and the Sicilian went limp. As the body sagged, the Executioner snatched at the BM-59.

Luigi had heard and spun. He was leveling his own weapon, but in his haste, one of his feet slipped and the barrel jumped off target.

Bolan fired first. He drilled a round into Luigi as the killer tried to raise his own weapon, fired another round into him as Luigi jolted to the first shot, added a third when the man refused to go down and a fourth because Luigi weakly tried to shoot even as his knees buckled and the spark of life drained from his cruel features.

Shouts broke out. Cardoni was calling Luigi's name over and over.

Bolan bent, patting Philio's fatigues. He found three spare magazines and crammed them into his pockets. He would have liked to help himself to whatever else might be worth taking, but loud splashing told him that the other Sicilians were rapidly approaching. He had to get the Camorran out of there and turn the man over to Brognola.

Plunging into the reeds, the Executioner ducked and double-timed to where he had left Falcone—only the man wasn't there. Bolan pivoted, thinking he had erred. But no, there was a reed Falcone had bent in two earlier. He was at the exact spot.

More bent reeds showed Bolan which direction the Camorran had taken. He rose onto his toes, and there to the southwest was the young tough, frantically scrambling onto solid ground.

Bolan bent and gave chase. As yet the Sicilians hadn't spread out to find him and Falcone, but they would once they got over the shock of discovering Luigi and Philio dead. He saw Falcone barrel into the pines, snapping a low limb. The man glanced back, spied Bolan and smirked.

The soldier threw caution to the wind. He crashed through the reeds, water lapping around him as he covered the final ten yards to the shoreline. A rifle cracked as he hurled himself up the bank, the slugs ripping into the spongy soil on his right. More rifles chimed in as he sprinted into the trees.

Falcone had left a trail of moist drops. Bolan flew into the forest, slowing only when the drops petered out. From then on he relied on broken twigs and branches and footprints to guide him. He counted on overtaking the Camorran quickly, but Falcone had more stamina than he bargained on. The trail led over a hill, into a ribbon of a valley choked with briars.

A deer trail wound into the heart of the thorny labyrinth. Bolan raced along it, rounding a bend and flying along a straightaway that ended at a ninety-degree turn. He took it with barely a break in stride.

Falcone was waiting for him. The clever Neapolitan had crouched just past the bend, and as Bolan came sprinting around it, he rocketed upward, his shoulder slamming into the soldier's midsection and lifting Bolan clean off his feet. The blow hurled Bolan into the briars. Instantly his legs and arms were entangled in clinging limbs, thorns tearing at his clothing, piercing his flesh.

Still bound, the Camorran resorted to his feet, giving a high hop and kicking at Bolan's face. The soldier jerked aside. Thorns lanced his cheek, but he was spared the brunt of the impact.

Falcone had outsmarted himself. His right foot was snared by the briars. He tried to yank it loose and land upright, but the clinging vegetation held him fast. He upended, his chest and head striking the ground, his leg still caught by the thorns. Cursing lustily, he shimmied backward and tugged furiously on his trapped foot.

Bolan was also trying to free himself, but he had a harder job of it. Every movement sparked pangs of agony. It was as if the briars were a living, breathing entity trying to digest him whole. He had to let go of the rifle to get more leverage. Exerting all the power at his command, he staggered from the prickly cocoon onto the trail, torn limbs hanging from him as if he were a tree.

Falcone had also pulled loose. Rising, he aimed a vicious head butt at Bolan's gut. The soldier sidestepped, his foot smashing into Falcone's shin, his hand chopping the Camorran's nape. That was all it took. Falcone fell like an anvil and lay momentarily still, his eyelids fluttering.

Bolan reclaimed the BM-59. A starling squawked to the northwest. He grabbed Falcone by the collar and dragged him into the maze, not caring if thorns bit at Falcone's legs and shoulders. His prisoner sputtered to life. Raging, he tried to stand.

"Let go of me, damn you! You can't treat me like this! I demand to speak to a lawyer!"

The request was so ridiculous that Bolan almost laughed. He pulled Falcone erect so sharply, the man's teeth crunched together. "Keep talking bigmouth. Let them know right where to find us."

The Camorran didn't seem to care. "Untie me. Let me go. We have a better chance if we go our separate ways."

The man had a point, but Bolan would be damned if he would admit it. Besides which, he was committed to taking Falcone in, and no pack of sham commandos was going to stop him. "Get going," he said, pushing Falcone ahead of him.

"You're an idiot, mister! Is holding on to me worth your life?"

Falcone wasn't moving fast enough to suit Bolan, so he drove the rifle's muzzle into the Camorran's spine. Falcone yipped and took the hint, grumbling fiercely.

"I'll never understand men like you! You'd die to uphold the law, and for what? Who the hell cares if you sacrifice yourself? The people on the streets? They won't lose any sleep over your death. Your superiors? If you die, they will just find someone to take your place. You are an expendable cog in a corrupt machine. You are throwing your life away for nothing!"

Bolan had heard the same lame argument before. Men like Falcone could never comprehend that there were ideals worth dying for, that upholding justice and defending freedom mattered more than the life of any one person. Falcone could never comprehend because he was too wrapped up in himself. He couldn't see that the highest form of human sacrifice was unselfish devotion to others.

A rifle cracked to the northwest and was answered by another farther west.

A signal? Bolan guessed. The Sicilians had split up, then. He put himself in their boots and concluded that two of them would enter the briars while the remaining pair circled around to head Falcone and him off.

"Faster," Bolan said.

A low growl rose from Falcone's throat. "I'm

doing the best I can! I'd like to see you do any better with *your* arms tied behind your back.''

The hardcase had another point. But Bolan had been stripped of his knife, and the soaked knots would be difficult to undo using fingernails. "I'll untie you when we can spare the time," he said.

"Should I kiss your feet now or later?"

The trail meandered on through the briars, twisting and turning at random. No other shots rang out, but Bolan sensed that some of the Sicilians were close behind. To make matters worse, Falcone's leg began to bother him again. The dip in the swamp had done more harm than good, and there were signs the leg was slowly swelling.

Close to twenty minutes of steady jogging brought them within sight of pines. Falcone immediately slowed, sucking in breaths, limping like a pirate with a peg leg. He was literally on his last legs and said as much. "I need to rest, big man. If I don't, you might as well shoot me and put me out of my misery. I'll never be able to keep up."

Bolan saw no evidence of the Sicilians. Once they were among the trees, he steered his prisoner to the west, halting when they were on the other side of a low jagged ridge. "Kneel," he directed.

For once Falcone was too exhausted to raise a fuss. Sagging, he hung his head, his chest heaving.

The knots were every bit as hard as Bolan knew they would be. He had to pry and pick and resort to his teeth to loosen the first one, and there were two others. He was bending to gnaw at the second when a whisper of sound snapped him around.

A Sicilian was visible through the trees. The gunner had to be sixty yards off, conducting a sweep pattern. And where there was one, another had to be nearby.

Bolan shoved Falcone flat. The Camorran began to protest, and Bolan clamped a hand over his mouth. "Your friends will hear. Do you want that?"

Falcone shook his head.

Releasing him, Bolan slid to a trunk wide enough to conceal him and rose into a squat. He propped the rifle against the bole, sighting on the Sicilian, who picked that moment to vanish into the undergrowth. Bolan lifted his head, gauged where the mafioso would reappear and shifted his sights accordingly. Over a minute passed, however, and the commando failed to show.

Bolan scoured the ridge. If the other Sicilians were out there, they were using their heads this time. It had become so quiet that he could hear himself breathe. Unexpectedly he also heard the tromp of heavy footsteps. It was unexpected because it came from behind him, not in front. He spun.

Falcone was on his feet and lurching into the woods. He didn't seem to care how much noise he made. Or maybe he wanted to make a lot, to draw Bolan and the Sicilians into conflict so he could make his getaway while they were occupied.

Bolan started after him. He took three steps, and had to fling himself for cover as the forest rocked to the blast of two autorifles. One of the shooters was near where the first Sicilian had vanished. The other was due east, or close to it. He raked the vegetation for telltale sign. Again the gunner to the east cut loose, a 7.62 mm buzz saw chewing up the tree above Bolan's head.

The Executioner dropped lower. Those shots had come much too close, almost as if the second Sicilian could see him much clearer than he could see the Sicilian. As if to confirm his hunch, the man fired again, a single round this time. The slug gouged a furrow in the earth less than an inch from Bolan's elbow.

The furrow angled down.

Bolan raised his gaze to the trees. At first he saw nothing out of the ordinary. Then an indefinite pattern resolved itself into a commando perched high in the fork of a pine. Bolan flipped to the left as the rifle belched lead. Another furrow sprouted where his chest had been.

Wedging the heavy rifle to his shoulder, Bolan settled a bead on the center of the camouflaged mass and fired. He couldn't be positive, but the Sicilian appeared to sway. The man fired again, hitting the dirt in front of him. Bolan responded in kind. Again the Sicilian was jarred, yet he continued the duel, unleashing two shots that came as close as any ever had to ending the Executioner's career. Bolan raised his sights a hair and squeezed.

The third time was the charm. The commando toppled, bouncing from branch to branch.

Bolan went to work the bolt. He realized the rifle was empty just as the brush to his left split apart and the other Sicilian sprang into the open.

# CHAPTER EIGHTEEN

*Los Angeles, California*

His name was Harold Stenbeck and he was assigned to the FBI field office in Los Angeles. It had always been Stenbeck's dream to work for the Federal Bureau of Investigation. Since his early teens his life's ambition had been to rise through the ranks and one day become as powerful as his idol, J. Edgar Hoover.

Stenbeck had worked his tail off in high school and college to keep his grades up. It had been daunting since he was a mediocre student at best, but in this instance plodding persistence paid off.

He had been a bundle of nerves the day he submitted his application. When word came back that he had been accepted for training, he had walked around for weeks with his head in the clouds.

It hadn't been long before reality brought Stenbeck crashing to earth. He had learned that his prospects for becoming director were on a par with his being elected President of the United States.

There were many underlying reasons. The most important of them was that the majority of his fellow agents had more on the ball than he did. They were sharper, more intelligent, more industrious. They hustled to earn promotions, whereas Stenbeck continued to do what he did best—he plodded.

Stenbeck liked to think that it all boiled down to the fact the FBI was a bureaucracy, and a bureaucracy was a lot like a well in that the strongest swimmers were the ones who made it to the top. Stenbeck never had learned to swim.

There was no denying, though, that luck played an important part also. An agent might stumble on evidence and break an important case. Or a wiretap intended to reel in guppies might snare great white sharks. Or maybe a stakeout might yield an unforeseen bonanza. All it took was one fluke, and an agent's career was virtually made.

So as Stenbeck toiled daily at his varied duties, he cherished the secret notion that one day soon his lucky break would come along, that he would find himself on the fast track to the top of the ladder and the fulfillment of his lifelong dream.

This particular day didn't have a promising start. Stenbeck had just sunk into his chair to tackle an overdue report when none other than the district supervisor had walked in and dropped a bombshell in his lap.

Everyone in the Bureau knew about the ongoing war between the Mafia and the Camorra. Word had come down from the top that every field office was to drop everything else and do whatever it took to cap the violence. Informants were badgered, sources plumbed. Desk-bound agents, men and women who hadn't been out in the field in ages, suddenly found themselves pounding the streets tracking down leads. It was an all-out effort, and few agents were spared.

Except, naturally, Harold Stenbeck.

He had asked—no, he had begged—to be assigned to the Organized Crime Task Force, as it was labeled. His superior had turned him down, saying, "Someone has to stay here and man the phones in case a crucial call comes in. And there is no one I would rather have handle it than you."

Stenbeck hadn't been fooled for a minute. He knew that his co-workers had a nickname for him that aptly summed up their opinion of him. "Gilligan," they called him. There was no need to ask why.

Now, holding the slip of paper that the district supervisor had handed him, Stenbeck blinked and cocked his head. "Are you sure that you want me to take care of this, sir? Mr. Jensen was quite insistent that I stay here and take messages."

The supervisor sniffed, as if he had detected a foul odor. "He was, was he? Well, Stenbeck, *I'm* giving you a direct order to get your lazy butt out of that chair and go check out the tip we received.

If it pans out, I'll let you make the arrests personally."

Stenbeck came out of his chair as if rocket thrusters were strapped to his posterior. "Yes, sir! I'm on it. You can count on me, sir. I won't let you down." He was out the door and hurrying along the corridor before he realized the supervisor was calling his name.

"Sir?"

"Racketeers don't make it a habit to welcome FBI agents with open arms. You might want to take your gun, just in case."

"Oh. Yes, sir. Sorry, sir. How careless of me, sir. It won't happen again."

"And Stenbeck?"

"Sir?"

"Quit acting like a suck-up. Groveling went out of vogue with the Middle Ages."

The address was a concrete company in north L.A. Vigoda Concrete and Masonry was a known front for the Mob, a legitimate business through which the proceeds of illegal activities were funneled. Money laundering, it was called. Five months earlier the Mafia had inexplicably pulled the plug and shut down the firm.

At the time the FBI had the company under twenty-four-hour surveillance. They were on the verge of making a major bust. All they had needed was a little more information to make their case airtight.

When the Mob closed shop, the FBI was left in the lurch. Months of hard work went up in smoke. Weeks of surveillance had been wasted.

Now came word that the company had started up again. A security guard at a neighboring firm had been asked to keep an eye on the place, and if there was any activity to report it to the Bureau. The private badge had leaped at the chance to play with the big boys. His call had come through the night before.

Harold Stenbeck circled the block once before parking at a supermarket and venturing back on foot. He wasn't the incompetent his peers judged him to be. Plodder or no, he knew proper procedure, and he wasn't about to blow what might be his lucky break. With everyone else wrapped up in the Mafia-Camorra war, he had the racketeering case all to himself.

It was to Stenbeck's benefit that he didn't look like a typical FBI agent. Thanks to TV and the movies, most people imagined agents as having computer-chip brains and the bodies of pro linebackers. In Stenbeck's case, he looked more like an animated scarecrow. He was tall and spindly, and his Adam's apple sagged so low that his own mother had often teased him about being careful not to trip over it.

Pulling up the collar of his jacket against the buffeting rain, Stenbeck went past the front of the building. Sure enough, lights blazed inside. But a

Closed sign hung on the front door, and the truck bays weren't in use.

Stenbeck took a right at the corner and walked to the alley that flanked the building. Acting as casual as he could, he strolled down it to a rear exit. Two stories up were large windows, the blinds closed. He was foiled again.

On a whim, Stenbeck tried the knob. He didn't expect the door to be unlocked, and he had started to turn away when it dawned on him that it had swung open. Startled by his good fortune, he hesitated. Procedure demanded that he call in. But what could it hurt if he took a teensy peek?

The hinges didn't creak. Stenbeck slipped indoors, his heart hammering like a jackhammer, his hand on the butt of his service weapon. He was in a dimly lit corridor that took him past several small rooms. An office ahead was bathed in light, the door ajar.

Stenbeck was almost there when he heard someone on the other side stir. He ducked into a storage room, barely breathing as footsteps scraped the corridor. Two men were talking.

"—be here by late tonight. The boss wants us to have everything ready for the sit-down."

"I just hope this one doesn't end like the last one did."

"No way. Those Camorran chumps don't know about this place. It's perfect cover."

"That's what everyone thought about the Moose

Head, remember? And we were lucky to get out with our lives.''

Stenbeck risked a peek. Two men as big as gorillas went to the rear door and exited. He glanced to his left and saw that they had left the office door open wide enough for him to glimpse figures moving about. It dawned on him that the gorillas had to be Mafia solders, and that for some reason the Mafia was about to hold a meeting at the concrete company.

Then a man filled the frame of the office door. He had one hand in a pocket and was puffing on a cigar. His expression was that of a pit bull at bay, a mix of latent savagery and extreme cunning. But for a few seconds there, with his back to the other men in the office, he let down his guard and his face betrayed worry. Something was eating at him, and he didn't want the others to know.

Stenbeck peered intently at that face, bothered by it. He felt that he should know the man, yet he was positive they had never met. In the recesses of his mind something clicked, and suddenly he realized who the man was. Any field agent who had ever attended a briefing on organized crime would know.

A shiver of raw excitement coursed down Harold Stenbeck's back. He was half inclined to pinch himself to verify he wasn't dreaming.

"Boss?" someone called out. "Don Castellano is on the horn. He says he'll be here by ten. Do you want to talk to him?"

"No," the man in the doorway said. "Just tell Joseph to be careful. Very careful. We can't afford to lose anyone else."

"Will do."

The man puffed a while longer, sighed and closed the door. Stenbeck was out of the room in a flash, streaking down the corridor with visions of a promotion swirling in his head. At the rear door he paused to make sure the gorillas were gone. It would be a shame to get caught when his future looked brighter than it had in ages. Satisfied the alley was empty, he slipped out and beat his feet to the street. Once he mingled with the other pedestrians, he willed himself to relax and beamed like an idiot.

Stenbeck couldn't help it.

For ages he had been praying for a stroke of luck, for things to finally go his way, and his guardian angel had come through.

Big time.

*New Jersey*

THE SICILIAN CRASHED out of the underbrush with his rifle already leveled. But he made a mistake. He shot from cover just a few feet from the Executioner, so close, in fact, that the soldier was on him before he could fire.

Wielding the paratroop rifle like a club, Bolan smashed the commando in the face. The man went down, his weapon skidding across the ground. Pouncing, the Executioner seized a sheath knife strapped to the killer's right hip, reversed his grip and buried the ten-inch blade to the hilt between the Sicilian's ribs. The man clawed at his neck, stiffened and expired.

Bolan quickly helped himself to the fallen rifle. He exchanged the partially spent magazine for a full one, then scanned the pines. Cardoni and the last Sicilian were nowhere to be found, but the shots were bound to bring them soon.

He remembered Falcone. Sprinting into the forest, he tracked the devious Camorran to the southwest. The young tough had been running flat out and left as much sign as a wounded elephant. Bolan adopted a jogging gait that could eat up miles without tiring him. He wasn't concerned about his quarry getting away. In the shape Falcone had been in, the man wouldn't get far.

Hundreds of yards later, the trees thinned and were replaced by a broad field. Waist-high grass was broken here and there by islands of rock. Bent stems revealed that Falcone had angled to the nearest, circled it, then went swiftly on to the next. The same pattern was repeated.

Bolan wondered if the Camorran had been searching for a place to hide. At the fourth outcropping he learned the truth.

Lying at the base of a jagged boulder speckled with drops of fresh blood was the rope that had bound Falcone. He had sawed it in two, slicing himself in the process. Now he had his hands free. He could make better time. And he would be that much harder to take prisoner again.

The bent grass brought Bolan to a rare band of deciduous trees, oaks, mainly, and a few weeping willows. He saw something on the ground ahead, beside the trunk of one of the willows, a brown object with an odd shape that he couldn't quite identify. He stepped closer.

Bolan blinked in rare surprise. It was a shoe, one of Falcone's. He was at a loss to explain what it was doing there. It hadn't been damaged and no blood dotted its surface. He bent to pick it up.

Too late, Bolan saw that the laces had been untied. Too late, he perceived what that meant and tried to straighten. The scrape of a heavy body on a limb above confirmed that he had fallen for one of the oldest tricks in the book. Since he had no time to dodge, he went limp to absorb the impact.

It came a heartbeat later. Falcone rammed into him like an express train, slamming Bolan to the turf and knocking the breath out of him. The soldier twisted and felt Falcone grab the rifle. He held on, refusing to relinquish it since to do so would prove fatal.

"Damn you!" Falcone raged. "You can't stop me now! I won't let you!"

The Executioner was pinned on his left side. He couldn't get enough leverage to toss the Camorran off, nor could he tuck his legs under him and push to his feet. His shoulders throbbed as Falcone tore at the rifle in potent rage, seeking to wrest it loose.

"Let go, damn it! I want this gun!"

Inspiration struck. Bolan let him have it. He abruptly released the rifle, and Falcone toppled backward, throwing an arm out to keep from falling. Bolan heaved up the moment the weight was off him. He tackled Falcone as the man tried to rise, bearing them both down. Falcone lashed at him with the rifle stock, clipping his temple. For a second or two the world spun. The Camorran, snarling like a wild beast, drew the stock back to strike another blow.

Although groggy, Bolan landed a blow first, a palm-heel thrust to the jaw that snapped Falcone's head back. A fist to the stomach, and the Camorran sagged, gasping, unable to lift the rifle more than a few inches.

Bolan shoved erect, yanked the BM-59 from Falcone's grasp and stepped back. The man had no idea how lucky he was that Brognola needed him alive. "On your feet," he ordered.

The soldier stepped back and covered the Camorran. He pushed Falcone to the south, saying, "I've put up with all I'm going to take from you. Keep your mouth shut from here on out." Falcone wasn't moving fast enough to suit him so he pushed the killer again. "The next stunt you pull will be your last."

For once the Camorran took the hint.

The better part of an hour went by before Bolan

spied a road. So many crisscrossed the Barrens that he couldn't be one hundred percent sure it was the one he wanted. He had Falcone stand still while he ventured into the open. There wasn't a living soul in sight, nor any parked vehicles.

Bolan beckoned and Falcone joined him. From the position of the waning sun, he estimated that they were west of where he had left his car. He started Falcone trudging eastward, their footfalls the only sound—that, and the Camorran's angry muttering.

The shadows lengthened. Presently the sun sat balanced on the rim of the world. Day would soon give way to night. Bolan didn't care to be stuck in the Pine Barrens until dawn with his prisoner. It would be nice, he reflected, if a Piney was to come along in a pickup truck and give them a lift.

On cue, an engine purred to their rear. Bolan moved to the side of the road and lowered his rifle so it wouldn't be clearly visible. He didn't want to scare off any Good Samaritans. Falcone stood a few feet away, as sullen as ever.

The vehicle came around a bend two hundred yards distant. In the fading light, with dust choking the rear half, it was several moments before Bolan saw that it was a car, not a pickup, and that it was a car he had seen before. Whirling, he shoved Falcone toward the trees. "Run!" he shouted.

The car's engine roared as the driver floored it. The dark sedan hurtled forward, its windows lowering. Three of the four men inside leaned out to take aim.

It was the sedan Bolan had shadowed all the way from New York City, the sedan containing the four triggermen who worked for Bruno Gaito. Bolan guessed that they had grown concerned when the Sicilians didn't return on schedule, and now they were patrolling the road, looking for them.

One of the gunners had an Ingram M-10 subgun. He opened up, but he was too far away.

Lead chopped into the road twenty feet from Bolan as he dived into the brush and spun. The car was bearing down on them at over seventy miles per hour. In the time it took him to turn, rounds were blistering the trees on either side. He aimed at the driver, barely visible through the tinted windshield, and emptied half his magazine.

Tires squealed as the sedan slewed to the right. A gunner in the front seat grabbed the steering wheel and spun it, but he overcompensated and sent the car hurtling sharply to the left. It went airborne, flying over a ditch and into the pines. Trees snapped like so many twigs. In a shower of leaves and busted limbs, it came to rest with the left rear tire off the ground. Otherwise, the car was undamaged.

Bolan ran toward it. The hardmen were spilling out the opposite side. He sent a slug through a window without telling effect.

The man with the M-10 popped up above the roof and blazed away. He couldn't see the Executioner, so he swung the SMG back and forth, spraying anything and everything to force Bolan to seek cover.

The tactic worked.

Bolan dropped into a hollow no longer than he was and hardly a foot deep. A hardman with a pistol made a break for the deep woods. Automatically he pumped the rifle to his shoulder, the shot bringing the hardman up short. It also drew the fire of the two soldiers still behind the sedan.

Bolan hugged the earth as the dirt from the rim of the hollow showered on top of him. He waited until the gunners' weapons cycled dry, then he was up and out of the depression and into the undergrowth before they could reload. One of them fired a few more shots at the hollow. Or so Bolan thought until he heard a thud and a moan.

The Executioner bore to the right in a half circle that brought him to the brush Falcone had disappeared into. He crawled a yard more and a pair of feet claimed his attention. Going farther, he parted high weeds.

The Camorran was on his back, his mouth working soundlessly, as if he were mute. His every breath was a monumental effort, his chest ballooning out, the three holes in his sternum oozing blood in a copious stream. His wide eyes found Bolan. He raised his head a fraction and seemed to want to speak. When he couldn't, a racking sob shook him from head to toe. He collapsed, his eyes glazing, his chest deflating with his dying breath.

The irony didn't escape Bolan. For once the Camorran had listened to him and not tried to run off. As a result, Falcone was dead and Brognola had lost a golden opportunity to learn more about the Camorra in general and Antonio Scarlotti's plans specifically.

Those Mafia goons were to blame.

Bolan slid on around the body, stopping close to the road. One of the triggermen was coming straight toward him and was blissfully unaware of the fact. He held his fire until the mobster happened to look right at him. It was the last sight the man ever saw.

Only one was left, the shooter partial to the Ingram subgun.

Backing into the pines, Bolan traveled forty feet to the east. A pine that resembled a tepee offered the vantage spot he sought. Slinging the rifle over his right shoulder, he climbed until he was high enough to see a considerable distance. He pinpointed Falcone's corpse and the body near the road. He could see the soldier he had dropped making a break, and the driver of the car slumped over the steering wheel.

But there was no sign at all of the man with the SMG.

All experienced snipers had one particular trait in common—exceptional patience. In Vietnam Bolan often had to lie or sit still for hours on end before his quarry showed itself. Once he hadn't moved a muscle for close to nine hours in order to bag an enemy general.

Now Bolan did the same. Only his eyes moved,

roving over the forest again and again. He missed nothing. Not the erratic flight of a small yellow butterfly. Not the robin that landed briefly on a limb near the car. Nor a caterpillar crawling on a leaf. Yet the gunner didn't show.

All that was left of the sun was a golden halo when a hand rose into view between the sedan and the road. It pushed a low limb aside.

Bolan swiveled the paratroop rifle.

The hand dipped, and a head rose in its place. The hardman scrutinized the terrain from right to left and back again. He examined every shadow, probed every bush. He was as thorough as it was humanly possible to be. He did everything he should have done except the one thing that would have saved his life.

He forgot to look up.

# CHAPTER NINETEEN

*Los Angeles*

Joseph Castellano had his driver go around the block four times before he allowed the limo to pull to the curb. The two trailing sedans immediately stopped to disgorge the six soldiers in each. Only when his men had formed a human wall on both sides of the rear door did Castellano emerge and hurry into Vigoda Concrete and Masonry.

Don Bruno Gaito was waiting to embrace him. "Joseph!" he declared warmly. "I can't tell you how good it is to see you again."

"The feeling is mutual," Castellano told his friend, surveying their surroundings. "But are you sure it is safe? Scarlotti fooled us once. He could do so again."

"Trust me on this," Gaito said. "Even the Feds wouldn't think to bother us here. They believe that we no longer use the place."

Ordinarily Castellano would have accepted his mentor's word without question. But the debacle at the lodge had taught him the value of paranoia. "I hope you're right."

Vigoda Concrete was a two-story building that reminded Castellano of a gigantic concrete blockhouse. The lower story was devoted to the loading docks, offices and conveyor belts that brought sacks of concrete and other products down from the second floor where they were stored. The place had a musty smell about it, and dust layered everything from the floor to the metal rollers.

"How many bosses will be here?" Castellano asked.

"Two Dons who were not able to make it to Chicago, and nine lesser bosses who stand to take over now that their own Dons have bought the farm," Gaito detailed. "The sit-down is slated for midnight. You're the first to arrive."

Castellano let himself be steered to an office where he was treated to a cup of piping hot black coffee. Sipping, he asked the question uppermost on his mind. "What about security, Bruno? I've brought fourteen boys with me. See fit to post them where you deem it best."

"I may just take you up on your offer," Gaito said. "But I'm not about to make the same mistake Fallini did. That peninsula of his was too open, too exposed. Anyone could get at us there." He indicated the exterior of the building with a wave. "Here it's a different story. There are only two doors in or out, not counting the truck bays. And they are kept closed and locked at all times. No one can get anywhere near us.''

Once, Castellano would have been content to drop the subject then and there. But he couldn't get the horrifying image of the nightmare in Illinois out of his mind. ''What if those lousy Camorrans try to bring the roof down on our heads? They blew up the garage. They may decide that the same stinking trick will work twice in a row.''

''I'd like to see them try,'' Gaito growled. ''Come with me. I have something to show you.''

Castellano was escorted onto the roof where eight gunners, dressed as painters, were on constant guard duty. Assigned two to a wall, they roved back and forth. They made it impossible for anyone to approach without being seen.

''The outfits were my brainstorm,'' Gaito said with a chuckle. ''From the street, they look as if they're working on the roof.'' He walked to the rear of the building, which was bordered by an alley. ''They've been up here an hour and no one has come anywhere near the joint.''

''But the sun has gone down. Soon it will be too dark for them to see much down below,'' Castellano noted.

Gaito's mouth tweaked. ''Do tell.'' He turned to one of his soldiers. ''Manny, show our guest what we have stowed under that tarp there, would you?''

The gunner knelt and pulled out a large black leather case. Opening it, he removed what appeared to be a pair of binoculars, except that they were twice the ordinary size and a strange closed metal tube was attached in the center. "Night-vision binoculars, Mr. Castellano, sir," he revealed. "We picked them up at an Army-surplus place. They're Russian made, but they still work like a charm."

"As soon as it gets a little darker, every man up here will put one on," Gaito said. "Feel safer now?"

"A little," Castellano admitted.

The New York Don clucked. "I never knew you were such a hard man to please, Joseph. Very well. Tag along and I'll show you what other steps I've taken."

It turned out that Gaito had done just about all that could be done to safeguard those who attended the sit-down. At every window were posted gunners with SMGs and grenades. Trip wires had been strung across the truck bays in case the opposition saw fit to bust inside. Four men outfitted with walkie-talkies, spaced at regular intervals, were assigned to walk around the block all night long, if need be. Four more in an armored sedan patrolled the immediate vicinity.

"So," Gaito said when they were back in the office and he was pouring a cup of coffee, "what do you think, my friend? Is there anything I've missed?"

Castellano couldn't think of a thing. The truth was, Gaito had outdone himself, demonstrating once again why no one had ever caught him off guard. The affair at the peninsula didn't count. That had been Fallini's show from start to finish. And even there Gaito had shown his foresight by having his car brought around in case of trouble. "You've done fine, Bruno. If those Camorran geeks try anything, we'll feed them their teeth."

"How many times must I say it? The Camorra can't possibly know about this place." Gaito paused. "What's that old saying? Oh, yeah. I remember." He laughed lightly. "We're as snug as a bug in a rug. They would need an entire tank brigade to break in here."

"Fortress Vigoda," Castellano said offhandedly.

"I like the sound of that!" Gaito declared. "Just let that scum Scarlotti show his face! It will be like the Alamo all over again, only in reverse."

TWENTY BLOCKS south of Vigoda Concrete stood one of the premier hotels in all of Los Angeles. Known as the Exeter, the hotel boasted a clientele who were the financial elite, the crème de la crème of high society. Bankers, corporate heads and movie stars routinely stayed there.

To Antonio Scarlotti, the Exeter was a slice of heaven on earth. Being waited on hand and foot suited him. He spent time in the hot tub, took a dip in the Olympic-sized swimming pool and relaxed in the ornate lounge. His men marveled that he could find time to relax on the eve of their crowning glory.

It was past six when Scarlotti returned to his room. He put in a call to the warehouse where his soldiers were preparing for the assault and learned that all was in order. As he rested the phone in the cradle, he glanced at one of his lieutenants. "Giovanni, have you heard from Falcone yet?"

"No, sir."

The news was mildly upsetting. Scarlotti had ordered Falcone to report in at five o'clock, and it was unlike the young firebrand to let him down. "If he hasn't contacted us within the hour, send someone to the nursery to investigate."

Giovanni took a notepad from a pocket. "The nearest people we have are two men in Atlanta. They're supposed to whack Sentelli if he shows his face at that hideaway of his."

"No one else is closer?"

"Sorry, boss. Everyone else is out here for the big hit."

It annoyed Scarlotti, but he had no one to blame except himself. He was the one who had ordered virtually every last soldier to converge on Los Angeles for the final assault on the Mafia's leadership. "Tell the pair in Atlanta to check on Falcone if we don't hear from him."

"Will do. Anything else?"

"No."

Giovanni turned to go, then hesitated. "Mind if I ask you a question?"

Scarlotti preferred to be alone to think, but he had his image to think of. He wanted his men to believe that he was always accessible, that he had an ear for their troubles any time of the day or night. He had found that it increased their respect for him.

Not that Scarlotti really cared whether they liked him or not. But he was a shrewd judge of human nature. And he had learned long ago that men were more willing to die for someone they respected than for someone they feared.

"You may ask one any time."

"It's about the guy who tipped you to the sit-down tonight. How did you get him to turn traitor? I know it wasn't for money. You said so."

Scarlotti folded his hands on his knee, looking every inch the imperial leader. "Every enemy has a weakness, my friend. The key to victory is to learn what that weakness is and exploit it. With some, like that weasel who betrayed Don Fallini, it is a matter of appealing to their greed. With the man here in L.A., all we had to do was appeal to the most basic of human instincts, self-preservation." Scarlotti snickered. "We held a gun to his head and convinced him that if he did not cooperate, there was nowhere on this planet where he would be safe from our vengeance."

Giovanni's disgust was evident. "He is a coward, then. He deserves his fate."

"The blame is not all his," Scarlotti declared. "Part of the fault must lie with his superior."

"How so, boss?"

There were few things Scarlotti enjoyed more than dispensing words of wisdom to his troops. He was fond of adopting the air of a benevolent teacher while secretly flaunting his knowledge in their faces. "An army is only as good as the person in charge. One of the most important skills a leader must have is the ability to read others as if they were open books. How else can he judge whether they are worthy of his trust?"

His lieutenant started to speak, but Scarlotti cut him off with a gesture. He didn't like being interrupted. "It is the leader's responsibility to pick men who will not let him down when the going gets rough. Bruno Gaito should not have picked this man to be a capo. Gaito is equally to blame for the treachery because this capo is only being true to his nature, a nature Gaito should have recognized."

The telephone jangled. Giovanni answered it, covered the mouthpiece and grinned. "Speak of the devil, boss. It's him. On line three."

Scarlotti's voice was soothing velvet. "Mr. Petrone! This is a surprise. I thought that I told you not to contact me again?"

"It's important," the mafioso declared.

"So important that you are willing to jeopardize

everything by calling me? What if your boss is listening in?''

"Relax, will you?" Petrone responded. "How stupid do you think I am? I'm calling from a phone booth six blocks from Vigoda's. Don Gaito sent me to a fast-food place to buy burgers for everybody."

The impudence of the man! Scarlotti thought. He made a mental note to make the turncoat suffer the torment of the damned before he died. "What is so important?''

"You have to call it off."

The laugh that burst from Scarlotti was as brittle as thin ice. "You must be joking, Dominic. Like it or not, we are committed. Tonight the Mafia topples."

"But you don't understand," Petrone said. "My boss has the place sealed up tighter than a drum. There are guys on the roof with night-vision devices, guys at every window, guys in the street. Even the bays have been wired to keep you out. Your men won't stand a chance. And I don't want you to blame me if something goes wrong."

"I thank you for the news, but it changes nothing. I have planned for every contingency," Scarlotti said. "As for blaming you, rest assured that I will not hold the outcome against you should it not go our way."

Petrone was loath to give up. "Don't you care about your men, mister? I'm telling you that they'll be chopped to bits if you hit us. You act as if they are nothing more than cannon fodder.''

Since Giovanni and other lieutenants were in earshot, Scarlotti put on a show for their benefit. ''How dare you!'' he bristled. ''Of course my men matter to me! Why else do you think I've gone to such lengths to minimize casualties?'' Out of the corner of his eye he saw all those present staring at him in frank admiration.

''Sorry I brought it up.''

Delighted by his subterfuge, Scarlotti now gave his underlings a demonstration of his power. ''Don't hang up yet, Petrone. Since you were kind enough to warn me about the men on the roof, it will be your job to eliminate them at the appointed time.''

''My job?'' Petrone practically yelled. ''What are you trying to pull? This wasn't part of our deal!''

''It is now.'' Scarlotti paused for effect. ''That is, if you still want to go on living after tonight.''

Petrone swore mightily. ''You're jerking me around, mister, and I don't like it. I could go to my boss and spill the beans. Then where would you be?''

Scarlotti chortled. ''You might ask yourself the same question. From what I hear, Gaito is not the trusting sort. How will he react when you tell him? Won't he be the least bit curious as to how you found out about the attack?''

The silence at the other end told Scarlotti that the informant was thinking the same thing he was, namely that Gaito would suspect Petrone of being a traitor. And they both knew how Gaito treated turncoats.

"I can't do it, I tell you. There are too many up there."

"How many exactly?" Scarlotti pressed him.

"Eight."

Scarlotti could imagine the worm wriggling in impotent outrage, and smiled. "I don't see the problem, Mr. Petrone. Sneak on up there with an SMG fitted with a silencer and you can do the job in seconds."

"What if I'm spotted going up or coming back down? What if someone makes the connection? Gaito would have me skinned alive."

"Then it is important that you not let anyone catch sight of you," Scarlotti said, and adopted his velvet tone again. "You can do it, Petrone. A smart man like you shouldn't have any problem."

The capo was crestfallen. "You don't know what you're asking."

Scarlotti beamed. He had won. "Considering that you are being rewarded with your life, I would say that you are getting off lightly."

"Yeah. Sure. I'll do it, but I don't like it."

The line went dead. Tickled at the turn of events, Scarlotti hung up and faced Giovanni. "Remember.

No one is to harm Petrone. I want the pleasure of disposing of the worm myself."

HAROLD STENBECK COULD hardly believe his eyes. Across the room were his immediate superior, the head of the L.A. field office, the district supervisor, a top Bureau official from Washington, D.C. and a big man with a no-nonsense attitude who had breezed into the building less than an hour ago and assumed total command.

Stenbeck had heard the newcomer's name mentioned. It was Brognola, but who the man might be and where he fitted into the scheme of things was beyond him. All that mattered was that his bosses treated Brognola as if the man were the President himself.

Suddenly the head of the L.A. field office beckoned. "Stenbeck, isn't it? Come over here."

Feeling queasy, the agent obeyed. He stood as rigid as a board, aware that the important personage behind the desk was studying him closely. "Yes, sir?" he squeaked, and flushed with embarrassment.

The big man seemed to smile without actually doing so. "At ease, Agent Stenbeck. This isn't the military, you know."

"Yes, sir," Stenbeck said much too loudly. "I mean, no, sir, it isn't. Sorry, sir."

The L.A. chief sighed and went to say something but Brognola silenced him with a glance. "Now, then," the big man said. "I'd like you to tell me everything you told your superiors earlier. Start at the beginning.''

Composing himself, Stenbeck did as he was bid. He paused when he got to the part where he had illegally entered the building. To cover himself, he fibbed as he had before, claiming that he saw Bruno Gaito at an upper window.

Brognola interrupted. ''And you're positive that it was him? You've looked at the mug shots again, and you're absolutely convinced there can be no mistake?''

''None at all, sir.''

Brognola pondered a bit. ''All right. Here is how we'll do it.'' Before him was spread a map of Los Angeles. The Vigoda Concrete company had been marked with a star. ''I want a six-block radius cleared. L.A. police will lend a hand. Go from door to door and get everyone out of there whether they want to go or not. We're not having a repeat of Atlantic City.''

Stenbeck saw that his superiors were hanging on the man's every word. In a way Brognola was a lot like how Stenbeck had always imagined J. Edgar Hoover being—forceful, intelligent, articulate, a born leader.

''The evacuation must be completed by nine o'clock,'' Brognola was saying. ''Our people must be in position no later than half-past. Based on the Camorra's performance to date, we can expect Scarlotti to hit Gaito sometime after midnight.

When it goes down, we move in and round up the whole bunch.''

The district supervisor whistled. ''It will be a war, with us caught in the middle.''

''Better us than hundreds of innocent civilians,'' Brognola said.

The head of the L.A. field office ruefully shook his head. ''It's too bad we can't take them down without any bloodshed. I'd love to get my hands on Gaito and Scarlotti and some of the other bosses.''

The Bureau official from Washington had a pertinent comment. ''In all the confusion it's entirely possible that they will get away. Days or weeks from now we'll have to go through the same thing all over again.''

Brognola looked up. ''I've taken steps to prevent that.'' His gaze drifted to a wall clock. ''An associate of mine by the name of Belasko is due here within the hour. He'll be our wild card, so to speak. It will be up to him to make sure that Scarlotti and Gaito don't escape.''

''How in the world can one man do that?'' the L.A. chief asked.

The big Fed ignored the question. ''Belasko is to be given a free rein. Whatever he wants, he gets. Treat his every request as if it came from me personally.''

The men exchanged glances, but not Stenbeck. He was mesmerized. Here was a man after his own heart, the sort of man he aspired to one day be.

"He'll need a liaison," Brognola added. "Someone from the local office."

The L.A. chief responded, "No problem. I'll assign one of my best agents. He's not here at the moment, but—"

"Why go to all the bother?" Brognola said, shocking Stenbeck by pointing at him. "What's wrong with Agent Stenbeck?"

"Stenbeck?" the L.A. head asked, somehow contriving to look as if he had swallowed his tongue.

"Is that all right with you, Agent Stenbeck?" Brognola asked.

All Stenbeck could do was nod. He was afraid that if he answered, he would sound as if he had just inhaled helium.

Brognola had a few more instructions to dispense. When he was done, he dismissed them. One by one the men filed from the room. Stenbeck was the last to go. He was almost to the door when the world as he knew it came to an end.

"Not you, Agent Stenbeck. I'd like a few words with you, if you please."

"Sir?"

"Close the door and come back here."

His skin prickling as if from a heat rash, his temples pounding like bongos, Stenbeck did as he was commanded.

"I want the truth, Agent Stenbeck."

"Sir?"

The big Fed rested his elbows on the desk and fixed him with a stare that held more curiosity than hostility. "I don't like being lied to. I want to know what really happened at Vigoda Concrete."

For a few seconds Stenbeck considered sticking to his story. Filing a false report was a serious breach that merited severe punishment. But something in Brognola's eyes stopped him. Somehow the man knew. He could feel it in his bones. So, against his better judgment he gave a true account, omitting nothing.

Brognola showed no reaction until the man was done. Then he nodded. "You showed commendable initiative."

"Sir?"

"If you hadn't snuck into the building, we would never have learned that Gaito was here."

Stenbeck wanted to pinch himself to verify he wasn't dreaming. "But I violated proper procedure."

"That you did. And it will be so noted in your personnel file. But you did the right thing, son, and that's what counts. That old cliché about rules being meant to be broken has some truth to it."

Half numb with astonishment, Stenbeck didn't reply.

"I understand that when it comes to computers, no one in the L.A. office can hold a candle to you."

Stenbeck's astonishment grew. It was true, but

how on earth had the man from Washington heard about it? "I just have a knack," he said lamely.

Brognola reached into his jacket, pulled out a wallet and removed a business card, which he extended. "Take this. Call me at that number in about two weeks. I'm always looking for a few good men and women to join a special operation, and you have the potential to fit right in." He closed the wallet. "That's all for now. You can go."

Harold Stenbeck left the office, went straight to his chair and sat there for the next ten minutes staring at the card. If anyone had bothered to look, he would have noticed that Stenbeck's face glowed like a Christmas tree.

## CHAPTER TWENTY

The Executioner stared out the window of the cab at the Vigoda Concrete and Masonry Company. "Go slow," he told the agent in the front seat. "But not too slow. We don't want to draw attention to ourselves."

"Yes, sir," Harold Stenbeck responded. He had donned a windbreaker in place of his sports jacket and wore a baseball cap. Chomping noisily on gum, he looked every bit like a typical cabdriver.

Bolan's trained eyes picked out the gunners on the roof, the gunners patrolling the block, plus more hardmen seated in a parked car near the entrance. No one could get in there without being spotted, yet that was exactly what he intended to do. It was 11:00 p.m. Brognola figured the fireworks would begin in an hour or so, which didn't give him much time to spare.

"Want me to go around the block again?" Stenbeck asked.

"Too risky," Bolan replied. He hadn't minded having the agent pawned off on him. Stenbeck knew L.A. better than he did, and it helped to have someone handy to serve as a buffer with local law enforcement. All Stenbeck had to do was flash his badge to get any policeman in the city to cooperate.

"What's next, then, sir?"

Bolan leaned over the front seat to point at a ten-story skyscraper. It reared catercorner from the concrete company and would overlook the roof. "Know what that is?"

"The Aztec Building, sir. The bottom five floors are devoted to business use. The top five are luxury apartments. Why?"

"Pull over and wait for me," Bolan directed. The agent promptly obeyed, then gave him the kind of look that made him think of a puppy eager for a bone for a job well done. "I shouldn't be long."

There was no doorman. A number of the businesses were still open, among them a flower shop on the fifth floor, according to the hours posted in the lobby. Bolan took the elevator, which only went as high as the fifth. He ambled down a hall to another elevator, but this one turned out to be private, for the exclusive use of the tenants who lived above. A key was required to activate it.

Stymied, Bolan went back past the flower shop and a bridal boutique to a stairwell. He thought that the door would be locked, but it swung inward at the merest touch of his fingertips. An inspection showed why. Someone at one time had jimmied the lock. Vandals, he figured, and started to climb.

The upper floors were quiet at that time of night. Few tenants were abroad. None of them was prone to use the stairs when there was an easier way to travel to the ground floor and back.

Experience had taught Bolan that the door at the top would be locked. But it, like its counterpart below, had been sprung at one time or another. It swung quietly open, and he stepped out onto the roof. A brisk breeze buffeted him. He caught sight of Santa Monica Bay far off in the distance.

Blocking Bolan's view of the corner that overlooked the Mafia's hideout was a structure that housed the air-conditioning machinery and other equipment. He began to go around, halting when he heard muffled voices.

Someone else was up there with him.

Bolan frowned. It would be just his luck for some kids or a couple of lovebirds to be enjoying the vista. Gliding to the corner, he saw two men with their backs to him. They were dressed in business suits, and one was peering down at the street through binoculars. Something about the man's posture jarred Bolan's memory, but it wasn't until the figure turned to address his companion that Bolan realized who it was.

Cardoni.

The Sicilian passed the binoculars to the other hit man, saying, "Your turn, Fabrizzio. My eyes are getting tired. I can use a break."

"Do you really think the Camorra will show?"

"Don Gaito believes they will, and it is his opinion that counts." Cardoni motioned at a pair of long leather cases propped against the low parapet. "I hope they do, though. We will pick them off like clay pigeons."

Bolan knew what those cases contained. He watched as Cardoni knelt, unzipped one and took out a high-powered rifle. The lighting was poor, yet adequate to reveal the fine, polished lines of a Weatherby Lazermark. It boasted a fancy walnut stock, intricate floral patterns on the grip and the stock and a Monte Carlo cheekpiece.

The Executioner had long been partial to Weatherbys, his favorite sniper rifle being a Weatherby Mark V, the predecessor to the Lazermark. Whatever else might be said about Cardoni, the man knew his guns. There wasn't a finer rifle anywhere.

The Sicilian took a box of shells from the carrying case. They were .460 Weatherby Magnum cartridges, the top of the line, their muzzle velocity rated at 2600 feet per second, with a whopping 2300 at a range of one hundred yards. A single shot could drop a rampaging rhino.

Cardoni inserted a round into the chamber, worked the bolt, then fondly patted the rifle as if it were a close personal friend. "I have not had a chance to test my new scope yet," he commented.

The scope he referred to was a passive night sight, a model similar in size and shape to the Hyper-miniscope Bolan had occasionally used during his Army stint, only this one had been modified for the Weatherby. Cardoni raised the rifle to his shoulder and put his eye to the scope.

"Beautiful, Fabrizzio. Just beautiful. It is as if it were broad daylight."

Fabrizzio made no attempt to unzip his case. He had stepped to the parapet and bent to see over the side. "There is a taxi parked out front."

"So? People come and go from this building at all hours."

"Maybe so. But have you noticed that there has not been much traffic the past hour or so? Is that not unusual for Los Angeles? The streets are supposed to be congested every minute of the day and night."

Cardoni snorted. "Your problem is that you watch too much television. Then you make it worse by believing what you hear." He nodded at sparkling skyscrapers to the south. "It is past eleven. Naturally the traffic is not as heavy as it was earlier."

"I still think it strange."

Bolan slipped a hand under his jacket to the butt of his Beretta. Cardoni didn't realize it, but Fabrizzio was right. Los Angeles police, at the urging of the Feds, were funneling traffic on major arteries away from the immediate area. Construction signs had been set up to hoodwink the public.

Cardoni focused on the concrete firm. "Someone has just come up on the roof. I think it is Petrone,

Don Gaito's capo." The Sicilian leaned out farther. "He is beckoning for the guards to gather around him. I wonder what is up."

"Maybe they are changing shifts," Fabrizzio suggested.

"No. They don't do that until midnight."

The Executioner had to attach a sound suppressor before he made his move. He saw Cardoni stiffen, heard his intake of breath.

"Mother of God! It cannot be!"

"What?" Fabrizzio asked. He had turned to the east and hadn't witnessed whatever Cardoni did.

"He killed them!"

"Who?"

"Petrone, you idiot! He just gunned down all the guards with an Uzi, and now he is hurrying below. The filthy cur! The stinking, miserable son of a—"

"We must alert Don Gaito!" Fabrizzio exclaimed, unclipping a radio from his belt. "Petrone must be working for Scarlotti. Do you know what that means?"

Bolan had paused, as taken aback as the Sicilians. The significance didn't escape him, and he quickly finished threading the suppressor onto the 9 mm pistol. Cardoni was still intent on the roof below and Fabrizzio was just raising the radio when he stepped from cover. The latter saw him first and spun, crying out as he clawed for a pistol.

"Cardoni! The one from the Pine Barrens!"

A single tap of the trigger and Fabrizzio acquired

a third nostril. He took an ungainly step backward and nearly pitched over the parapet.

Cardoni had also whirled, the Weatherby arcing around. Since he already had the rifle tucked to his shoulder, all he had to do was squeeze his finger.

Bolan was a fraction faster. He pumped two slugs into the hit man, both in the mouth in case the Sicilian wore Kevlar. Cardoni was dead on his feet, but he didn't go down. He shambled forward a half stride, tripped over his own feet, then fell. Bolan sprang, grabbing the Weatherby before it hit, sidestepping the body as it rolled against him.

Stepping to the parapet, Bolan trained the scope on the roof of Vigoda's. Eight bodies were sprawled in attitudes of violent death. The door to the roof had been left open. No one else had appeared, so those inside weren't yet aware of Petrone's treachery.

To date, the Camorrans had demonstrated a penchant for conducting their attacks with military precision. They operated according to a set timetable, just as any elite unit would do. Scarlotti always coordinated their assaults down to the smallest detail. So it was unlikely that the slaying of the roof guards was a chance event. It had to fit into Scarlotti's master plan, and that could only mean one thing.

The attack had to be about to begin.

Bolan scanned the street. Two Mafia gunners patrolled the front sidewalk. They were trying to be inconspicuous, but the bulges under their jackets and the radio one carried were dead giveaways. Two more were on the north side of the building. They had stopped so one could light a cigarette.

Few pedestrians were abroad. Down the street from the concrete firm an elderly couple and a teenager were waiting for a bus. Farther off a scruffy man rummaged through a trash bin. A car went past, heading east.

Then, five blocks away, several vehicles swung into the street from a side road and rumbled in Bolan's direction. He had to tweak the scope to see them clearly. His jaw muscles twitched. They were moving vans, rental trucks from one of the leading agencies in the country. They rode bumper to bumper at a lumbering crawl, giving the illusion of being three segments of a giant yellow caterpillar.

Bolan remembered the moving trucks the Camorra had relied on before. He remembered the peninsula firefight, and the blast that nearly claimed his life. He remembered Oklahoma City, and he knew what was going to happen just as surely as if he had X-ray vision.

The lead truck gained speed, its gears grinding. The other two slowed, forcing a car that came up behind them to brake.

Meanwhile the Mafia gunners had paused at the far corner. One glanced down the street at the oncoming vehicles but didn't act the least concerned.

The first truck passed the homeless man sorting through trash. Again the gears growled. It was doing over forty and still gaining speed. The other trucks were a full block back and falling farther behind every second.

Bolan fixed the scope on the windshield. He could see the driver hunched tensely over the steering wheel. His finger curled around the trigger, but he held his fire. He wanted the truck to pass the bus stop so the bystanders wouldn't be harmed when it veered out of control.

A new element intruded itself. A woman and a little girl out walking a dog had appeared on the corner nearest Bolan. If they kept going, they would reach the vicinity of the truck bays about the same time the moving van did.

Bolan was keyed as tight as piano wire. He leaned forward as the truck sped past the bus stop, drawing curious stares from the elderly pair. It was now doing close to sixty miles per hour. He fired.

Being hit by a .460 Weatherby Magnum was like being hit by a sledgehammer. The driver was slammed back against the seat. Everyone below looked up at the roof of the Aztec. Consequently none of them saw the driver slump over or the truck stray from its lane into the other. The mobster with the radio talked urgently into it.

The truck was still doing over fifty. Bolan went for the front tires. Blowing them out, he reasoned, would bring the vehicle to a stop that much sooner. His next shot ruptured the tire on the passenger's side. The truck should have angled back into the proper lane. Instead, it slanted toward the sidewalk. It was now less than a block from the concrete firm.

Bolan tried to get a shot at the other front tire, but the vehicle weaved wildly. It bumped up onto the curb, flattening a mailbox in its path, then fishtailed onto the street. Not once did it lose speed. There could only be one explanation. The dead driver's foot was wedged on the gas pedal.

The two gunners had finally awakened to the real peril. They opened up on the cab, autopistols cracking in a beating cadence that had as little effect on the hurtling vehicle as slingshots would have on an elephant.

At last Bolan saw the driver's side tire. The Weatherby thundered, the stock punching his shoulder. The tire burst, and the moving van began to slow. Only it was too little, too late. The truck had too much momentum. It jumped the curb a second time, sheared off a traffic light in a spray of crackling sparks, arrowed across the intersection and plowed into the corner of Vigoda Concrete and Masonry.

The explosion was everything Bolan had feared it would be.

A fireball engulfed the lower half of the building. It devoured the two gunners as they turned to flee. It caught the woman and her little girl flat-footed, reducing them and their poodle to cinders. Every window in every building for blocks in all directions shattered. Vigoda's seemed to rise into the air and settle back again, flames, smoke and dust spewing from the gaping crater that marked the center of the blast.

The truck bays had been reduced to splintered shards, the metal doors mangled, a jagged hole over thirty feet wide where the corner had been.

Inside, Bolan imagined, Gaito and company would be blinded by the smoke and fighting for a breath of air. They were momentarily helpless, just as Scarlotti had planned.

With flawless timing, the other two trucks barreled onto the scene. One braked at right angles to the building. The other did the same to the left. Immediately the rear doors were thrown open, and from out of the vans swarmed dozens of Camorran hardmen. The staccato beat of autofire sounded like fireworks compared to the devastating explosion.

Bolan wasn't idle. He picked off two Camorrans before they could reach the building. He noticed that they had formed into two prongs, and that their advance was being directed by a tall figure who stood in the shadow of one of the trucks. A lieutenant, Bolan assumed, until the man strode into the open.

It was none other than Antonio Scarlotti. The big man had decided to personally take charge of the final assault on the Mafia.

Bolan shifted. He centered Scarlotti in his sights. But before he could end the Neapolitan's bloody reign of terror, a cloud of smoke drifted between them. He held the Weatherby steady so that when the cloud moved on, he would be ready. Seconds that seemed like minutes went by. The sluggish breeze pushed the smoke past the truck.

Scarlotti was gone.

Sirens wailed in the distance. The Feds were closing in. Bolan set down the Weatherby and ran to the stairs. He would be more effective below, in the thick of things. Taking the steps three at a time, he sped toward what he hoped would be a showdown with the Naples Butcher.

One way or the other, the wholesale slaughter was going to end.

JOSEPH CASTELLANO'S ears hammered so severely, he could hardly hear. Blinded by acrid smoke, racked by a fit of coughing, he stumbled from the main office and leaned against the wall to get his bearings. Nonstop automatic and pistol fire echoed from the corner of the building. Men were screaming, cursing and gurgling their death rattles.

Castellano's own soldiers were among those dying, but he didn't think to go help them. His only thought was to get out of there, to save his own hide. He took a few halting steps, trying to determine whether it would be safer to go out the back way. Evidently not. More gunfire rocked the alley.

"Damn!" Castellano swore.

"Joseph? Is that you?"

Don Bruno Gaito materialized out of the smoke.

His eyes were watering, and he was coughing just as violently as Castellano, but he was otherwise unruffled. "I don't know how they found us, but they did," he said as calmly as if they were seated in his study sipping brandy.

"We're trapped!" Castellano said bitterly. It was the Moose Head all over again, only worse. None of them would get out alive.

Incredibly Gaito smiled. "You should know me better than that, Joseph. Have I let you down yet?" He snagged Castellano's sleeve. "Follow me. You'll learn something."

A pair of soldiers fell into step behind them as the two Mafia leaders raced through the smoke-filled building toward the northwest corner. They came to a large crate that barred the aisle. To Castellano's utter amazement, Gaito pulled on the outer edge, and the front of the crate swung open as if it were a door. He was hustled into another aisle, one he hadn't even known was there, then to the rear of the building.

Sets of clothes had been piled on top of a cardboard box. Neatly folded, many bore insignia and patches. There were also hats.

Castellano picked up a shirt. "Police uniforms!" he blurted.

Gaito chuckled. "What better cover? Find one that will fit and hurry up and change. I have a spare car stored in a garage three blocks from here. We can be at the L.A. airport in forty-five minutes."

"But how will we get out of the building? The Camorrans won't hesitate to gun down cops."

"Where is your faith, Joseph?" Gaito asked sternly.

The soldiers also changed. Shortly, to all intents and purposes, they were four of L.A.'s finest. Gaito squatted at the corner. Lying beside it was a large screwdriver. He inserted the tip into a hairline crack three feet above the floor. Prying vigorously, he loosened a square section of wall about half the size of a refrigerator door. His gunners had to help lower the heavy slab to the floor.

"Once we're out, don't stop for anything," Gaito cautioned. "My men will take care of any trouble."

The two soldiers went out first; Castellano stayed close to his friend. As he straightened, he saw an empty intersection on their right. To their left was the alley. He didn't need to look to know that a pitched battle was taking place.

"Now!" Gaito barked, and bolted across the street. His men flanked him every step of the way.

Castellano spied several unmarked cars with flashing overhead lights speeding toward them from the south. He thought for sure that the driver of the first one would stop to question them, but the three vehicles sped on past to the front of Vigoda's and squealed around the corner.

"What did I tell you?" Don Gaito said. "It worked like a charm."

They cut across to the next street. People were

on their stoops or staring out windows, drawn by the din. A heavyset man with bushy sideburns hailed Gaito. "Hey, Officer! What on earth is going on? It sounds like World War III."

"Mind your own business," Gaito snapped, then winked at Castellano. "You can stop sweating, Joseph. We're safe now. By morning we'll be in New York. For a while we'll lay low and rebuild." He smacked his right fist against his left palm. "The Camorrans haven't won yet. Not by a long shot. You'll see."

Castellano began to believe that his mentor was right. Maybe they did have a prayer, after all. "If only someone would nail Scarlotti," he said absently.

"It's only a matter of time, brother. Only a matter of time."

ANTONIO SCARLOTTI knew that his carefully planned assault was going all wrong, but he couldn't fathom exactly why.

First a Mafia sniper had somehow guessed that the moving vans were more than they appeared to be and had slain the driver of the first truck. Scarlotti would have called off the attack then had the bomb truck not slammed into the concrete company anyway, opening a way in.

The Camorrans had poured from the vans under the cover of thick smoke, only to encounter withering fire from within. The Mafia shooters were putting up stiffer resistance than Scarlotti had counted on.

Even more aggravating were the wailing sirens. Scarlotti heard them as he ducked into the building on the heels of his men. It sounded as if the entire Los Angeles Police Department were converging on the site. Yet how could the police have responded so quickly? Scarlotti had calculated that it would take half an hour for the cops to arrive in any force.

Nearby one of his men went down, riddled in the chest. He saw two others lying a few yards away. His strike force had spread out, but his gunners were unable to envelop the enemy in a pincer movement as he had counted on doing. Nor had the men he sent around to the rear of the building been able to break inside.

Too much was going wrong too fast.

The trademark of a competent leader was the ability to adjust to the ebb and flow of combat. On the spur of the moment Scarlotti came to a tactical decision. Grabbing a lieutenant, he shouted in the man's ear, ''Give the signal! Fall back to the trucks! We are getting out of here!''

The lieutenant was out the opening in a flash. Within moments a horn blared and kept on blaring. It was the arranged signal for the strike force to regroup at the vehicles.

Scarlotti started out. Already the sirens were much too close. It was possible the police would throw up roadblocks to cordon them in before they could get away. The prospect chilled him. He had worked too long and too hard to be foiled when he was so near to achieving victory.

"Scarlotti! Scarlotti! Wait!"

Out of the smoke heaved Petrone, the capo who would sacrifice his own mother to preserve his miserable existence. Scarlotti smiled grimly. Fate worked in mysterious ways. He would be able to salvage something from the fiasco. "What do you want?"

"Take me with you! Drop me off when we're in the clear. It's the least you can do. You owe me, mister."

"That I do," Scarlotti said, giving his wrist a sharp twist to activate the spring in the special rig up his right sleeve. The hilt of his prized stiletto molded to his palm.

Petrone never saw it coming. A flurry of SMG fire had caused him to partly duck and turn. He was facing front when Scarlotti drove the stiletto into his abdomen and sliced upward. A high-pitched squeak was the only sound he made. He did attempt to aim his Uzi, but his legs were already folding.

Scarlotti jerked the stiletto out and wiped it on the capo's jacket. "I'd like to stay and watch you bleed to death, but I must run."

Fully one-third of the Camorrans were outside and more streamed from the building every moment. Protected by a living phalanx, Scarlotti headed for a truck. Suddenly a gunner on his left took a round in the chest. It couldn't have come from Vigoda's. Scarlotti glanced up the street.

A skinny man was shooting at them over the hood of a taxi parked in front of the Aztec.

"Kill him," Scarlotti said.

A hailstorm of lead pockmarked the taxi, shattering every window and the side mirror. The skinny man dropped from sight as scores of holes blossomed in the doors and fenders.

Scarlotti walked to the truck and climbed in. Per his instructions, the drivers had stayed with their vehicles. "Remember the escape route I showed you, Kossa," he told the man behind the wheel.

More Camorrans were backing onto the street, but there were still too many inside. The sirens were almost on top of them. If they didn't make their escape soon, it would be too late.

In confirmation three unmarked cars swept around the corner near the Aztec and zoomed toward the trucks.

THE EXECUTIONER reached street level just as total mayhem exploded.

Three carloads of federal agents screeched onto the scene. Unfortunately for them, the Camorrans were spilling en masse from Vigoda's. Twenty to thirty guns spit lead in an earsplitting crescendo. The lead car took the brunt of the barrage, the driver and another agent in the front seat dancing in their seats as if in tune to the metallic music. Without anyone to guide it, the car howled up over the curb and plowed into the front of the concrete firm.

The other two drivers swerved their vehicles broadside, and the agents leaped out to engage the Camorrans. They were hopelessly outnumbered, their feeble firepower barely slowing the Camorran retreat.

Bolan took all this in as he raced to the taxi. Harold Stenbeck was on his knees, wearing a peculiar grin. The cab had been riddled.

"Are you all right?" Bolan asked.

"Never better," Stenbeck said, and laughed. "I always wanted to see some action. Think this qualifies?"

Bolan heard a truck engine rev and moved to the rear bumper. One of the moving vans was in motion, making straight for the two cars that blocked the street. The other rental truck was still taking on gunners.

All this time the wail of sirens had risen to a fever pitch. Reinforcements would arrive at any moment. But it might not be in time.

The lead moving van swiftly gained speed. The few FBI agents left tried to stop it, but they were still under fire from Camorrans streaming from the building. The driver pointed the truck at the gap between the two sedans. At the last moment the agents scattered.

The truck rammed into the cars like a bright yellow tank into a papier-mâché barrier. With a rending of metal and glass, it smashed both from its path and shot on down the street. In seconds it was at the intersection. Stenbeck popped up to snap off a few shots.

Bolan had another idea. As the truck came abreast of the cab, he darted to the taxi's front door, flung it open and slid in behind the wheel. The key was in the ignition. A flick of the wrist and the engine turned over. He threw the cab into gear.

"Wait for me, Mr. Belasko!"

Stenbeck dived onto the seat next to Bolan as the taxi leaped forward. He didn't want the agent along, but it couldn't be helped.

The gunners were pulling down the van's wide rear door. It made sense. Dozens of men armed to the gills would be a dead giveaway. At the next corner, the truck bore to the right.

Before taking the same turn, Bolan looked in the rearview mirror. The second moving van, crammed with hit men, was almost to the Aztec when four more unmarked sedans arrived in the intersection. It rammed into one of them and stalled. Camorrans jumped from the back as federal agents scrambled from their cars. The last Bolan saw, it was the gunfight at the O.K. Corral all over again. Only infinitely worse.

The first moving van stuck to the speed limit, which surprised Bolan. He felt that the Feds or the police would show up at any moment, but neither did. "Get on the horn and let your office know what is happening," he directed Stenbeck.

"Right away, sir." He snatched the microphone from the rack under the dash and pressed the transmit button. Three times he tried to raise the L.A. field office. Three times the speaker crackled with static in response.

Stenbeck bent to examine the radio. He ran a hand behind it and hissed in anger. "Bullet holes. No wonder it won't work. What do we do now?"

"We don't lose sight of that truck," Bolan said. It was paramount. This was the closest anyone had come to nabbing Antonio Scarlotti. He wouldn't let the opportunity slip through his fingers.

The moving van came to a major artery and blended into the traffic flow, traveling northward. Bolan stayed so far back that he stood a real risk of having his quarry give him the slip, but it was either that or have the Camorrans spot him—if they hadn't already. In due course the truck turned onto a side road. A sign revealed that they would soon enter the San Gabriel Mountains.

Another glance in the rearview mirror showed Bolan a helicopter making a wide sweep over the area the truck had passed through. A minute or two sooner, and the police would have spotted the van.

Stenbeck was gnawing on his lower lip. "Mr. Belasko, how many Camorrans would you estimate are in that truck?"

"Thirty. Maybe more."

"And there's just the two of us."

Bolan looked at him. The Fed was more hyper than fearful, under the potent influence of surging adrenaline thanks to the rush that always afflicted someone during a first time in combat. Bolan remembered his own initial experience well. "I'm not about to commit suicide, if that's what is worrying you."

"No, sir. Not at all. I merely made an observation. To tell you the truth, I've never felt more alive in my whole life. My entire body is tingling."

"It'll pass," Bolan said.

"Too bad. A man could become addicted to a feeling like this."

"Some do. They're the ones who wind up being mercenaries."

"You, sir? Do you feel it every time?"

The Executioner was honest with the novice. "Not anymore. A cool head counts for more in the heat of combat than having our glands in overdrive. When a person is all keyed up, he's more prone to make mistakes. And mistakes in my line of work are usually fatal."

"What exactly is your line of work, if I might inquire?"

Bolan was spared from having to answer by the moving van, which unexpectedly pulled off the road four hundred yards ahead. A green sign informed Bolan that they were approaching a campground. He immediately pulled onto the shoulder and killed the lights. "I'm going the rest of the way on foot. You head back into L.A. and let Hal Brognola know where I am."

"That's not right, sir. There are too many of them for you to take them on alone. I should stay and help."

"It wasn't a request. It was an order," Bolan stressed. Drawing the Beretta, he turned and smashed the overhead light, then opened his door and slid out. "Don't turn the headlights back on until you've gone around that last curve we passed." He scrutinized the young agent's anxious features. "Are you okay to handle this?"

"No problem, sir." Stenbeck moved over and gripped the steering wheel. "But I still think it's wrong for me to leave you."

Bolan started to close the door.

"Sir?"

Mildly peeved that the man wouldn't go along quietly, Bolan said, "Don't make a federal case out of it, Harold. You're to do what I say and that's final."

"It's not that, Mr. Belasko." Stenbeck produced a Smith & Wesson 410. "I thought you might want to borrow this."

Extra firepower always came in handy. Bolan accepted the loaner, along with two spare magazines. "I'm grateful. Now get moving. Tell Brognola that

I'll do what I can to keep the Camorrans from going anywhere.''

Nodding somberly, the FBI agent started the cab, wheeled in a tight U-turn and headed back toward Los Angeles as if he were driving the Indy 500.

Bolan jogged up the road. Traffic was sparse. No other vehicles had gone by in minutes. The yellow truck was dimly visible, parked among trees well into the campground. He passed a sign that let people know picnic facilities were available. A little farther on, he came to a field that bordered the campground. Since the Camorrans were bound to be watching the entrance, he slanted into the high grass and made for the yellow outline of the van.

As the soldier drew closer, he was surprised to see a number of vehicles parked at the campsite. There were two vans, several pickups and cars. Campers, he guessed, innocents who would be caught in the line of fire if he engaged the Camorrans. Then it occurred to him that no tents had been erected, and that all the vehicles were parked near where the van had stopped. Coincidence? He doubted it.

Bolan paused at the edge of the field. Figures were clustered around a picnic table not far from the truck. He saw no strays, no lookouts. Pine trees gave him the means of getting a lot closer. Soon he heard the murmur of excited voices. A match flared off to the left, alerting him that there was at least one guard.

The members of the Camorran strike team were almost as keyed up as Agent Stenbeck. Understandably. Their attack had gone sour, and they had lost fully half their force. They were upset by the setback, but they dutifully grew silent when someone climbed onto the picnic table and raised both arms.

It was Antonio Scarlotti.

"Friends!" the Camorran leader began. "Tonight the Fates have not been kind. The few Mafia leaders left are still alive, and it appears that many of our brothers have either been killed or taken into custody by the Americans." He paused. "But it is not the end of the world. We have the Mafia reeling. It will be simple for us to finish them off, just as it will be simple to have our ranks replenished by a phone call to Naples."

Bolan was scouring the campground. The only vehicles present were those near the moving van. So there were no bystanders to contend with. He could do as he pleased.

"We will rest a week or two," Scarlotti informed his followers. "Then we will hunt down Bruno Gaito and Joseph Castellano and put an end to this farce. By the end of the year, the Camorra, not the Mafia, will be the supreme criminal organization in this country."

Bolan circled to the left. The lone lookout was facing the entrance. Stalking to within ten feet of the unsuspecting killer, the Executioner tapped the trigger once. The suppressor's cough wasn't loud enough to be heard over by the picnic table.

The lookout was convulsing when Bolan claimed the man's Uzi and three magazines that went into a back pocket. He headed on to the moving van, hiked a leg onto the step and peered in the open driver's window. The keys had been left in the ignition.

Dropping the Uzi on the seat, Bolan gripped the edge of the roof and levered himself into the cab. He rolled down the passenger's-side window to reduce the danger from flying glass once the Camorrans realized what he was up to and came after him.

He had to work fast. There was no guarantee that he would survive, but the sacrifice was worth it if he stopped the Camorrans from escaping. Otherwise, the war would rage on. Countless innocents would suffer.

Bolan steeled himself, then turned the key. At the engine's first rumble, heads turned. He could imagine their fleeting confusion as they wondered which one of them had started the truck. He checked the side mirror, saw a Chevy van twenty feet behind him and shifted into reverse.

Someone shouted as the moving van lurched backward. Bolan spun the wheel furiously to angle it just right. He was doing about thirty when the rear bumper slammed into the side of the Chevy. The moving van was bigger, heavier, a colossal battering ram powered by hundreds of horses under the hood. It buckled the Chevy van like an empty tin can.

Instantly Bolan shifted into first gear and veered toward a pickup. Camorrans were running to intercept him, but they were forty feet away when he rammed into it with a rending crash, flipping the pickup onto its side. The unmistakable scent of gasoline filled the air, letting him know that the pickup's fuel tank had been ruptured.

The first shot sounded as Bolan looped toward the second van, a Ford. Suddenly rounds were drilling against the passenger's door and punching through the windshield. The Executioner ducked, shards whizzing over his head.

"Stop him!" someone roared above the autofire. It sounded like Scarlotti.

The truck's grille caught the Ford in the front fender and jarred it against a tree, folding it in on itself like an accordion. Bolan shifted again. He heard one of the front tires grinding against either the bumper or the fender, but the damage wasn't enough to slow him. He drove in as small a circle as the big rig permitted, aiming at three parked cars.

Some of the Camorrans had caught up. Lead peppered the windshield, hammered his door. Two men appeared alongside the cab, trying to fix a bead while running. He snatched up the Uzi, poked it out the window and triggered a short burst, chopping both off at the waist.

The rental van neared the cars. Slugs smashed

into the roof and into the seat beside the soldier. He hunched over the wheel, wishing the truck had the acceleration of a sports car instead of a tank. It sounded as if he had been caught in the worst hailstorm of the century. The cab and the van were being pounded mercilessly. It was only a matter of time before a lucky shot scored.

Dozens of Camorrans were close behind when Bolan sheared into the first car, reducing it to twisted wreckage. He did the same to the next. As he rolled toward the last, one of the others went up in a spectacular fireball that enveloped the tail of the moving van and some of the Camorrans. Their screams mingled with the stench of burned rubber.

Bolan slammed into the last car. The cab jumped, tilting wildly. He was thrown against the passenger's door. Lunging, he tried to regain the wheel and was flipped back when the truck became airborne. He braced for the impact, but nothing could prepare him for the bone-wrenching crunch. Like a human table-tennis ball, he was bounced against the dash and the doors. He flung his arms out for support, which wasn't there.

Just when he thought it couldn't get any worse, it did.

The truck's left side rose into the air and kept on rising. Bolan snagged the steering wheel, but it didn't keep him from tumbling onto his shoulders as the cab came to rest on its right side. Something thudded against his chest. Groping, he grasped the Uzi.

Strident yells were proof the Camorrans were almost on top of him.

Galvanizing into action, Bolan tucked his legs under him and leaped. He caught hold of the lower edge of the driver's window and propelled himself out of the cab. A few bullets spanged off the fender as he dropped and bolted, the mystery of the crash explained by a ditch he hadn't known was there.

Coming to some pines, Bolan whirled and fired into the moving van's fuel tank. Gunners were coming around both ends of the overturned behemoth, and they had nowhere to take cover when the truck exploded. Drenched in flaming fuel, three fiery scarecrows swatted in vain at the flames that were devouring them alive.

Bolan dived behind the pines. He slapped a new magazine into the Uzi and rolled into the open in time to catch a knot of Camorrans who had wisely given the truck a wide birth. Some of them fired at the same moment he did. Dirt flew into his face; wooden slivers stung his cheeks. He saw five of his foes go down, and the rest sought cover.

From near the destroyed cars rose the voice of Antonio Scarlotti, vibrant with primal fury. "I want him dead, do you hear me? Whatever it takes, he must pay!"

Bolan rose and ran toward the entrance to the campground. He would make his stand there. One way or the other, the Camorrans weren't getting past him while he still breathed. How many were left, he had no idea. Twenty, at least. More than enough to do as Scarlotti wanted.

He sprinted across a strip of grass onto asphalt. A few of the hardmen fired, but the only damage they did was to trees lining the road. Turning, he zinged a few slugs in their direction to discourage them long enough for him to reach the turnoff.

Bolan dropped into a ditch, crouched and waited. The Camorrans had lost sight of him and most had slowed. The impetuous ones paid for their folly when he emptied the magazine in a crisp arc. Four or five more collapsed to the ground, never to rise again.

Back among the trees, a pickup that the soldier hadn't damaged growled to life. Headlights stabbing the night, it wound toward the entrance. Gunners were in the bed, and others leaned out the windows.

The pickup swerved around a bend and bore down on him. He made no attempt to hide when he was bathed in the glare of the high beams. Fingers working feverishly, he inserted the Uzi's last magazine. The gunners cut loose, shredding the top of the ditch as he fired into the pickup's grille, into its hood, into its windshield. Those inside were the fortunate ones. They died instantaneously.

The pickup veered into the far ditch. With the driver dead, there was no one to steer it back out, no one to right it when it began to roll. Those in the bed attempted to spring to safety but only one succeeded. The others were crushed like so many stick dolls when the pickup rolled over them.

Bolan discarded the Uzi and drew the .44 Magnum Desert Eagle. An inky form heaved out of the bushes, snapping off random shots. A single blast of the Desert Eagle punched the hardman into oblivion.

Camorrans were zeroing in on the ditch along a wide front. One man couldn't possibly hold them all at bay. Yet Bolan drew the Smith & Wesson and waited for them to get closer, until they were so near that he couldn't miss. Then he rose and fired with ambidextrous precision, the .44 and the .40-caliber S&W booming like twin peals of thunder. Charging Camorrans fell as fast as they presented themselves, yet there were still more than he could drop no matter how hard he tried, no matter how good he was.

One reached the ditch.

Bolan expended the last round in the Desert Eagle, dropped it and unlimbered the Beretta. He fired at two men to his left, at two more to his right. The Camorrans were seconds away from overwhelming him. More reared directly ahead. He was staring into their muzzles when the entire tableau was flooded by bright light that riveted the hardmen where they stood.

A helicopter came from out of nowhere, the

*whump-whump-whump* of the rotors punctuated by the booming of a heavy-caliber machine gun. Camorrans toppled like ten pins.

Cars screeched into the turnoff, sirens wailing, FBI agents adding their firepower to the helicopter's. Somewhere someone bellowed through a bullhorn for the Camorrans to lay down their arms while they still could.

It all happened so swiftly that one moment Bolan stared eternity in the face, and the next he was in the clear and the gunners were either scattering or dropping in bloody piles.

A tall shape rose up out of the ditch almost at his elbow. "You did this!" Antonio Scarlotti snarled. "You ruined everything!"

A stiletto flashed. Bolan, turning, felt the blade rasp across the Beretta, knocking the pistol from his hand. He extended the Smith & Wesson and squeezed the trigger, only to hear the dry click of an empty weapon. The stiletto lanced at his chest. He blocked it with a forearm, pivoted, then rapped the Smith & Wesson against his adversary's temple.

Scarlotti staggered, dug in his heels and tried again, aiming a wicked cut at Bolan's throat.

Letting go of the pistol, the Executioner caught the Neapolitan's wrist in both hands even as he jumped straight up and rammed his knee into the man's elbow.

Scarlotti cried out, the stiletto falling from his stiffened fingers. It never hit the ground.

Bolan palmed the hilt as it fell, spun on the balls of his feet and drove the blade into the butcher's ribs. Scarlotti gasped, clawing at his arm. Holding firm, Bolan twisted the knife, and Scarlotti jerked as if to an electric shock.

"That's for all the innocents," Bolan said, stepping back.

The Camorran turned a stupefied expression on the Executioner, tried to say something and gave up the ghost.

The firefight was already winding down. FBI agents were rounding up wounded Camorrans and herding those who had surrendered toward waiting vehicles. A man as thin as a beanpole detached himself from the activity, rushing to the ditch. "Are you all right, Mr. Belasko?" Harold Stenbeck asked.

Bolan merely nodded. Wiping his brow, he climbed out and stared down at the body of the man who had been responsible for so much death and destruction. "You came just in time," he commented.

"Thank the chopper crew, not me," Stenbeck said. "They had the moving van under surveillance the whole time, but the pilot held off until enough agents to handle the Camorrans got here. I ran into them shortly after I left you."

Bolan inhaled the cool mountain air. Another

battle had been won. The forces of evil had suffered another setback, but it was only for the moment.

Tomorrow was another day.

Tomorrow the war would go on.

# James Axler

# OUTLANDERS™

# DOOMSTAR RELIC

Kane and his companions find themselves pitted against an ambitious rebel named Barch, who finds a way to activate a long-silent computer security network and use it to assassinate the local baron. Barch plans to use the security system to take over the ville, but he doesn't realize he is starting a Doomsday program that could destroy the world.

Kane and friends must stop Barch, the virtual assassin and the Doomsday program to preserve the future....

One man's quest for power unleashes a cataclysm in America's wastelands.

# A preview from hell...

## JAMES AXLER

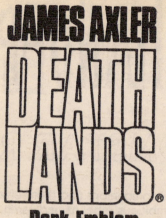

# DEATH LANDS®

## Dark Emblem

After a relatively easy mat-trans jump, Ryan and his companions find themselves in the company of Dr. Silas Jamaisvous, a seemingly pleasant host who appears to understand the mat-trans systems extremely well.

Seeing signs that local inhabitants have been used as guinea pigs for the scientist's ruthless experiments, the group realizes that they have to stop this line of research before it goes too far....